GUARDIAN

GUARDIAN

DIARY OF A DARK MONSTER™ BOOK ONE

MARTHA CARR
MICHAEL ANDERLE

THE GUARDIAN TEAM

Thanks to our beta reading team

John Ashmore, Kelly O'Donnell

Thanks to the JIT Readers

Diane L. Smith
Dave Hicks
Wendy L Bonell
Peter Manis
James Dyer

If we've missed anyone, please let us know!

Editor
The SkyFyre Editing Team

CHAPTER ONE

The night was dark and forlorn. The wind tugged at Henry's leather jacket. He leaned forward and forced the Ninja to go faster, a request the vehicle obliged with a high-pitched roar.

The thing was fast, and that almost made him sad. He could barely get it up to speed, and he was already approaching his destination. He would work it out later running with his pack through a nearby forest.

At this time of night, Washington State Road Three was a dark and desolate stretch of asphalt following the edge of Sinclair Inlet. Distant lights sparkled on the water. Their beauty distracted him for a moment, and the speed wobbles kicked in.

Henry forced his attention back to the road, squeezing his knees together and tightening his hands like he was trying to regain control of a bucking bronco. The muscles in his thighs were strong from the years of shifting into a wolf. A bone-crunching metamorphosis. He pushed the thought away.

No way he was going to let himself wreck the Ninja. Not so soon, anyway.

Up ahead, he finally spotted the prey. A truck full of goods about to be stolen.

He was on his way home from a cruise around Port Orchard when the call came in from his old friend, the watchful gnome, Lexus. A gang of smugglers was on their way north. Toward home. Probably trying to get on the nine o'clock ferry to Seattle, where they could offload their hot wares and disappear.

The last boat of the day. Tired security guards. No one paying much attention because they were looking forward to being home. The perfect time to make a run.

Not on Henry's watch. He slipped easily from business owner by day to not-so-friendly neighborhood vigilante by night. It was his way of making something good come from being kidnapped and forcibly changed into a hairy creature.

He winced at the memory, grinding his teeth. *Damn the dark families.* He revved the engine, twisting the handle and pushing the bike to go even faster. Anything to drown out the memories. He'd work it out another time. *Or not at all.*

It was almost scary how fast he caught up to the semi. It was hauling relative ass, going ten over the fifty MPH speed limit. It might as well have been standing still. The Ninja's tires chewed up the pavement, zooming up on the rear of the semi before the driver could glance in his side mirror.

Henry grinned, hoping they could somehow see his bared teeth through the opaque face shield on his helmet.

Yup. I'm here. Take it in.

Henry was looking forward to seeing these guys flinch, then watching them scramble and do their best to refocus. *It won't be enough.*

The man in the passenger seat rolled his window down, stuck his hand out, and waved Henry forward.

"You want me to go around, huh?" He accelerated, lurching forward. "Well, what goes around comes around. Didn't your mother ever teach you that?"

He maneuvered into the slipstream, the area of broken airflow behind the semi. The truck did the work, pushing against the drag. It was a large vehicle, acting like a wind-sail as it tore down the road. Back here, in the space immediately behind it, Henry was hit with almost no drag at all. The effect allowed an increase in the Ninja's top speed. Within a second, he was right behind them, his front tire almost bumping the bottom edge of the trailer.

He saw their next move coming.

These guys aren't as stupid as I thought they were. "Time for a little fun."

They figured out pretty fast that he meant trouble. The driver hit the brakes. The semi's tires screeched. Henry reacted, but he had given himself zero maneuvering space. His front tire slotted neatly under the trailer and his face smacked hard against the back of it. *Fuck.* He sipped in air, letting the shifter energy pass through him. Enough to keep him upright, but not enough to cross the line and transform.

Henry braked and backed off a little, reaching up to lift the cracked face shield. It didn't help much. He could still barely see anything. The thin stream of blood down his face wasn't helping.

He gritted his teeth, an involuntary growl rumbling deep in his chest. Dark fur momentarily crawled across the back of his neck, receding just as quickly.

Now I'm pissed. It wasn't their first mistake, but it was by far their worst.

Reaching up to the collar of his riding jacket, he stuck a finger inside and felt along his neck until he found the button on the center of his necklace. It was another Lexus invention. One of hundreds over the years.

He pushed hard, the small, round cylinder pressing against his skin. A funny feeling spread over his head, a fuzzy pins-and-needles sensation as the energy discharged, creating an equalizing of pressures. The lines of his face blurred into a grotesque mask, shielding his identity from onlookers.

Lexus claimed it was harmless, but if Henry wound up with a brain tumor ten years from now, he'd know why.

Until then, he'd keep kicking ass.

Case in point, quarter to nine at night on a lonely stretch of road. Just him and the semi-truck. At least two drug-running doofuses. Probably more in the trailer.

Henry reached back, grabbed the curved handle of a black umbrella, and pulled it out.

The passenger in the truck put his head out the window and laughed. "What's that, your grandma's umbrella? It's not even raining, jackass!"

"I know, right?" Henry called. "I hate it when people say it never stops raining in the Pacific Northwest. But you never know when a good umbrella will come in handy."

He held the handle like a gun and aimed the umbrella's tip at the truck's rear tires. A tight squeeze on the handle caused a concussive *bang* and a strong recoil that kicked the umbrella up into the wind, almost ripping it from his grasp.

The projectile flickered red in the night, splitting in two. Each piece embedded itself in the rubber of the back tires, heating up. The tires quickly deflated, melted into goo, and sloughed off onto the road. The bare rims ground on the pavement, tossing up a shower of sparks that fell around Henry like sideways rain.

He gritted his teeth and narrowed his eyes, ducking his head as he swerved through the fiery shower that pricked at his skin and jacket.

The truck driver fought to keep control as Henry set about making his job harder. He swerved to the left, coming dangerously close to scraping himself along the concrete divider. With the left front tire in his sights, he squeezed off another round.

The projectile found its mark and opened into a fan with sharp, tiny hooks that rotated upon contact. In a few seconds, the tire was completely gone. So was any hope the driver had of getting away.

The truck lost traction and fishtailed, smashing and scraping the divider on one side and kicking out over the train tracks on the other. The back wheels caught and pulled the truck to a stop with the front wheels slowly spinning.

Henry seized the opportunity, stopped, and pushed down the kickstand on his motorcycle. He stepped off and paced up the road toward the floundering semi, pulled an inset toggle switch on the umbrella's shaft, and aimed again.

He shot the door on the back of the trailer. No fancy bullets this time, only a standard projectile the size of an arrowhead, fired with incredible aim. It hit the latch, causing it to spring open. Several men tumbled out, getting road rash as they flopped and rolled to a stop.

Henry jumped back on the Ninja and raced up toward them, delivering a few swift kicks to fragile jaws before speeding onward toward the truck.

It had stopped with the trailer wedged almost sideways across two lanes. Henry navigated through the other flotsam that had ejected with the men in the back. The shattered remains of a bunch of statues, all depicting various religious figures. There were a lot of Buddha, a few of the more recognizable Hindu gods, and hundreds of good old Jesus. They were all made out of the same dry, crumbly material.

Henry had seen it before. The drug trade was always coming up with genius new ideas to hide and disperse their products. Nowadays they had even more tools at their disposal and the ability to transmute their products into completely new materials. This stuff looked like any other flimsy pottery, but it was pure fentanyl. Dangerous to even be around.

Sneaky. "Not in my town," he growled, tasting the coppery blood trickling down his cheek.

He parked the bike again and casually strolled up the side of the jackknifed trailer. The passenger was scrambling out, bleeding from a contusion as he clumsily yanked an FN Five-seveN pistol off his belt.

Henry clicked the toggle on his weapon again and delivered a shock blast to the center of the thug's chest before his opponent could get off a round. The lean, wiry man stiffened and a second later, went completely limp. He folded over like overcooked lasagna, banging his face on the ground.

The driver came around the front of the truck, his AR-15 blazing. Henry dove for cover, rolling beneath the trailer and quickly coming up on the other side. The driver was coming toward the back, but Henry was ready for him. He sent out a shockwave and watched with satisfaction as the driver hit the dirt with the same unceremonious thud.

Henry walked over, staring down at the unconscious idiot.

"Tough luck, asshole." He wiped his face, staring at the blood on his fingers. "If it makes you feel like any less of a failure, you did manage to make me bleed. You can think about that while you're rotting in jail for the rest of your life. It's the small victories, right?"

As he headed back toward the bike, he glanced in the truck's side mirror to ensure his little run-in hadn't damaged anything. When he stared at his reflection, he saw everything as it should be. His black leather jacket hugged his broad shoulders. His new matte black helmet was purchased yesterday and already covered with dings and scrapes, not to mention the shattered face shield.

When he looked at the reflection of his face, he saw the false, tortured image. His eyes, nose, and mouth pulled in different directions and blurred. The effect was eerie. For a lot of criminals in the Pacific Northwest, it was something that would give them nightmares for the rest of their miserable lives.

"Still working. One less thing I broke...this time," Henry muttered.

He kept the techno-magic illusion up as he returned to check on the other thugs. Two of them were out cold from the kicks to the face. The third was crawling along, trying to reach a gun lying in the middle of the road.

Henry took a short run and stepped on the man's back. "Not so fast, buddy. You're hurt. You should rest. Get your strength back. No, no, I insist."

He pushed down, squeezing the guy's diaphragm against the road. The thug let out a satisfying groan as he kept struggling futilely. Meanwhile, Henry pulled a phone out of his pocket and pushed a red button near the top. Another Lexus add-on that the gnome called a wolf signal.

"I sent an anonymous tip to the local cops that a bunch of morons got themselves into an accident. Don't worry. They'll find a nice, cozy room for you to stay in that will be secure from any outsiders. Complete with bars for doors and a bright light that never shuts off. Have fun."

Shutting the phone off and shoving it into the Faraday pocket Lexus had sewn into his riding jacket, Henry turned on his heel and headed for the Ninja. He whistled as he got on and started the engine, heading up the road. His keen canine hearing picked up a faint sound from the front wheel. "Should hold long enough." Hard-won experience from too many crashes.

He started over, whistling the song once more.

"Damn, what the hell song is that? Lexus will know."

There was a soft chiming in his ear. The inside of the helmet face shield lit up with glitchy emojis as the shattered screen tried its best to display caller information.

Henry grunted and pulled off to the side of the road, glancing over his shoulder to make sure he was still alone.

He could already see the police lights flashing in the distance. The Ninja had taken him a full mile beyond the stranded semi. Not nearly far enough.

Henry pulled out another phone and saw the name "Reese" pop up on the caller ID. A shady wizard and former Silver Griffin agent. *Must be trouble.*

Henry answered the call. "Talk to me."

"Is that really how you answer a call? I knew you were a cliché, Neumann, but fuck me…"

"Yeah? Never."

"Fair enough. Does fuck you work for you?"

"Not at all. Why are you calling me? I'm supposed to be the one contacting you when I need help." Henry looked over his shoulder again. The lights were still in the distance. There was no way they would be able to catch up to him anyway. Not until they got that truck out of the way. "I'm kind of in the middle of something."

"Actually, I have it on good authority that you finished your most recent business transaction." There was a noise in the background, a soft whimpering.

"Tell me that's a horror movie playing in the background, Reese."

"Of course, Neumann."

Henry started to say something, but Reese barged ahead. "Tell me they were magicals. I can be there in fifteen, maybe ten. I'll have them in Trevilsom Prison and off your hands before anyone knows anything."

Henry sighed in annoyance, wiping dried blood off the

bridge of his nose. "Sorry, Peanut Butter Cup. No magicals this time. Just your garden-variety drug smugglers."

"You know, these cartel types are dumb motherfuckers. A few magicals would make this more of a fair fight."

"Magicals don't get into the drug trade unless there's another angle besides money. You know that, Reese."

"I do indeed. One of these days though, that angle is going to appear. Keep an eye out. You take care, Neumann. And if you think calling me the name of a delicious snack is an insult, think again."

Henry looked out over the dark waters of Sinclair Inlet. The only lights he saw now were a few dim ones on the far side. The security lights at Kitsap Marina. "I never mean it as an insult. You're just so sweet, is all. And you come in a monster two-pack. A wizard and a Kilomea. How is your bigger, uglier half doing, by the way?"

"I thought you were in the middle of something." Reese laughed. "Red is doing well. Now go. The night isn't going to police itself."

Henry hung up without saying another word and raced into the darkness.

CHAPTER TWO

Flying along the outskirts of Bremerton, Henry took mostly main roads as he headed northwest and up into the neighborhood of Rocky Point. Rocky Point Road was the only thread that traced the peninsula's length, bristling with side roads that climbed up into the isolated reaches of the hills.

Henry took the road almost to the end, the Ninja gliding up and down the gentle slopes, then turned off before reaching the terminus. Giving it a little gas to get up the steep slope, he found his way to Circle Drive via Hope Street. Here, the houses thinned out and dense trees brooded over the road, forming a dark tunnel through the night.

It wouldn't be the only dark tunnel he'd be taking.

At the highest point of Circle Drive, there was another offshoot called Faith Circle. Past that offshoot, a thin track that could scarcely be called a road angled off into the trees.

Henry took the track, killing his speed and letting

himself bounce along, laughing as he followed the cone of his headlights down through the trees. This was a hiking trail he had blazed himself, which his neighbors commonly used. It was safe to assume none of them were out at the moment. If they were, he believed they would see him coming and jump out of the way.

Past all the switchbacks, the trail finally ended down near View Drive. Henry revved the engine to climb onto the gravel road, then turned left and followed it down.

Finally, he came to a driveway blocked off by a steel gate.

Looking both ways, he punched in a code at the gate, waited for it to open, and drove through.

High above him, resting not far from the mouth of the hiking trail, the dark shape of the Neumann mansion rose against the sky.

Dead ahead, the driveway vanished, swallowed up by the mountainside. Henry wove through low-hanging branches festooned with damp moss and entered the tunnel. It was unlit, a necessity for stealth, so he slowed down and relied on the headlights and his muscle memory. He knew when he was getting close. Hooking a sharp left turn, he let the tires squeal as he erupted into the dark cave that formed the mansion's hollow roots.

Suddenly he was in a high-tech area, surrounded by racks and shelves that held all the cutting-edge devices he'd gotten his hands on. Everything he could ever need to bring down his targets. Weapons, suits, various gadgets.

Past that, he rolled into the parking area. Here, between several other motorcycles and electric cars, he slotted the Ninja into an empty space and killed the engine. Finally pulling the sweaty, bloodstained helmet off, he hung it on a nearby rack and strolled into the computer area.

Looking up, he let his eyes wander through the artificial constellations. The huge high-res planetarium screen was linked to astronomical databases and showed a revolving display of the night sky.

Lexus was standing at one of the computer banks, dunking a butter cookie into a cup of tea. The gnome looked up at Henry, no hint of alarm or worry on his wrinkled face.

"You may need stitches."

"Nice to see you too." Henry approached the tin of cookies and grabbed one for himself. "You shouldn't eat too many of these. They're nothing but calories."

Lexus adjusted his waistcoat, pulling it tight around his midsection. "Still plenty of room. That is a pretty nasty gouge. Did someone get a headbutt in?"

Henry scoffed. "Give me some credit, old man. The only person who could hurt me like this is me."

"So, you did something stupid?" Lexus pulled the tea bag from his cup and tossed it into a trash can. "Why am I not surprised? One more question...do I even want to see the Ninja? I didn't hear any sputtering or rattling sounds when you pulled in, so maybe it's better than I expected."

Henry tossed another cookie back, savoring the buttery texture as it dissolved between his teeth. "Now you're commenting on my driving skills. For your information, the Ninja is fine. I might have bent the front a bit. Rode a bit wobbly. Oh, and the front rim got a little crushed. Other than that it's fine." Henry reached for another cookie. "What? Don't give me that look."

Lexus smiled. "You might be the most wasteful human in existence."

Henry looked down at the older man. The gnome looked like a distinguished old professor in the small body of an eleven-year-old child, complete with a neatly groomed beard and a set of spectacles that Henry was sure were only for show. They were far too small and always perched right at the tip of the gnome's nose.

Henry tugged off his jacket and headed for the small med bay, where he grabbed a gauze pad and pressed it to the wound on his forehead. After mopping away the blood, he gently probed the wound with his fingers. Head wounds always bled a lot, no matter how small they were. This one was a tiny gash. No need for stitches.

Maybe he would visit his sister tomorrow and get a professional opinion.

From the control area, Lexus seemed to be greatly engaged in whatever he was watching.

"There you. Yes, you've about got it… He's in!"

Henry headed back over, his curiosity piqued. "What are you watching? Football?"

"No. Far from it. This is something much more entertaining. Yes, they've about got it." Lexus turned to Henry with a calm smile. "It looks like you have visitors, Master Neumann."

Henry looked past the gnome to the bank of screens. A half-dozen of them were security feeds. On one of those, an angle of the first floor east side hallway showed a dark shape slithering through a window.

Henry roared with anger and rushed for the steps. "You could have said something, Lexus!"

The gnome's voice echoed after him. "Oh, they weren't much of a threat at first. Just loitering around outside. I assumed they were looking for a spot to smoke. They look like teenagers to me."

"They'll look like corpses pretty soon," Henry grunted. He pulled a few armaments off the walls, along with a fresh vest—something in bright colors. Intimidation might solve this problem for him with no need for violence. It sounded more efficient but much less fun.

When he returned to the screens, Lexus had taken control of the camera feeds and was following the invaders through the house.

"They must think you're an easy mark. Or out of town. There's something to be said for at least leaving a security light on. It isn't as if people can't easily see the giant mansion on the hilltop."

Henry watched the invaders without responding to the quip. He mostly paid attention to how they moved in a rather tight formation with plenty of hand signals rather than verbal communication. The effect was spoiled when one of them ran straight into an armchair and fell to the floor with such an impact that they almost heard the *thud* way down in the cave.

Lexus smiled. "This isn't their first foray. There's organized chaos at work here."

"Teenagers? Organized?" Henry shook his head, then pointed at something on the screen. "No! Don't touch that. You'll blow your face off."

Lexus *tsked*. "I've told you a million times to put your toys away, Henry. Look here..." He panned past a kid jumping up and down on a couch to another. This one looked like a girl. She was moving carefully, her eyes scanning everything.

"They're looking for something specific. Maybe. Maybe not. Are they children looking for a fun place to party? Or are they part of a well-executed plan? It's hard to say. But they have some sort of magical ability. Unless you didn't notice that none of your sensors tripped."

Henry scowled.

"Kind of genius," Lexus went on, grabbing another cookie. "Use magical teenagers to do your dirty work and leave chaos behind." He pointed again, this time at the couch-jumper who was now doing cartwheels through the room, knocking things over. "To cover up…something."

Henry shoved the cookie tin away. "What makes you think there's someone behind them?"

The gnome shrugged, eying the tin with a sad frown. "I've been around almost a thousand years, Henry. A group of teenagers like this can't organize much other than a walk to the store to buy more snacks. But who knows? Maybe this is a first. A gang of rowdy youths with a brilliant plan."

Henry watched the couch-jumper as she spun through the house, kicking end tables and knocking pictures off the walls. He let out a deep growl, causing Lexus to crack up.

"Funny that you come off as the grumpy old man here. Don't you remember how wild you were as a child? Even before you became a shifter, I would have sworn you had the spirit of a wolf inside you. Except back then you didn't need to grow fur and fangs to be a pain in the neck. Let me tell you a story…"

Henry groaned again, adjusted his vest, and snugged up his necklace while the gnome launched into the tale.

"Picture old Lexus as a child…nearly a millennium ago. When your civilization hadn't even been dreamed up yet. As a world of nearly ageless beings, Oriceran doesn't move as quickly as Earth. Eons pass without much new happening unless some lousy Atlantean decides to start a war."

Lexus hobbled to the side on his cane, making eye contact with Henry as he pulled several more cookies out of the tin. "Even so, everything looks different when seen through young eyes. One day, I was exploring the woods looking for the Gardener of the Dark Forest when—"

A loud *crash* from the screen brought the story to a wonderfully premature end. Henry and Lexus looked over to see the teenage girl reaching through a broken glass case to grab the object inside.

It was a smooth stone, flat and rounded, about the size of the girl's head. Etched into it was the shape of a lion and a lamb, facing one another. To the untrained eye, it looked like it might have come from a museum gift shop or someone's Etsy page. Henry's blood ran cold when he saw it.

Lexus, however, immediately changed his focus to something else. He finally looked toward the vehicle parking area. "The Ninja looks clean. Did you really manage to bring something back in one piece? I applaud you." He narrowed his eyes, looking closer. "Never mind. The fender is missing." He shrugged. "Still, a vast improvement in your driving skills or common sense. I'll take it. Give them hell, Master Neumann!"

Henry was already long gone, running through another

tunnel that had been bored through the hill. This one was smaller, narrower, and lit with glowing neon. He found a set of stairs and vaulted up them three at a time. In the draft of cool air rising from the cave, he felt the hairs on the back of his neck move. They were growing longer, coarser. Henry let out a low growl, trying to force the transformation down.

"I don't need that," he groaned. "Just need to stop them..."

He slammed through the door at the top, swung out a bookcase, and sent the volumes on the shelf flying to the floor. It was a hidden entrance to the cave. Pulling out the palm-sized device Lexus had nicknamed the egg due to its shape, he pointed it up into one corner of the ceiling in this room and hit a button. An alarm went off, screaming through this corner of the house.

A couple of teenagers suddenly sprang up from their hiding places and darted for safety. Or at least toward someplace where the terrible noise wouldn't damage their sensitive young ears.

One of them was the girl, cradling the stone artifact to her side. He caught a glimpse of her hair. A few locks had fallen out from the confines of her hood and knit hat combo. Dark hair, starting to go silver at the tips.

"Drow," Henry said. He gritted his teeth, knowing what would happen next.

In the already dimly lit room, a new pocket of darkness popped into existence as though bleeding through from some dark parallel dimension. The girl leaped into it and vanished.

Henry took a chance, sprinting toward the shadow. He

barreled straight through it, hoping to feel his shoulder hit something soft. Hoping to catch her before she was gone.

Instead, he was spat out on the other side as the shadow dissipated into the air. He tripped, hit the floor, and slid on his hip. Claws grew from the ends of his fingers, digging into the dense Persian carpet and causing him to stop.

He looked back, scanning the room. The girl was gone. The rest of her crew had somehow followed her into the shadow, or they had run for their lives, escaping through windows.

Henry sighed, aimed his egg again, and hit a different button. The lights came on, illuminating the destruction in the room. Pillows had been slashed, the stuffing thrown everywhere. A crystal decanter, a gift from his sister on his previous birthday, was in shards on the floor. At least it seemed like the one artifact was all that was missing. If they were garden-variety thieves, which was increasingly unlikely, they had glossed over such obviously valuable items as the original Monet on the wall in favor of a simple carved rock.

Except they had a Drow. A magical being who at least knew enough about her heritage to use shadow magic. They knew what they were doing. Mostly, at least.

Henry cursed and hobbled back downstairs, nursing his bruised hip. It seemed like diving full force into a shadow pocket without knowing what he'd hit wasn't the smartest idea.

Lexus was exactly where he had left him, standing at the screens. The cookie tin, which had still been a third of the way full when Henry ran off, was now empty.

"That looked like it hurt," the gnome commented. "It's

not often that someone bests you, Henry. Especially not in your own home." He arched an eyebrow, scratching his chin in thought.

Henry could only grin. "Not bested, Lexus. At least not entirely. Those kids were fast, but I'm smarter. Didn't you know I put a GPS tag on that relic?"

It was Lexus' turn to smile. "Brilliant, Master Neumann! Leaving it on display was a stupid idea, but at least you thought to tag it. Of course, I knew. I was more referring to the part where you fell on your ass."

"Hah hah." Henry squatted, trying to loosen up his legs. "Who was that girl, anyway? The rest of those kids were wild idiots. She was the leader. A Drow."

"Yes, I noticed. Whoever she is, she is clever. As for your GPS tag, Henry, she seems to have already found it and removed it."

"Damn!" Henry ran for the screen that showed the GPS signal, an unmoving blip outside the house. "How did she know it was there?"

"Another good question. One that must wait for an answer. In the meantime, I believe it's time to get myself to bed." The gnome moved away from the screens, leaning on his cane more than usual. Even with the extra support, he was limping.

Henry rushed to the older man's side, grabbing his arm for extra stability. "You're supposed to be retired, Lexus. All this time in a cold, damp cave can't be good for you."

"Chasing criminals all around the Pacific Northwest can't be good for *you*. We both have our jobs to do. Besides, who says I'm not retired? This is an amusement for me. I love supporting you on your runs and tinkering with your toys."

"You do a lot more than that." Henry gestured around the cave at all the strange and unique items. Things that had no copy on Earth or Oriceran. "You came up with all of this."

Lexus nodded and smiled, but there was weakness in his eyes. "Yes, and it's kept me young. Kept my mind moving. But no one is immune to time, Henry. No one."

CHAPTER THREE

The red Ducati glided through the night, reflecting street lamps and headlights. Henry held on tight for the ride, taking the corners slower than usual. After what happened to the Ninja the night before, he was in no hurry to wreck another one of these magnificent machines. It was only a matter of time, so why rush it?

There was a seedy bar off Perry Ave. on the north side of Bremerton. Not a place he enjoyed visiting, but sometimes it was necessary to slum it for a little while. Henry took the lesser-used Manette Bridge across the Port Washington narrows and made his way through side streets to reach his destination, the Alphabet Inn, a popular place for alcoholics and betting junkies.

As always, the parking lot was packed. Henry made an ugly face as he scanned the rows upon rows of rusted-out beaters. He pictured what the parking lot would look like a couple of hours from now. A bunch of drunks stumbling out, yanking their doors open without a care in the world what they hit.

So he made a wise choice and parked the Ducati up the road at the animal shelter. It was closed for the night. No security cameras. No problem with leaving the two-wheeled beast there for a short rest.

Henry tucked his helmet under his arm and strolled over to the Alphabet Inn.

It was pandemonium as soon as he walked inside. A wall of noise that almost seemed to push him back. The thick stench of cigarette smoke and stale beer. An emaciated man of indeterminate age immediately approached him, asking if he was looking to score. Henry planted a hand firmly on the guy's chest and shoved him away.

"Not sure exactly what you're offering. I know I don't want any of it."

He kept walking. A second later, his sixth sense tingled, and he whipped around in time to dodge a swing from the scrawny dealer. By inches, he missed having an empty bottle smashed over the back of his head.

Henry didn't get the chance to retaliate. A bouncer instantly grabbed the dealer by the throat and choke-slammed him to the floor. The huge bouncer glanced back at Henry.

"Looking for Sammy?"

Henry nodded. "Got some business."

The bouncer smiled. "He's at his usual post. Good to see you again, Neumann. You keeping out of trouble?"

Henry adjusted his riding jacket. "Hell no."

"Yeah, me neither. Life's too short, right? Head on back."

The crowd parted for Henry the rest of the way. He

strolled right through the middle of the place, completely unafraid and unchallenged. Really, he almost forgot he was even there. Something the bouncer said made him start thinking of Lexus.

Life's too short.

No one is immune to time.

Henry shook his head to dispel the dark thoughts. It didn't work, and he felt like an idiot for letting this bug him. He knew the lifespan of gnomes. Lexus had lived a long life and, as far as Henry knew, a happy one. There was no reason to be sad that it was coming to an end. Why get broken up about inevitabilities?

Except for the fact that it would be such an abrupt change. Henry had only been a part of Lexus' life for a small percentage of it, but he knew the old gnome would have been devastated if something happened to him.

On the flip side, Lexus had been a part of Henry's life for a much greater percentage of it. Losing him would be like losing a parent. Or, more accurately, like losing a part of his soul.

It didn't bear thinking about. The problem was, Henry knew it would force him to think about it a lot. Probably much sooner than he was afraid of.

It wasn't like him to stonewall a pretty girl, but he wasn't in the mood. So when one approached him, a gorgeous blonde who didn't fit the surroundings, he surprised himself by walking straight past her.

He didn't like this place. Get in, get out. That was the idea.

There was a VIP area in the back behind a set of

curtains. Sammy was sitting back there on his usual stool at the private bar, sipping a martini in a dirty glass. Two fidgety young guys stood beside him. One of them was counting out a wad of cash, his hands shaking so bad he kept losing his spot. Finally, he set the money down, and the two of them rushed away like they realized their flies were down.

Sammy let out a dry rasp of a laugh and spoke without turning around. "First-time betters. Virgins. Damn, I feel sorry for whatever girl ends up being their first time."

Henry approached the bar and sat. "Virgins? Those guys must have been in their thirties."

"Yeah, so?" Sammy slid his empty glass away and rapped his knuckles against the counter. "Maybe if they win big on this bet, they'll be able to afford one of my girls. Probably not, though. They thought they'd be clever and bet on the underdog. Psh." A bartender appeared out of nowhere, gracing Sammy with a fresh drink and whisking away the empty glass. "No way Ortiz is taking out Pendergast. No *way*."

Henry shrugged. "I have no idea who the hell Ortiz and Pendergast are."

Sammy gave him a look of supreme disgust, dipping his fingers in the martini and flicking some of it at Henry. "The two biggest fighters in MMA right now? Really? What, you don't got cable TV at that big ugly mansion of yours?"

"Cable? How old do I look? Ninety?"

Sammy grinned, showing a set of very grimy teeth. "So, you're not here to put a bet down. Clearly. Not that you need to. What'd you ride in on tonight, huh? A fucking unicorn?"

"Those don't exist." Henry narrowed his eyes, trying to remember if Lexus had ever told him any story about a horned horse. "I don't think."

"Jeez, my granddaughter sure thinks they do." Sammy rolled his eyes. "You shoulda seen her last birthday party. Unicorn this, unicorn that. Oh my lord. She even asked me to have a tea party with her and Bubbles, her favorite stuffed unicorn. Imagine me having a tea party. Huh? Hey, bartender! We got a guest here!"

The same guy reappeared, looking ashamed. Henry waved him away. Sure, he was thirsty. But he didn't trust anything about this bar, much less the drinkware or the cleanliness of the taps.

"So…" Sammy plucked the olive out of his martini and smashed it between his teeth. "I guess you're probably not here to get some horizontal refreshment, neither. So what is it? Information?"

Henry smiled. "You're good, Sammy. Maybe you should ditch this disreputable job and become a nice, friendly fortuneteller instead. I'd hate to have to crack your skull someday."

Sammy reached out, knocking a fist against Henry's dense, firm chest. "Yeah, I'd hate that too, kid. Probably crack my head like a damn peanut, right? So, what is it?"

Henry was about to talk, but another group of squirrely looking guys came up.

"Um… Sammy, sir? We'd like to put down some money."

"Yeah? Who on?" Sammy nudged Henry and mouthed the name "Ortiz."

"Five hundred on Pendergast," the head weasel replied.

Sammy winced. "Smart kid. What's the name?"

The "kid," who was probably in his late thirties, gave his information. Sammy took it down, sticking the cash in an envelope already bulging dangerously. He turned to look at Henry, but there was someone else there now, a young woman licking her lips nervously with a small stack of bills in her hand.

"Are you the bookie?" she asked.

Sammy sighed. "That's me. What'll it be, sweetheart?"

He didn't bother looking at her. Henry did, and he saw by the look in her eyes that she was struggling. Something was going very wrong in her world. She placed her bet. Henry side-eyed her the whole time, picking up on cues.

As soon as she stepped away, he almost opened his mouth to talk. Then a third party arrived right on cue, a goofy-looking kid. Actually a kid this time, probably no older than nineteen or twenty. He marched right up with forty dollars in his hand.

Without even letting the kid talk, Sammy shook his head. "Beat it. I don't need you."

The kid's face fell. "I've got good money here, mister. I'm a young, budding entrepreneur, and—"

"Lemme guess," Sammy interrupted. "You made a few bucks selling lemonade or mowing your neighbor's grass, and now you're looking to double up so you can afford a new Game Boy. See this?" He held up the envelope, which was already stuffed with thousands of dollars. "You think I need your pocket change, twerp? Get out of my face."

The crestfallen kid quickly backed away, his head hanging low. Henry hoped he remembered to tuck those twenties back into his pocket before some lowlife swiped them.

"Anyway, as we were saying…" Sammy reached behind the bar and pulled up a bowl of mixed nuts. He started munching, offering Henry some and receiving a headshake in response. "You were looking for some knowledge. Man's eternal quest, right? Always more shit you want to know. Why is the sky blue and all that. My granddaughter asked me that question the other day. You know what? I told her I have no idea."

"It has to do with the diffusion of electromagnetic energy in the atmosphere." Henry had second thoughts, reached for the nuts, then had third thoughts and brought his hand back empty, remembering a statistic about hand-washing at bars. "I need to know more about a gang."

"Yeah? Who are we talking about here? Those nocturnal weirdos in the city, what do they call themselves?"

"The Midnight Collective." Henry shook his head. "No. I'm not going after them. Not yet, anyway, and not at all unless they decide Seattle's too small a stomping ground and leak over into my domain. I'm after a gang of kids."

Sammy laughed, or maybe it was more accurate to say he wheezed in a way that sounded painful. Like air slowly let out of a balloon. "Kids? What the hell are you after *kids* for? And why are you suddenly looking at me like I got a dick growing out of my face?"

"You don't? Oh, that's just your nose." Henry set his helmet down on the bar. "My bad. Look, you don't need to know why I'm after them. Maybe it's better if you don't."

"Except I probably already do." Sammy fished a crushed pack of cigarettes out of his coat pocket, stuck one between his chapped lips, and lit it up. "They broke into your place, I'm guessing. Looks like they're getting bolder with who they go after. Moving up to bigger targets. You know, that kind of upward momentum and confidence is the kind of attitude we should be happy to see in the younger generation, don't you think?"

"Unless it involves them stealing my shit. Then all I want to see is their sad little faces in a mugshot. So, I guess this wasn't their first rodeo…"

Sammy scoffed. "Far from it, my friend. They've been jacking people all over town. And they've got a pretty smart MO. Make it look like a random act by a group of idiots. Party it up. But that's all part of the scam, right? Don't tell anyone I told you this, but every time they break into a place, only one or two items end up missing. Always something of big value. There's something else going on here, Henry. Someone big is pulling the strings on this one. Mark my words."

Henry waved in front of his face to dispel the wretched breath. "Oh, yeah. Consider them marked."

He left Sammy to drink soon after that and strolled back outside. Along the way, he found the worried young woman who had placed the bet earlier, whispering encouragement in her ear and discretely handing over a thick wad of cash. He had no idea what kind of trouble she was in. Maybe it was self-inflicted. Either way, he knew the kind of pain that showed in her eyes. He had felt it firsthand.

He left the bar and strolled up the road toward his Ducati.

Who the hell could be behind this op? Who could have enticed a bunch of teenagers with their whole lives ahead of them to act as their boots on the ground? Henry had been a teen once. He knew that stupidity and recklessness went with the territory. But this went beyond that.

Add one more thing to the growing list of problems in Henry's life.

CHAPTER FOUR

"I think that went rather well," said the voice of Lexus. Henry was on his way home from the Alphabet Inn, weaving around parked cars as he raced through the darkened streets. "I'm going to need a shower after that. I had no idea you were listening in, old man."

There was soft laughter through the earpiece. "That's my job, isn't it? To make sure you do yours properly? I'm not going to be around forever, but I'd still like to do everything I can."

"Stop talking like that." A green light went yellow then to red ahead of him, and Henry coasted to a stop. "We don't know how much longer you have. The age range is pretty big, right? Could be another twenty years. Maybe more."

"Let's not kid ourselves. Reality doesn't care about our feelings, Master Neumann. I suppose you know that better than anyone."

Visions of suffering flashed through Henry's mind as he gunned it through the green light. Memories of agony, shattered thoughts of torturous pain. Images of dark and restless nights spent tossing and turning through endless nightmares.

"I suppose I do." He turned a corner too sharply, nearly ditching the Ducati into a retaining wall. He came upright again, his heart thumping. He didn't want to trouble Lexus with yet another wrecked ride, nor did he want to visit his sister the surgeon for anything other than a few questions. "That's enough bad energy for one night, huh? How about we do something fun tomorrow?"

"Like catch the kids who stole that artifact?" There was a crunching sound. Lexus had gotten into more cookies. "Is that the kind of fun you mean?"

"Not quite. More like actual fun. Maybe even something that a normal person might do. And I won't take no for an answer."

"Well, then..." More crunching sounds. "I suppose I won't waste your time or mine by trying to talk you out of it."

No one is immune to time.

At 8:35 the next morning, Henry pulled onto the lower deck of the Bremerton ferry in the souped-up Lamborghini Aventador. The top was down so they could soak in the sun, and it was impossible to miss the looks they got from the other people getting out of their cars. That suited Henry just fine. If they were staring at the car, they might not notice that the older man hobbling along on his cane was much tinier than he ought to be.

"Nice ride, bro!" a young guy said. "Can I get a picture?"

Henry tossed him the finger guns. "Go ahead. You can even touch it if you want. Don't worry. Believe it or not, this is one of my cheaper rides. Good for a nice casual cruise around."

"No way, dude. If I had this ride, I'd never bring it on the ferry! What the hell kind of money do you have?"

Henry walked away and let the question float there. The kid was probably looking for a cool answer. Movie star, maybe, or sports hero. Somehow, telling people you were working to solve the energy crisis made them less likely to want your autograph or have your babies. Lexus usually liked to blame the dumbing down of America.

They climbed onto the upper deck and ambled around as the ferry hummed into life and started forward, leaving Bremerton behind in a swirling white wake. It was a beautiful clear day. A young couple with their two young kids were all excitedly pointing at something out in the water.

Lexus approached the railing, narrowing his eyes to stare out into the distance. "A pod of whales. Is that a humpback? My eyes aren't what they used to be."

Henry smiled, pulling out a pair of binoculars and handing them over. Lexus's eyes lit up. He grabbed the binoculars like they were the last cookie in the tin.

"Yes, a humpback. I knew it! Magnificent creatures." He pulled the binoculars down, staring at Henry suspiciously. "Wait a second. Why do you have these? People don't usually grab a set of these whenever they leave the house."

Henry patted the older man on the back. "What, you don't see my routine every morning? I go around grabbing all the stuff I need. Wallet, keys, phone, binoculars."

"If that's true, I'm less observant and you're even more insane than I thought." The gnome glanced over his shoulder. "I smell coffee. Shall we?"

"After you." Henry gestured at the doors to the inside section.

As they walked away, the young girl at the railing pointed and laughed. "Mommy, look at the funny little man!"

The mom quickly shoved her daughter's arm down, whispering harshly, "We don't say things like that, sweetie..."

Lexus, ever the incorrigible ham, turned and waggled his fingers at the child, who kept right on laughing despite the look of total horror on her mother's face.

"What a wonderful little girl." Lexus laughed as they entered the galley. "Everyone agrees on the fact that Atlanteans are the only magical race indigenous to Earth. I think that's incorrect. Humans are magical too, in their way. Through their imagination and their sense of wonder. It's a shame most people lose that when they grow up."

"We lose everything eventually," said Henry. "Like you said, no one and nothing is immune to time."

"Happiness dies." Lexus reached out, tapping on a glass case that displayed a traditional mask crafted by a local Native American tribe. "But so too does sadness. So too does pain. And so too does evil. Remember that always, Henry."

Henry looked away, fighting the tears that came to his eyes. He saw something strange happening to his right. Two young men with blue face tattoos stood very close together and acted shifty. Henry's sixth sense told him that some kind of trade was about to go down. Or maybe it already had. By the time he and Lexus ordered their coffees, the young men had parted ways, filtering off into different areas of the ship.

Henry's chauffeur was waiting for them past the gangway on the Seattle side. Henry traded keys with him.

"The black Lexus." The chauffeur smiled at the gnome. "As usual, sir."

"Good. Take care of the Lambo, Hugh. Wipe off any greasy prints you find on it. I might have given some kid permission to touch the doors."

Hugh nodded, heading back inside to wait his turn to board.

Henry and Lexus walked through the terminal and down into the parking lot. The gnome was already sniffing the air and patting his belly.

Henry hit the unlock button on his key fob, using the beeping sound to track down the right car in the crowded lot. "We'll get fish and chips later. After we work up an appetite."

"I thought we already did." Lexus opened the passenger door and hopped in, performing a clumsier, creakier version of the move a small child did when entering a car. "It had better be Ivar's. They have the best fish and chips. Besides, I like feeding the seagulls."

"Yup. Nothing better than loading those birds up so they can shit all over the place where people eat. Seattle's finest tradition." Henry drove out of the lot and headed north along the waterfront. "Nothing beats their tartar sauce, though."

"Don't forget the clams." Lexus reached into the glovebox and giggled like a schoolgirl when he saw the stash of granola bars. "Peanut butter chocolate chip! Obviously the best flavor. This should tide me over. Where are we going, anyway? Pike Place Market?"

"Maybe later. If you want more fish to go with your fish. Just be quiet and let me drive. Actually, never mind. You were telling me a story the other night when those kids were rampaging through the house. Bad timing, by the way. But I'd like to hear it."

Lexus stared longingly through the window as they passed Ivar's Fish Bar. "Forget it. You don't want to hear that tale. It was only an old man's reminiscence."

Henry almost argued, but then he realized there was no way Lexus would turn down telling a story. Not unless he didn't want to tell it. The old gnome was in a strange mood. It would have been hard for an outsider to tell, but he was quieter and more introspective than usual.

Henry drove and let the city pass them by.

It was a decently long drive to get where they were going. Long enough for Lexus to spout out about fifty different guesses. All of them were wrong. When they pulled into a field where a hot air balloon was waiting for them, though, it became obvious.

"So, this is why you brought the binoculars." Lexus gave Henry a strange look. "You know I don't like flying."

"That's because your only experience was when the witch sicced her pet gargoyle on you." Henry parked the car and shut off the engine.

Lexus went green. "It grabbed me by the arms and carried me a mile into the sky. I thought I was going to die that day."

They got out of the car, and Henry waved to the guys waiting by the balloon. "You deserved it, though. That's what you get for sneaking into her garden and stealing all her best flowers."

Lexus hobbled toward the balloon, cringing from the shameful memory. "I wanted to give them to the girl I liked. What was her name? I don't remember. I suppose that goes to show it wasn't worth it."

"Or maybe it's because that was all ancient history. Literally."

Lexus made a few more complaints, but once the balloon lifted and he got over the initial fear he glowed like the young, daring gnome he used to be. Soon enough they were treated to an amazing panoramic view. The glittering city, the waters of Puget Sound, and the vast glory of the rainforest with Mount Rainier rising high above, its peak covered with an eternal snowfall.

Henry took in the sights and enjoyed them, but this wasn't for him. This was for Lexus. Seeing the old gnome so happy and animated yet shriveled and gray filled Henry with equal parts of joy and sorrow.

He knew how time worked. He knew what a son of a bitch it could be and how it eventually ravaged everything. He wished he could gain control of it, at least for a little while, and live this day all over again.

His phone buzzed in his pocket. A notification from his shifter app.

It seemed like someone was organizing a run.

CHAPTER FIVE

Henry leaned against a tree, his heart beating faster from the expectation of pain. The transformation was already trying to start. With his newly enhanced eyes, he could make out the sign standing in the dark thirty feet away. **Olympic National Park—Hoh Rain Forest.**

Quite a jaunt from home, but well worth it. Details jumped out of the darkness. The dark, alien trees covered in their blankets of green moss. The rich smell of decay in the air. The subtle scratching of a small animal making its way through the undergrowth. He pulled out his phone and checked the app one last time. Red dots filled the area around him, converging on a central location.

Henry pushed the transformation down, quickly dropped his gym bag, and stripped off his clothes. He folded each garment neatly and tucked them away, using this meditative process to keep the change at bay.

Eventually, though, it was time to open the floodgates.

His heart rate skyrocketed as he let the change rip through him. Immense pain filled his body from the stretching of skin, the grating of bones, and the powerful bulging of muscles. This was the part he feared—the sheer agony. It was over almost as soon as it began. He crossed a threshold into a place where everything felt right. His mind was finely tuned, his body was full of power and grace.

The wolf that once was Henry, bristling with a stripe of silver fur down its spine, reared back and howled mournfully across the night. Without waiting for a response, he took off into the trees. His reflexes and his sight worked in perfect harmony. He flowed through the forest almost like liquid, moving silently, darting under logs and leaping over boulders.

A chorus of howls soon joined the call he had sent out. Dozens of them sounded from all corners of the night. Henry no longer needed an app to tell him where to go. He followed the howls and his instincts. In a moment, he was suddenly aware of another wolf sprinting alongside him. Then another, and another, until the majority of the pack ran on either side.

<hr>

Clint dropped the joint onto the ground, backing slowly down the road. The first howl sent chills through his body, a primal fear overtaking him. As soon as he heard the other howls, he quickly turned and ran back toward his car, coughing the smoke out of his lungs.

He dropped the keys and fell to his knees, his hands scrabbling wildly through the dirt. He found them and opened his car, jumping sideways into the front seat and tucking his feet up safely as he reached out to pull the door shut, certain that at any second a wolf would grab hold of his ankles and shake him around like a chew toy.

Eventually, he sat up, shaking his head and laughing at the thrill. "Musta been coyotes. There aren't wolves out here, right? Coulda swore that sounded like wolves." He thought back to the joint he had dropped only half-smoked. "Shit, maybe I should lay off the weed for a bit. Hearing things."

Nothing would ever feel as freeing as this. Sometimes, late at night while he was cruising the main roads of Bremerton on one of his motorcycles, Henry was able to come close. Still, the power of a machine, a separate entity beneath you, was no match for feeling that power in your muscles and surging through every cell of your being.

Like liquid shadows, the other wolves fell in and out around him. Some mavericks went off on their own and came back in. Others stuck around, following each other close. In this way, the pack made its way through the untamed wilds, occasionally leaping over a narrow hiking trail. At one point they crossed through the headlights of a parked ranger vehicle, but the ranger himself was fast asleep, napping on his patrol.

Eventually, Henry sensed that he was nearly alone. Only one other wolf was beside him at the moment, a massive gray one. The alpha of the pack, a shifter named Hatch Latham. Other than Lexus and his sister, Hatch was one of the only other beings in existence who knew all of

Henry's secrets. He had been there since the beginning, suffering right alongside Henry as the dark families put them through the first transformation.

He and Hatch didn't talk much these days. They barely needed to. They had already been through everything together. They had already suffered through ten lifetimes of pain at each other's side.

It was a new moon, Henry noticed. The opposite of the full moon that movies and books all seemed to think his kind needed for the transformation. It was dark in the forest tonight, and yet nothing was lost to his vision. Every last bug and rodent leaped into view. Any animal with half a brain turned and ran as soon as they caught wind of the pack's presence. But a hunt wasn't what they were after now.

They wanted nothing more than a chance to stretch their legs—and their minds. A run like this was the very best place in all of creation to reflect on your life, to consider your problems. The forest at night was akin to a church. A sacred place where a shifter could commune with the universe.

Tonight, there was more to ponder than ever before. Henry was right in the middle of a huge project at work. The largest of his whole career. Quite possibly his magnum opus, the legacy he would leave behind. Other than all of the criminals he stopped, of course, but if things went according to plan no one would ever connect him to any of that.

There was also the small problem of the missing artifact. Saying that the Pictish stone was dangerous was an understatement, and in the hands of a bunch of children...

Chances were those kids would never be able to figure out how to use the artifact. Even with a young Drow who was already well-versed in shadow magic leading them, it seemed unlikely the stone would be trouble in their hands.

Unfortunately, it wasn't their hands Henry was worried about.

They had a boss, someone behind the scenes. It could be someone they were loyal to or someone paying them a bunch of money. Either way, Henry was afraid the stone would change hands very soon. What happened with it after that was anyone's guess.

All he knew was that Lexus was afraid. The old gnome was good at hiding it. He had almost ten centuries of experience under his belt, and putting on a calm mask was easy for him. But Henry knew Lexus too well to be fooled.

Such a shame that he might spend his last days terrified of a future he would never see.

The only course of action, then, was to get the stone back before anyone got hurt.

All of that seemed so far away right now, though. Out here, sprinting through the wilderness with the pack, Henry could almost forget his problems. There was nothing but the kiss of the wind, the tickle of leaves flowing past his snout. When he shifted, it wasn't only his body that changed. His mind changed as well. Things became simpler. He didn't lose sight of his goals, fears, or desires. It was simply easier to control things.

He ran alongside Hatch. The wolves looked at one another, starlight reflecting off their eyes. Everything they might want to say passed between them with that simple glance. They weren't the only shifters around, but in a way, they were still the last of their breed. Hatch knew who he was even in wolf form, and Henry knew who he was.

Out of their original group, those turned by the dark families in that horrific chapter of Henry's life, all had either gone AWOL or died out over the years in some bloody battle.

As for the rest of the wolves around them tonight, they could be anyone. The bag boy at the grocery store. The old lady who worked at the library. Hell, one of them might even be someone famous. An actor or a rockstar.

Out here, they were all the same. Sure, there was a pack mentality. The alpha and the followers. Other than that, none of them held a higher station than any other. They were like one organism spread across many bodies. A single mind with a single purpose.

Run and be free.

All good things come to an end. Eventually, everyone had to return to reality. One by one the wolves began to leave the pack. The forest became emptier and quieter. Finally, it was Henry's turn to break away. He got his bearings and ran back toward the entrance to the woods, finding his trail and following his nose. At the same time, he paid close attention to his surroundings. The last thing he wanted was for some other wolf to see what came next.

It was unlikely to happen. They all had an understanding and a desire to keep this beautiful and terrifying part of their lives from interfering with who they were the rest of the time.

When he was close to where he'd stashed his clothes, Henry started to transform back into a human. It was like a balloon deflating. Henry was a strong guy. He kept himself fit with the gym area in the cave. Still, coming back into human form was always jarring. For a moment you felt as fragile as a twig.

By the time he reached his bag, naked in the night breeze, he felt like himself again.

"Whoa, dude…"

He turned and saw the stoner standing there, the cherry at the end of his joint glowing in the dark. Other than that, he could make out nothing other than a silhouette with his now-human eyes. The skunky smell of marijuana was plain, though.

The stoner took a puff. "Are you really naked right now, man?"

Henry unzipped his bag and pulled his clothing on. "None of your business."

"Hey man, it's cool. I'm all about getting back to nature and all that cool shit. But *dude*, I gotta say this a shock for me. What are you, a Wiccan or something? Are you in, like, a sex cult?"

Henry shot the guy a look. "Who's asking?"

"The name's Clint." The stoner lifted his foot and snubbed out the joint on the underside of his shoe. "I guess I shoulda listened to myself an hour ago and left. But man, I thought I heard wolves, and I kinda wanted to investigate. Did you hear any wolves?"

Henry stared at the guy. "Do you think I'd be running around in these woods naked if wolves were around? Get a grip. And do yourself a favor and cut back on the wacky tobaccy."

"Hey, man, it's legal now. You want some? You got any money? Shit ain't free. Not like it grows on trees. More like on little bushes or some shit, right?" Clint let out the perfect spaced-out stoner laugh.

Henry figured the guy wasn't a danger to anyone except maybe himself. He picked up his bag and headed back down the road toward his bike.

Next stop, Seattle. If he drove fast, he could make it to the hospital before his sister's late shift ended.

CHAPTER SIX

After a brief stop at the hospital Starbucks, where he half-expected to find his sister, Henry headed deeper into the building and approached a nurse's station in the section where his sister worked. Before he had a chance to page her, Aspen appeared.

People often said she was pretty much the female version of Henry. That was an outsider's perspective. They looked almost identical, but the similarities didn't go much deeper than that. Where Henry was impatient and brash, Aspen was calm and steady, traits that served her well in her role as a chief pediatric surgeon.

It took a special kind of person to be a surgeon, but the work on children was a whole different ballgame. Sure, Henry was bringing new scientific innovations to the world, but he felt like his job and contribution to the world paled in comparison with hers. Of course, Aspen didn't see it that way. She seemed to have it in her head that Henry was a hotshot who thought he was better than anyone else, and that was why he was living in the mansion while she stayed at a small apartment in the city.

Henry could never come up with the words to convince her otherwise, to let her know that deep down he was still a scared kid caught in the clutches of the dark families, and the thought of changing his life any more terrified him.

In the end, she was his sister, and he was her brother. He didn't think she would ever forsake him, no matter what, and it was that stability he needed now more than ever.

Henry held out the Starbucks cup. "Your favorite."

She took the cup and brought it to her lips, blowing through the little sipping hole. "A latte. Better be with almond milk this time."

Henry sighed. "I got it with coconut milk *once*, kid, and that was because they ran out of almond. Are you busy or what?"

"Let me see." She checked her watch. "The first ferry from Bremerton doesn't leave for another hour, which means you had to drive all the way around. That's a long way."

He thought back to his run through the rainforest and the reckless speed he used to get here in time. And she thought he was only coming from Bremerton. "You have no idea."

"I guess you didn't do all that driving just to buy me a coffee." She popped the plastic lid off, sipped, and made a face. "You'd think after all those lawsuits they'd stop giving people coffee that was the same temperature as lava. Tasty, though. Good job, you little whippersnapper."

"Hey, you're younger than I am."

"Yet somehow you're still my little brother. How does that work?" She blew on her coffee, making waves in the foam that came dangerously close to spilling over the side of the cup. "So, what is it? You want to talk?"

Henry looked around at the silent, desolate halls. "Not here. Do you have time to go for a walk?"

"Got nothing else scheduled. No emergencies. Sure, we can take a little stroll around. But if I get paged, I'm shoving my coffee at you and hightailing it back here."

They started walking down the hall. "No deal. I don't care if some kid comes in here with a fence post through his chest. You're mine for the next fifteen minutes."

She made a face. "Dark! Don't joke about that kind of stuff. I know you've suffered a lot, but that doesn't give you the right to give me flashbacks here."

"You're right." Henry pushed down the anger, the urge to tell her she had no idea what suffering was. "I only want to talk to you."

"Then talk."

Henry glanced around again. There was no one here, but that only made the vibe of the hospital even eerier. He wanted to wait until they were outside.

They went out through the atrium, walking under some crazy hanging art installation of stained glass fish. Exiting through a side entrance, they headed out onto Penny Drive, a road that led straight through the hospital campus with offshoots and footpaths heading every which way.

Henry and Aspen walked in a random direction and soon strolled in the middle of a green-painted bike lane.

Henry kept looking over his shoulder, which made

Aspen laugh. "Don't worry. No one's out riding their bikes around at this time of night."

"I don't know. This is Seattle after all." As soon as they reached a spot where there was a sidewalk, he hopped up onto it. "A lot of weirdos in this city."

"There's one more every time you decide to grace us with your presence." Aspen took a long slurp of coffee. "So, how's life?"

"Um…" He chewed his lips, trying to figure out what to tell her. "I just finished another run. It's been a while, and I needed to stretch my legs. The Hoh Rain Forest this time."

"Mm!" Aspen hummed around a mouthful of foam. She swallowed. "Beautiful place. Kind of spooky. I'd love to go back, but the life of a surgeon doesn't have a lot of time off. And it's soooo far away. I'd never make it there and back, not if I wanted to do any proper hiking. Did you see Hatch?"

Henry nodded, glancing behind him at a pair of head-lights. "He's doing fine, seems like. Not that we do a whole lot of talking."

"Maybe you should. Catch up a bit."

Henry shrugged. They were heading toward lights, but they were still in the middle of the campus with trees on either side. A dark little hideaway. "I don't know. It would just be us reminding each other of everything we lost. Not really worth it, you know?"

He must have been acting fidgety because she suddenly reached out and touched his arm. "Is everything all right, Henry?" She laughed. "Silly question, right? When's the last time everything was all right? Probably not since we were kids, before…" She sighed. "What I'm trying to say is, I poke around inside people's bodies for a living. I do things to save lives. You can't get much more high-pressure than that. So whatever you're dealing with, I can help share the burden. You know?"

"Yeah, I know." He didn't think telling her about the break-in was necessary. She was a human, untainted by magic. He couldn't help that she knew all about his life as a shifter. He wouldn't want to change that, anyway.

There were things she didn't need to know. Namely, there were artifacts in the world with another power, and in the wrong hands, they could easily bring about the end of everything.

He decided to change to a different subject. "It's Lexus. He's getting old."

Aspen tipped her coffee cup back, trying to get the last of the foam. "He has been ever since you've known him."

"I mean, he's getting *old*. He's slowing down a lot, and he keeps talking like he knows he doesn't have much time left. I'm worried."

Her hand had never left his arm. Now, she squeezed it tighter. "I don't suppose a human doctor would be much help for him. Not with…whatever his physiology is. Not that I wouldn't mind getting a look, but I would think he needs someone from Oriceran. Someone magical. A magic doctor. Is that a thing?"

"It is, but Lexus won't hear of it." Henry kicked a piece of trash, a plastic bag, then cursed when it wrapped around his foot and stayed there. "He says there's nothing wrong with what's happening. Every road ends, and no journey is complete unless it *has* an ending, yadda yadda…"

He swore again, tearing the bag away with his hand and

throwing it as hard as he could. It went about three feet, then drifted slowly back to the ground.

"*Fuck!*" he shouted. "Stupid piece of shit, get out of here!"

He ran at the bag, kicking and punching it as it fell.

"Yup, I can tell that run did you a lot of good." Aspen came over and rubbed his back. "You know, Lexus isn't wrong. It's not like he can live forever. Unfortunately, Henry, death is a natural part of life. Believe me, I wish it wasn't, but I have to face reality every day. Eventually, you're going to have to face reality with Lexus."

Henry shook his head, caught the bag, and shoved it into his pocket. "There has to be a way. It's like he's sick of living. Like he's giving up. He's not fighting."

"Because he already fought and won." Aspen patted his back. "He got to live a long life, and he probably already lived longer than he would have otherwise. Because he found you, and you gave him purpose. There's nothing wrong with shuffling off this mortal coil when the time comes. The only thing that matters is what we do along the way.

"I can tell this whole pep talk isn't doing anything. I have an idea. How about we have dinner together, the three of us?"

Henry was in the middle of thinking the proposition over when Aspen's beeper went off.

"Shit." She pulled the device off her belt and looked at it. "I have to go. Look, Henry, I don't want to go to bed tonight, or I guess this morning, worrying about you. You need more friends."

They hugged quickly. Henry forced himself to smile. "Says the chick who pretty much lives at work."

"Whatever. Just take care of yourself. I think you really should catch up with Hatch. Probably do you both some good." The last words were delivered as a shout over her shoulder as Aspen jogged away, headed back to her post.

"Yeah, maybe." Henry headed in the opposite direction, out toward the main road. He pulled the bag out of his pocket and stuffed it into the first trash can he came across.

This was a quiet area of Seattle. Other than the ambulances that sometimes screamed through, it was usually a restful place. Small houses and apartment buildings lined streets shaded by evergreen trees and the sky always seemed to be overcast, even on the warmest summer day.

At the moment, everything was silent. The night still reigned, the cool nocturnal breeze blowing down the road. Henry almost felt the urge to turn again, to run wild here in this playground, to take ownership of the night and preside over it in his bestial form. But the world couldn't know what he was. He didn't care so much about himself, especially now when Lexus' days were numbered.

He cared about Aspen. She deserved a normal life.

He spent a lot of time wondering where he would be and what he would be doing if she didn't exist. His life would be vastly different without that one remaining connection to the human world. He might have gone feral, racing off to some hidden corner of the Earth the way so many of his brood had done. Instead, he remained caught between two worlds. He and Hatch Latham, stuck in a moment in time.

There was at least a small amount of comfort in stagnation.

Now that the stone was in the wind, Henry hoped he could set things straight and get back to whatever passed for an ordinary life.

CHAPTER SEVEN

It took a long time for Bechtel Stryker to get used to that empty feeling inside himself. Centuries, in fact. What do you do when someone has stolen such an important part of who and what you are? He could speak from experience on that. First, you got mad. Then you fell victim to a long period of sorrow and dejection. For him, it had lasted nearly a hundred years.

Then you fell into some state halfway between. The anger still burned but was controlled. A faint ember deep inside that, at a moment's notice, he could stoke into a raging blaze.

The sorrow was still there too, for what he had lost and would never regain. He was closer than ever to finding the stolen essence of his people, but the world as it had been, bloody and dark and so beautifully *simple*, was dead forever.

Or was it?

Stryker smiled as he made his way through Pioneer

Square, his jeweled walking stick clicking over the herringbone-patterned bricks. On a bench near the totem pole, a homeless man sat crying as he searched through a tattered old bag.

Stryker approached the man, smiling. "Nice night, isn't it? Although it doesn't seem very nice for you. What seems to be the trouble, my friend?"

The homeless man looked up, his toothless mouth hanging open. "Damn kids. Stole all my panhandling money. Some assholes told me Colman Beach was a good place to beg. Nuh-uh." He sobbed again, turning the bag upside-down and shaking it. Something fluttered out, a small rectangle of white paper.

Stryker crouched to pick it up. It was from a fortune cookie. He read it aloud. "'Something wonderful is waiting just around the corner.' Somehow, I doubt that's true. This world is an unforgiving place, is it not?"

"It is, mister. It is." The homeless man rocked back and forth, completely miserable.

"Colman Beach you said?" Stryker looked vaguely east, narrowing his eyes. "Quite a distance. I assume you must have walked it. Those shoes of yours are in rough shape." He gestured at the flapping bits of rubber clinging to the man's feet by a few leather shreds. His grimy toes were poking out the ends.

Over the years, many different mental health institutions had closed down in Seattle. The rumor was that most of the patients had simply been let loose on the streets. The homeless crisis in the city was only getting worse over time, not better. Simultaneously, the profits of the mega-rich were skyrocketing. Corporations were making more money than ever before.

And people liked to tell Stryker this world was worth preserving.

He smiled sadly as he stood and pulled some money out of his pocket. "This is fifty dollars. I trust you'll spend it wisely. On second thought, I know you'll probably waste it on momentary pleasures. Either way, it's yours."

He slipped the money into the man's bag.

"Oh, thank you, mister." The guy tried to grab Stryker's hand, but he pulled it away. "Thank you, *thank you.*"

"Don't grovel to me. We're all men trying to find our way in this world, aren't we?" Stryker tapped his walking stick on the ground. "We're all trying to find our way back home. Except we can never find it. It's gone forever. A man can never stand in the same river twice, and he can never really go home either."

The man was staring up at him curiously. "Are you a professor or something?"

"No. Just a fellow trying to find his way underground."

The homeless man's eyes lit up. "Yes! Underground. You'll want Bill Speidel's. It's right over there. Right behind you!" He pointed at a building not far away.

Stryker turned to look. "Ah, yes! There it is. Thank you very much. That piece of information was worth fifty dollars at least."

He walked away, skipping past the front of Bill Speidel's Underground Tour. He already knew exactly where he was going, but it was best to let the homeless man think he had been a big help. It would stop his incessant blathering.

Stryker went around the back and into the alley,

making a disgusted face at all the trash and filth that had accumulated there. He found a set of stairs going down to a locked door. With a single hammer-like blow of his fist, he shattered the lock and stepped through the door.

He whistled as he made his way through the dark. The only light down here was what bled in through the grates overhead from street lamps and building lights, distant and dim. This was a place of shadows and dripping water. Most of the city's homeless were too terrified of the law to enter this underground domain, so it was pretty much a free range.

The farther Stryker went, the deeper into the past he got. His eyes adjusted to the deepening dark, the magic in his blood turning the place almost as bright as day. The ancient stone walls were plain to see, along with the rusted implements of the past piled up wherever they had fallen in their decay. There were signs of fire everywhere, scorch marks and soot.

Soon enough he broke free into places that no one had entered in a hundred years. No one except for the intrepid band of youngsters that now called this place home.

He found them in a small alcove they had kitted out as an entertainment room, using power hijacked from the street above. Sandbags on the floor protected the TV and gaming consoles from the ravages of the water that trickled through the place constantly. They gamed in the dark, with the volume turned down low.

"Good evening," Stryker announced, taking his jacket off and hanging it on a nearby peg. "The only way I could find to get down here was a locked door in the back of Bill Speidel's. How do all of you get down here?"

A young male Drow stood and approached. "That's our secret, old man. We survive by hiding our actions from the world, so don't start thinking we'll tell you everything."

Stryker stared at the young man. When the teenager looked like he was on the verge of pissing himself, Stryker smiled.

"Fair enough. You have to protect yourselves. Although I do hope you'll learn to respect me more, Wexell. After all, my money is the only thing keeping you from begging for food in the streets. Or stealing it and getting caught.

"You're different, Wexell. Just like your girlfriend over there. 'Different' doesn't work out so well. The world will always try to crush you. It's up to us to crush the world before it has a chance. On that note, show me what you've procured."

The teenagers all scrambled, suddenly animated. They gathered up their wares. In the meantime, Stryker took another look around the place. The kids had managed to gain all kinds of ill-gotten goods over the years. They weren't stealing power with any ordinary cable or conduit. They were using a magitech antenna, sucking the juice straight out of the air. Another antenna was in use to get a Wi-Fi signal, but Stryker assumed they were probably getting that from whatever coffee shop stood above them. There was no shortage of those in Seattle.

In a moment, they'd laid out all of the items at his feet. Someone switched on a lamp so he could see better. Stryker scanned the items. They were all quite beautiful and interesting, including an egg sculpture that radiated peculiar energy. Stryker thought it might be Fabergé, but more likely it was a knockoff.

"Interesting. Which is my code word for 'not what I'm looking for.'" He touched the egg with his toe. "This, though… You might want to look into selling it. If it's real, you can get a pretty penny, even if you go through a fence. Still, not what I want. Did you not find anything else? Come on, now. I asked for artifacts, and what is *this*?"

He indicated an ugly beige slab.

Another Drow came forward. The girl, Ellie. As much as Wexell tried to act tough, Stryker had an idea that she was more of the leader of the group. As soon as she stepped up, the rest of the scared kittens took several steps back and looked away.

Ellie blew a lock of silver-tipped hair out of her eyes. "That's an Atari 800 computer. It's old as hell."

"Relative to you, maybe." Stryker reached out with his walking stick and tapped her on the arm. "I know what it is, sweetie. It's worth nothing to me. You can buy one on eBay for less than a hundred bucks, and it won't be covered with mouse turds. I assume you have something more for me?"

Indeed, she held something under her arm. It looked like a boring old stone. Maybe they used it for a doorstopper. But Stryker was desperate.

As soon as she turned the thing over, he grinned. He stepped forward and took it from her hands, feeling the weight, running his fingers over the engravings.

It looked right. The right style, probably the right era. It was close.

"Very good." He handed it back to her. "Very, very good. Keep looking. Especially for anything that remotely resembles this piece."

Ellie narrowed her eyes. "Don't you want it?"

"No, you keep it." He looked around. "Nice place you have here. Bone-chillingly cold, ugly, and desolate. But nice nonetheless."

He laughed and stepped out of the room, whistling again.

Wexell went to shut the door, shaking a little. "What did he mean by that? Is he trying to make us feel bad about ourselves, or what?"

Ellie scoffed and waved it off. "Guys like that are always trying to make you feel bad about something, right? Forget him. We'll keep taking his money and doing what we do."

She looked down at the stone in her hands. Funny. It seemed like nothing to her. It *looked* like nothing. So, why had she grabbed it in the first place? She was glad she did because Stryker liked it. Still, the question remained.

It was a feeling she got when she was close to the thing. A little tickle, not strong enough for her to analyze. Apparently, the big man felt it too. He knew something about this stone, and he wasn't letting on what that was.

There was something special about it.

"Whatever." She turned away from the door. "Who's hungry?"

A chorus of excited voices went up, and they all rushed together into the next room. This was the only spot in their underground domain that had adequate ventilation and old pipe going up to street level, so they used it as a kitchen. Wexell lit the camp stove, and Benjie started opening cans.

The smell of frying Spam soon filled the space, but Wendy ruined it a moment later when she cracked open one of her cans of sardines and stunk everything up.

"Gross!" Benji said. "What is that, mustard sauce? Fish with mustard! Who eats that?"

Wendy flicked some of the yellow sauce at him. "I do. And you're gonna eat my fist if you don't shut up. This crap's good for you. Omega 3s and shit like that."

"More like oh, mega *deez.*"

"Deez?" Wendy tilted her head in confusion. "Deez what?"

Ellie quickly clamped a hand over Benji's mouth. "You don't want to ask that question, trust me."

Once they'd cooked the food, a delectable array of canned meats, Minute rice, and cheese product from a spray can, it was back to the entertainment area to continue their game. There was a tournament bracket going on in a fighting game, and this was the final match between Benji and another kid named Davis. They all squeezed in together by the TV, trying to keep their excited shouting to a minimum.

"You don't think we're gonna have to move out of here, do you?" Wexell asked.

Ellie glanced at him. "Why do you say that?"

It was hard to see much of Wexell's expression. The only thing she saw was how the TV light reflected off his eyes. "I don't know. This Stryker guy... he's different. He's on some kind of quest, you know? He isn't just looking for money."

"I guess not. But hey, if things start to change, maybe it'll be for the better. We've been stuck down here for three years now. Sunlight's already hard enough to come by in this city, and we're spending most of our time underground waiting for night to fall so we can go robbing houses. Maybe…"

"Maybe what?"

The game momentarily stole Ellie's attention. Benji, who had been ahead at first and poised to win the tournament, had suddenly choked. Now, Davis had landed a few big hits on him, bringing his health bar down dangerously low. The atmosphere in the room went tense. Ellie noticed that her hands were getting warm and sweaty.

She looked at Wexell. "Maybe it's time we stopped working for guys like Stryker and figured out how to work for ourselves. We could move up in the world. We really could."

He shook his head. "That's a pipe dream, El. Always will be."

She was about to launch into a speech, but all of a sudden she felt like she'd laid both hands on a hot stove burner. She yelped in pain and dropped the stone to the ground, where it landed with a heavy thud, still radiating massive amounts of heat against her leg.

Ellie quickly grabbed a nearby towel, doused it with water from a bottle, and wrapped it around the rock. There was a hiss, a puff of steam, and suddenly the heat went away. The stone went from burning hot to room temperature in a few seconds.

Benji had paused the game, and everyone was staring at her.

"What the hell was that?" someone asked.

Ellie wondered the same thing. She found her bag and stuffed the stone inside. Apparently, letting it sit in your hands was a bad idea.

It was time to learn more, and she knew Stryker wasn't about to tell her anything.

CHAPTER EIGHT

The clouds were low over Seattle today, their wispy streamers wrapped around the plate glass and steel of Neumann Tower. Henry headed into the lobby, finally pulling down his hood and removing the hat and sunglasses. He took his hoodie off and, in a few seconds, transformed from a random grunge punk on the streets to a spiffy business person.

"Morning, Mr. Neumann," the older woman at the front desk said. "It's a nice one isn't it."

Henry took his coffee from her with a smile. "If by 'nice' you mean gloomy and ominous, it sure is. A beautiful day by Seattle standards. A day for new happenings, don't you think?"

He pointed at her dramatically as he headed for the elevators.

She pursed her lips. "Yeah, maybe. Like, maybe I'll finally get a raise. Right?"

Henry laughed. "Anything's possible, Glenda! Let's find out how this latest gambit works out for us, huh?"

The smile dropped off his face as he entered the elevator. The smile was a mask like any other, easily pulled on and off, a way to hide. For men like Henry, every day was Halloween. Every day was a masquerade ball. No one needed to know the constant turmoil inside, which was at a fever pitch now.

It did seem like a day for happenings. Henry hoped he was wrong about that.

The elevator climbed toward the heavens, stopping a few times along the way to let people on or off. Henry shared banter with his employees, putting his sunglasses back on so he could discreetly glance at their nametags and use their names in the conversation. There was too much going on at Neumann Technologies these days and far too many people wandering the halls for him to remember all their names.

The old days were dead and gone.

At the top floor, Henry stepped off the elevator and into his private domain, an office space that took up an entire floor. The security stations spread throughout the lower floors were only nerve bundles, tertiary pieces of the puzzle. The brain of the operation was up here. From this place, Henry could control the whole building.

It was his custom to walk a lap around the place before settling in at his desk. He moved slowly, taking in the views through the huge windows. Through the thick cloud cover, he caught small glimpses of Puget Sound and the city streets below him. The tops of the other tall buildings around Seattle jutted through, a floating forest of monoliths in the sky.

Henry let his thoughts wander away from Lexus and

the break-in at home. It was easier to do now that he was in his real happy place, the quiet vastness of his office, where he was free to stop being Henry Neumann the secret shifter and instead become Henry Neumann the brilliant inventor.

He reached his desk and leaned down to turn his computer on. His eye caught something sitting on the back corner of the desk surface. Did he get a new paperweight? Did Susie, his assistant, bring him one he hadn't asked for?

Henry stood back up to get a better look. His eyes went wide when he saw that it was the stone that the girl had stolen from his house. He would know those etchings anywhere. The lion and the lamb, their lines sharp and crisp despite centuries of aging and weathering.

Now that he knew it was there, he could almost feel the strange power radiating from it. Despite his shifter curse he had no real magical aptitude, but some forces couldn't be denied or ignored. In the case of the stone, the aura it gave off was so subtle he could almost chalk it up as psychosomatic. Except he realized that he had felt it since he left the elevator, despite not knowing the stone was here.

The soft hum of barely contained power. If his theories about the stone were correct, it might contain every bit as much energy as an atom. If the right person found it and figured out how to split it, the force might obliterate his world as he knew it.

Henry was already facing the storage locker behind his desk chair when the lights in his office suddenly went dim. Shadow leaked in from nowhere, swirling and overlapping into areas of stark black like a light show from a nightclub in hell.

A large puff of smoke appeared, bobbing around aimlessly. It stopped on the other side of the desk, and the Drow girl stepped out, staring straight at Henry. Her hands were at her sides, but she held no weapons. However, he knew she might have something concealed in her jacket.

Henry had already reached into his locker, past the extra suit jackets, and into the hidden compartment at the back. He held a sword ready, watching the girl.

He licked his lips. "How'd you get in here, anyway? My security…"

"Isn't set up to detect magicals," the girl finished for him.

Henry laughed. "Actually, it is. Do you think I'm some kind of a moron? That I'd leave myself vulnerable to attack?"

The girl shrugged and reached out to play with the Newton's cradle on the desk. "I guess you need to beef up your defenses against shadow magic. Ditto for that big ugly thing you call a house over in Bremerton."

"So, it is you."

She looked at him like he was an idiot. "No shit. How many kids my age are running around disappearing and reappearing from puffs of smoke? I thought you were supposed to be smart. You know, a hero of science. All that crap about 'saving the world from itself.' The energy crisis and stuff."

She laughed and spread her hands.

"You don't need the sword, by the way. If I wanted to fight you, I probably would have appeared at your back.

The element of surprise. Just saying. The name's Ellie, by the way."

"Cool. Good to know." Henry took a step back, maintaining his stance. "But I'll just hold onto it for now. Can't be too careful when I've got weird little Drow ninjas warping around."

She laughed, pulling a Post-it note off his monitor. "So, you know what I am. Cool. By the way, don't forget to call Steve back at noon."

She flicked the note away, letting it flutter to the floor like the world's most boring confetti.

Henry gritted his teeth. "Fuck Steve."

She raised her eyebrows. "If that's the way you swing, bro, go for it. I might be a pain in the ass, but I have an open mind. By the way, you asked the first most obvious question already. How did I get in here? But you didn't follow it up."

"Fine." Henry stood straight, lowering the sword but keeping his grip tight on the handle, his muscles tensed and ready for a potential fight. "Why are you here?"

"Great question. It's about this lump of crap." She picked up the stone and tossed it over. Henry jumped out of the way, barely avoiding having his toes smashed. "I noticed how you didn't bother trying to catch it. So, you already know this isn't any ordinary rock. It isn't going to crack or break that easily. What else do you know about it?"

Henry bent and scooped up the rock, grinning at her and ignoring the low-level hum that radiated through the bones of his hand. "I know it's heavy. Probably weighs about as much as your ego. Or the load of shit you'll leave in your pants when I decide to come after you. Hey, why is it warm?"

She shrugged. "You tell me, battery-man. You specialize in this kind of thing, right? It's been doing that sometimes when I touch it. Getting warmer like that. Doesn't it do that for you?"

He shook his head, marveling at the stone. It was already going cool in his hands. "Did someone get hurt?"

Ellie smirked and stuck her chin out, the perfect picture of the defiant teen. "I dunno, old man. Here's a better question for you. Why do you leave dangerous shit like this lying around?"

He jerked both hands toward her, pretending like he would throw it at her. She flinched and danced away, the shadow already rising to swallow her. He laughed, pointing at her, and she strode forward again with a pissed-off expression.

"Lying around, huh? I call bullshit on that. Last time I checked, I could put things, even dangerous things, anywhere I wanted inside my house. If some dipshit kid decides to break in and gets herself into trouble, well, that's her problem. It was even in a case."

Ellie scoffed, stepped around the desk, and laid her hand atop the stone. "Dude, it's not like this thing is just some loaded gun, right? It's more than that. I think even you know that."

He felt the heat growing. Right when it reached the point where it was starting to get painful, she took her hand away, and it cooled down.

"Weird." Henry shook his head. "Okay, I see your point. Playing the grumpy old man doesn't cut it when stuff like this is in the wind. Probably should have put in a safe or something, right?" He shook his head. "Lexus has been trying to tell me that for years."

Ellie retreated to a safe distance, crossing her arms. "Your car talks to you? Or is Lexus a person?"

"Doesn't matter. As far as I'm concerned, you're a petty thief. A lowlife criminal. You caught me off-guard and mind-tricked me into answering some of your questions, so now it's my turn. Who sent you to my house?"

"A guy." Ellie raised one eyebrow, challenging him. "Next question."

Henry sighed, pulled out his desk chair, and sat. He was annoyed and ready to start breaking things, but he no longer felt threatened. "If you won't tell me, why are you here? You have to realize there's a thing called the law of equal exchange. I help you, and you help me. If you don't want to give anything up, why should I? Why are you here?"

She tapped her foot impatiently. "I already told you. I need to know more about that stone."

"The one you stole." Henry grinned. "I guess you're accustomed to getting something for nothing."

He stared at her, waiting patiently. Sure, she was fast. She was cunning. And she had magic. But she was a kid, and one thing kids didn't have was patience. He was going to wait her out and hope she started talking.

He noticed a tickle along his arms, the strange sensation of his hair standing on end. His wolf sense was kicking in, warning him that there was something he was missing.

Ellie finally cracked, just a little. "I need it."

"The information or the stone?" Henry asked.

She sat on the edge of the desk, kicking her feet. "Both."

"Why would I give anything to you? Especially the stone. It's mine, and it's dangerous. You can talk all you want about how I should keep it in a safer spot, but the fact of the matter is it was all fine until you broke into my damn house and fucked everything up."

"Language, dude. I'm just a kid." She smiled, but the expression fell away as her eyes wandered back to the stone. "I need it."

"You already said that." He kept staring at her with a perfect poker face. He was giving nothing away unless she could somehow discern something from a face of stone. Honestly, she was doing almost as well. Plenty of sardonic smirks and wrinkled noses, but she had no real tells.

What the hell was she thinking?

Just when he was starting to doubt his strategy, something changed. Ellie let out a long-suffering sigh, then laughed and shook her head.

"Okay, here goes. The sob story. Except I'm not telling it to make you feel sorry for me, it's just the truth. Me and these other kids my age, we're kind of a family. We have nothing else but each other. Sure, we have some magic capabilities between all of us. But all of that just helps us evade people. We have no way to fight for anything better or to defend ourselves."

Henry kicked his feet up on the desk. "Let me guess. You make your living by stealing shit and selling it."

"Sort of. Have you heard of the magical dark web?"

"Sure. I know a thing or two about that." He knew more

than a thing or two and spent hours every week scouring it with the help of Lexus. She didn't need to know all that.

"Okay. So, we find work there. It's enough to eke out an existence, but we're not doing much living, you know? I'm trying to get us into a better spot. Maybe it's naïve of me to say this, but I want to make the world a better place. So I'm trying to take jobs from the good guys, or at least the not-totally-evil guys. This new dude kind of seems like he fits in that category. And no, I'm not going to tell you more about him. So don't ask."

"I wasn't planning on wasting my breath."

"So, anyway, I stole this stone from you. Except then it suddenly went haywire and almost melted down in our hideout. It could have killed me. It could have killed my friends, and that's even worse." She bit her lip, looking vulnerable for the first time. "I need to know what I've gotten myself into. I need to understand. I was born into magic, but I feel like I'm completely cut off from it. It doesn't feel right."

Henry sat forward, the chair creaking under his weight. He set the stone on the desk. "You've got guts, Ellie. Equal parts brave and stupid. Kind of like me. I can admire it. But I can't let you have the stone. It's way too dangerous. I can at least tell you that it comes from an ancient culture. One that died out a long time ago. I have no idea what it's capable of, and that's the truth."

He grunted, already angry at himself as he grabbed a pen and wrote on another Post-it note. He handed it to the girl.

"It's my phone number. One of them, anyway. If you get

into any water that's too hot to pull yourself out of, give me a call, and I'll be there. No questions asked."

She took the note, staring at it in disbelief. "Why are you giving me this?"

Henry shrugged, resting back in his chair again. "I know I probably seem like some ivory tower asshole, but I care too. I have my boots on the ground just like you. If you're really one of the good guys like you're telling me, I don't want you getting yourself hurt."

She was about to say something else, but they heard a door opening. Henry's assistant, Susie, walked in holding a stack of files which she promptly dropped on the floor.

"Oh my God, Henry, I'm sorry," she said. "I know I didn't let her in. How did she get past me? Should I call security?"

Henry shook his head. "You should call her a cab and pay for it with the company card."

"No need for that." Ellie stood fast, rushing out of the room. "I'll catch you later, battery-guy."

The door shut and Henry and Susie stared at each other awkwardly. He tore his eyes away, scooting toward the desk to finally get to work. Suddenly, he realized there was a suspiciously empty spot on the desk where the stone had been a moment ago.

"Shit!" He stood and sprinted out into the hall. The elevator doors stood open at the end, but there was no sign of Ellie. Nothing other than a shred of black smoke dissolving into the air.

CHAPTER NINE

Henry winced as the Ducati bumped up and over the uneven pavement, the wheels briefly losing traction in a gummy seam of tar. It was raining, unsurprisingly, a warm summer sprinkle that fell from a strangely clear sky. Evening was fast approaching. Far away, past the lights of Bremerton, the ferry was visible but shrouded in the fog of distance on its way across the Sound.

Henry was here, at the southwest edge of town. He rode past the post office and an ugly white and orange building on the left. On his right was B&B Auto Repair, an elongated building lined with garage doors set back a mere car length from the road.

Careful not to slide on the slick asphalt, Henry turned and rolled to a stop just beside the junky old truck of the owner, an old friend of his. He killed the engine and stood, pulling his helmet off. He realized now how quiet the late afternoon was. Most of the businesses were closed for the day, and there was no traffic on the road.

The only sound was the soft hiss of rain on the pavement, almost like meat sizzling in a hot pan.

Henry went past the garage doors to the small glass door of the lobby and knocked. Someone moved inside, unlocked the door, and pulled it open.

Hatch Latham peered out, the suspicion on his handsome but weathered face turning to pure joy.

"Henry, you old bastard! How the hell are ya?"

"As good as I can be." Henry looked over his shoulder, scanning the area. "Are you gonna let me stand out here in the rain?"

"Sorry, sorry!" Hatch stepped back, holding the door open for Henry to enter the dark lobby. "Just getting over my surprise. It's not every day a billionaire rolls into your shop. I figure a guy like you can pay someone else to fix up your wheels."

Henry shut and locked the door. "I'm not here about the Ducati."

"No?" Hatch rubbed his chin suspiciously. "I don't buy it. The thing must be wrecked in some way, right? How many bikes have you screwed up so far this month, huh?"

"Just a couple, no big deal. It's good to see you too, Hatch. Got anything good in?"

"When do I ever?" Hatch scoffed, leading the way into the garage. "This is a grease pit, not a BMW dealership. Mostly work trucks and old cars that should have been retired ten years ago."

"Speaking of which, I see you're still in that same busted-up Ford." Henry gave his friend a playful punch on the shoulder. "It's kind of ironic, isn't it? You run a garage whose whole job is keeping vehicles in top shape, and you're driving around in that piece of shit."

Hatch flipped the lights on, revealing the grease-stained garage in all its glory. A couple of bays held cars that were staying overnight. "That piece of shit is going strong and purring like a kitten, thank you very much. See, I told you. Nothing good. Unless you call a '73 El Camino 'good.' I guess it is vintage. And you don't see too many of them in Washington. Hey, wait a minute…"

He suddenly turned to Henry, the hairs on his tanned arms standing up. "Why are you here, anyway? You haven't been to see me in months."

Henry picked up a giant socket wrench and tested its weight. "What are you talking about? We just went on a run the other day."

"Yeah, and it was a hell of a run. But us meeting there was incidental, right? Not like you came just to see me. So what's the deal? You need to borrow some money?" Hatch laughed, reached into his wallet, and pulled out a couple of five-dollar bills. "Here, this should take care of about half a down payment on a new particle accelerator or whatever the hell you might need. I expect prompt repayment as soon as your stock goes up another thousand percent."

"Quit being a smartass. I know it's fun, but still. Can't a guy swing by and visit an old friend?" Henry set the wrench down and grabbed a random rag to wipe the grease off his hands. "I know this isn't really that kind of friendship. It's more. When you go through what we've been through together, Hatch, it does one of two things. It can break people apart, or it can bring them together and make their bond as hard as titanium."

Hatch pointed in his face. "Don't get sappy on me, Neumann. You aren't a tree. We both know you don't drop by for random visits. Not holding it against you. Just stating a fact. That's not the kind of guy you are. Or maybe it's not the kind of life you lead. Too busy, right?"

Henry sighed, stepped over to the El Camino, and ran a hand along the hood. The metal was dusty and pitted. "You don't know the half of it."

"Yeah? I can probably take a guess. Tell me what's up."

Henry turned to his friend, taking a breath, tasting the motor oil and rust in the air. "There's this artifact. I think it's Celtic in origin. Maybe Pictish. The provenance isn't well-established. Earliest record has it at the National Museum of Ireland in Dublin. From there it went into private collections but never stayed put for too long. It built up a bit of mythology. Supposed to be bad luck. One of the owners even claimed it set his house on fire."

Shit, that might be possible now, he thought.

"Sort of like that spooky-ass painting." Hatch shivered. "With the little boy and that weird doll thing standing next to him."

"Kind of. Except not very interesting, visually. This artifact's a stone. Probably from a river bottom, given how smooth and rounded it is. There are carvings in it. A lion and a lamb."

"Hm…" Hatch squatted, thumping the El Camino's tires with his fist. "Kind of weird, isn't it? Did the Celts even know about lions?"

"Probably. They originated on mainland Europe, and they fought with the Romans. Ever seen that statue, the Dying Gaul? What I'm trying to say is, they were fairly worldly. Even in ancient times, knowledge spread pretty well. Even across cultures. Anyway, the carvings aren't the weird thing about the stone."

He gave Hatch an abbreviated version of what he knew. The strange properties of the stone, its humming energy, the way it got hotter when Ellie touched it. He had no idea what might cause that last part. Maybe an ancient enchantment. Hopefully not so ancient that no one alive knew anything about it.

By the time he reached the end of the story, they had migrated from the garage into Hatch's cramped office, where they sipped cold coffee from a pot that had been brewed who knew how many hours ago.

Hatch stared into space for a while, fidgeting with the mouse connected to his ancient computer, complete with a beige CRT monitor.

"You know," Hatch finally said, "I'm not the guy to come to for this stuff. Our fun little vacation with the dark families was enough for me. I try not to dig around in the shadowy corners of reality if I can help it."

"I hear you, Hatch." Henry set his coffee aside, wincing at the sour flavor. "Sometimes you can't help it. For me, this is one of those times. I'd really appreciate your help on this."

The other man reached out, and they shook hands. "Just like old times, huh? The two of us lone wolves. Well, not really lone, but you get what I mean."

"Sure I do. Lone, but together. A couple of loners in the night. Not that we were always alone. Have you heard from any of the others lately?"

Hatch frowned, his eyes losing their usual spark of joy.

"Nah. Not for a long time. Who knows where they are? Who knows if they're even alive? Man, this coffee tastes like shit. You hungry?"

It was a classic Hatch method of moving the night along, of keeping constant momentum, so Henry wouldn't be able to come up with an excuse to get away. Luckily, Hatch claimed to have a place in mind that was nearby, and by "nearby" he meant down the street and across the intersection of National and Arsenal.

Henry had driven past Cookie's Clubhouse several times but never felt the urge to go in. It wasn't that he had the stuck-up palate of a billionaire. He didn't enjoy the atmosphere of bars. Too many people acting stupid, too much noise. Too messy.

Thankfully, Cookie's was quiet at this early hour of the evening. However, it was just about pulsating with latent potential. Some guy with a guitar was getting ready on the karaoke stage, testing the mic and strumming a few chords to check his tuning. A gaggle of waitresses had gathered at the bar, talking in low and reverent voices. There wasn't any work for them at the moment, yet they were all here, racking up the hours. It could only mean one thing.

Cookie's was about to be packed.

Hatch led Henry to the bar, then held up two fingers. Just that. Two fingers, not a word spoken. Maybe there was a bit of a friendly nod, a waggle of the eyebrows. The bartender approached them a few moments later with two bottles of the cheapest beer known to humankind. Or at least the cheapest beer that came in glass.

"You like drinking this stuff?" Henry took a sip and cringed even harder than he had at the old coffee. "Good thing it's ice cold. If it wasn't, it'd taste like I licked a skunk's ass."

Hatch nudged him in the ribs. "Yeah, you would know what a skunk's ass tastes like. Don't insult my beer, Neumann. It's piss, sure, but it's good American piss. So drink up and enjoy. I'm buying."

"Good. I wouldn't want to waste my money on this. I thought you asked me if I was hungry."

"Yeah. So?"

"So, why are we drinking and not ordering food?"

Hatch gave him a funny look. "You telling me you never say 'fuck it' and decide to drink your dinner? I thought all single guys did that from time to time."

Henry grinned, forcing back another swallow of beer. "I drink my dinner sometimes. A nice green smoothie blended up by Lexus. He knows what I like."

Hatch shivered so hard he almost spilled his beer. "What is that, like kale and shit? Disgusting. You're a wolf, Neumann. You have all the goddamn money in the world. Shouldn't you be eating rib eyes every night?"

Henry shrugged. "Only when I need the protein. This place has food, right?"

Hatch laughed, gesturing to the communal plate of fries the idle waitresses were sharing. "Sure, it has food. All the classic food groups; grease, grease, and more grease. The fried mac and cheese triangles are to die for. Literally." Hatch thumped his chest and made a pained face. "If you decide to get an order, I'll split them with you. If you eat the whole thing, you'll probably need to speed over to your sister for an emergency bypass surgery."

"No dice. She's a pediatric surgeon."

"Yeah, and you're a big baby, so it works out. Hey, I'm sorry, bartender. I didn't mean to badmouth the food." The guy behind the bar just smiled, shook his head, and sidled away. The air was filled with the deliciously rich aromas of grilled burgers and fries fresh out of the fryer basket. "I am getting kind of hungry. But hold on. Let's wrap this business up first. Bartender!"

The guy came back, looking vaguely annoyed now, but in a humorous kind of way. Hatch must be a regular here. A regular pain in the ass, the bartender would probably say.

"Yeah, whaddya want now?" he asked, setting down the glass he'd been drying off.

Hatch jerked a thumb at Henry. "My friend here has a ton of money burning a hole in his pocket. He wants to know what your most expensive whisky is."

The bartender had the answer ready. "We've got Johnnie Walker Blue Label back here. Been working our way through the same bottle for about five years. Knowing you, Hatch, you do not want to ask how much a glass of that costs."

Hatch clapped, rubbing his hands together. "Great! He'll take a glass. Two fingers, neat."

The bartender glanced at Henry, took in his brand-new riding jacket and the expensive watch on his wrist, and poured the drink without a word. He slid the glass over to Henry, who nodded his thanks. He raised the glass to his nose and took a whiff.

"Smells like whisky." He set the glass back down. "You know I'm not a drinker, Hatch. And this is probably a twenty-dollar glass of booze."

Hatch broke down laughing, slapping the bar and throwing his head back. "Twenty dollars! Hey, everybody, this guy thinks two fingers of JW Blue only costs twenty dollars!"

No one else laughed. A few people cringed, giving Henry looks of solemn concern.

"Forty dollars?" Henry ventured, looking at the bartender. The other man raised his thumb toward the ceiling. Henry made another guess. "Fifty?"

Hatch threw an arm around him. "More or less. I guess you can probably afford it, though. No, don't worry, I'm not trying to bankrupt you *or* get you drunk. I'm trying to give you a piece of information in a way that sticks. Now take a sip."

Henry took a tiny drink of the whisky and shrugged. "I guess it's good. Very smooth. I kind of expected it to taste like engine degreaser."

"Are you kidding me, Neumann? That's primo scotch. For a billionaire you sure are uncultured. Look here… Like I said, I'm not the kind of guy to go to if you want information about artifacts. I might know someone who *is* that kind of guy. The trouble is, he's a weirdo. Even weirder than you. He's a recluse, and he hates visitors. Even if the visitor is someone he likes, which would put them on a very short list. Here's the trick, though. You bring him a bottle of the good stuff, and he might let you in. He might even talk to you. Got it?"

Henry nodded, sliding the rest of the whisky over to Hatch. "Here you go. No sense wasting this on me. You can have my beer, too."

Hatch grinned, pulling the beverages toward him. "What a friend, Neumann. What a friend."

CHAPTER TEN

Stryker spent the day strolling around Bremerton, and he learned a thing or two about the city. The first thing he learned was that the downtown area—at least at the time of day he visited it—felt like one of those episodes of *The Twilight Zone* where a man slowly realized he was the last human left on Earth. Everything was quiet and deserted, with no sign of the people he had come off the ferry with.

Stryker continued through the downtown, his walking stick *clicking* on the pavement. He tapped out the melody of a song, something old whose name he had forgotten. He wondered if he had heard it somewhere in Europe, maybe at the Berlin State Opera during his obsession with what people now called classical music back in the nineteenth century.

Eventually, he entered the suburbs, where children played in yards and people walked out to check their mailboxes. He waved at a few of them, sharing greetings. At one point, as the morning wore into the afternoon, he stopped long enough to ask someone where to find a particular address.

"You want that old place?" The man stared at him dubiously. "Well, you're gonna want to catch a ride. That's a few miles away."

Stryker smiled, tapping out a little ditty with his stick. "Just tell me where it is, and let me decide how I get there. If you don't mind."

That was how he found himself standing at the bottom of the hill hours later, staring up. The manor silhouetted itself against the darkening sky. Stryker had taken his time getting there, and the hour was almost right.

By the time he got up there, it would be time.

He began the hike up the hill, his ancient bones protesting but his powerful muscles allowing him to scale the slope like a mountain goat. He avoided the footpath, opting for the steeper sections. It reminded him of his home. His *original* home, among the fog-filled valleys and windswept cliffs.

As he came close to the house, he raised his walking stick and held it like a spear with the top pointed out. With no hesitation, he approached a window and jammed the walking stick into it. The diamond embedded in the top caused the glass to shatter with little effort, although it broke into large, deadly shards. Stryker clicked his tongue disapprovingly as he carefully slipped inside.

"No safety glass. I did this gentleman a favor by shattering his window. He really ought to upgrade things around here."

Stryker adjusted his suit jacket and looked around, admiring the fine wood paneling of the hallway, along with the paintings and sculptures set back in alcoves. The place was clean if a bit dusty around the edges. There was a smell of Pine-Sol in the air. Someone had recently mopped the hardwood floors.

Piano music drifted from somewhere nearby. Stryker turned and moved away from the sound, taking off his shoes and setting them on the floor near the broken window. He entered a large library room filled with dozens of art pieces and relics. He tried to empty his mind, letting himself become attuned to whatever magical energy was floating around the place.

He felt small tugs here and there. There was plenty of latent energy hiding in this room, ready to be unleashed by the right person. He was not the right person for any of them. He was looking for a specific signature, something that felt familiar and *right*, but he didn't feel it yet.

Time to move to a different room. He started across the library, toward the next branch of the hallway. However, two things happened to clue him in that his easy stroll through the place was about to be interrupted.

First, the distant piano music stopped. The player had quit and could be anywhere now. Perhaps they had heard Stryker enter the house.

Second, and most importantly, one of the bookshelves had swung out from the wall like a door.

Stryker turned to face that bookshelf as it opened wide enough to reveal a dark tunnel with a staircase carved into the earth. Someone was standing there, someone large and broad, their shoulders dramatically rising and falling as they breathed deeply. Their eyes almost glowed in the dim light.

Stryker struck his best pose, planting his feet wide and using his walking stick to point. "You must be Henry Neumann. Tech billionaire. I must admit, I expected you to live in a more modern type of home than this. Glass and steel, all flat planes and austerity. Complete with an AI voice assistant that can hear you in every room."

"And who the fuck are you?" the man growled, stepping into the light.

Stryker recognized him for sure now. It was hard not to. His face had been plastered on plenty of magazines and Internet posts in recent years. Henry Neumann, the thirty-five-year-old genius who was revolutionizing the energy industry. It would be a shame if he had to die here tonight, but Stryker's mission was a little more important.

At least to him.

"Who I am is not your concern, Henry. It's unfortunate that you had to interrupt me. If you allow me to continue, I'll take what I came here for and be on my way."

Henry took another step forward. Stryker sensed a lot of tension in the man. The tension of a battle taking place inside him. Henry was trying to reach some decision or come to some tactical conclusion.

There was something new in the room now. A magical energy Stryker hadn't felt before. It felt feral, violent, and dangerous. He wanted to look around to spot the relic, but the energy suddenly dissipated.

That was when Henry sprinted forward.

Stryker dodged the billionaire easily. He danced out of the way and spun, slamming his walking stick against Henry's back. The instrument looked light in Stryker's hands, but it weighed a good thirty pounds.

Henry felt the full brunt of it. Grunting in pain, he stumbled forward and caught himself on the arm of a couch. He acted like he was about to stand, but when Stryker came toward him, he dropped farther toward the floor and swept his leg in a clean arc.

Anyone lesser might have failed to react in time. The kick would have taken their feet from under them, giving Henry the upper hand. Stryker leaped over the sweeping leg and came down on one foot. His other foot was already up and out, kicking toward Henry's head. The blow connected with great force, snapping Henry's head back and splitting his eyebrow.

Blood spattered Stryker's foot, and he looked at it with pursed lips. "You're lucky I took my shoes off. I would have billed you for getting blood on them. Are you going to stay down now, Neumann, or should I keep going? You're a handsome lad and obviously in good physical shape, but I promise that you're no match for me."

Henry clawed his way back to his feet and turned to face his enemy. Stryker could swear he saw the man's eyes glinting again in that strange way, but the illusion quickly vanished.

Henry lifted his fists. "I could tear you apart, fancy-pants, but I don't want to have to clean your guts off my floor. Let's see what else you've got."

"Oh, I've got plenty. Sadly for you, you won't live to see all of it. Not unless you smarten up and concede."

"No chance!" Henry dashed forward again like a dumb bull. Using the same strategy that hadn't worked for him before.

Or maybe not. Stryker dodged again, but this time

Henry quickly diverted in the same direction, meeting Stryker and punching him hard in the jaw.

It was Stryker's turn to stumble back. He took two steps away, reaching up to touch his jaw. That punch had felt much harder than anything he had taken in a fight over the centuries.

He nodded respectfully. "Good hit. You must use a protein supplement. You probably have a home gym as well. Let me guess…it's in the basement."

Henry shook his head, more beads of blood flying out of his split brow. "Do you always talk this much when you get caught breaking into someone's house?"

"Only when I'm trying to keep them distracted."

Henry hadn't noticed Stryker's hands moving behind his back. He had twisted the handle of his walking stick and pulled it away, revealing the needle-thin, razor-sharp blade hidden inside. He lunged forward like a fencer, jabbing the blade toward Henry's gut.

This was it. Stryker had him, and he knew it. Time seemed to slow down, adrenaline coursing through Stryker's veins as the death blow approached.

Something spun into view from the side. A metal serving platter. It hit the side of Stryker's blade and shoved it aside. The momentum of his lunge carried him forward, and his shoulder struck Henry's musclebound chest.

Stryker recovered, hit the floor, and rolled in the direction the platter had come from. He saw a tiny older man standing there, dressed in an equally tiny bathrobe. Stryker stabbed out without thinking, his anger taking over. The blade went straight through the older man and out the other side, causing blood to blossom and spread through the terrycloth of the robe.

It was hard to hear through the pulsing heartbeat in his ears, but Stryker detected a scream of fury and pain from Henry. He withdrew the sword and stood, whirling on his heel and running out of the room.

———

Henry turned to watch the invader flee the library. He roared, his muscles tensing, racked with pain as the transformation began. He was going to chase the man down and rip him apart. Slowly. He would let him watch as he tore away little pieces of his body.

He felt to his hands and his knees, howling as emotions boiled inside him. A moment later, he heard a small voice behind him.

"Henry..."

He turned, his half-wolf eyes glimpsing Lexus. The old gnome was lying on his back on the floor, one hand held tight to his wound. Blood welled up between the fingers, more pulsing out each time his heart beat.

Henry came back to human form, feeling his torn clothes settling limply over his body. His pants fell to the floor as he raced toward Lexus, falling to his knees.

"Let's get you downstairs, old man. To the medical bay. I can stitch you up and..."

Lexus shook his head, a tear forming on the corner of each eye and dripping toward the floor. "No use. You can barely manage to suture your injuries, Henry. I won't let you turn me into a pincushion."

They shared a solemn laugh. Henry grabbed the gnome's hand and held it tight.

"Then I'll call Aspen. She can be here fast. I'll even ask her to take a helicopter."

"No, Henry. Even if she hopped in a fighter jet, she wouldn't get here soon enough. It's too late, and we both know it. Please don't fuss around and waste whatever time I have left. Stay with me."

At first, Henry nodded. He soon went against Lexus' wishes and lifted the gnome off the floor. Lexus grunted in pain and tried to complain, but he didn't have the strength to summon a single word.

"Relax, old man." Henry carried him down the hall, careful not to bump him against any corners. "I'm only bringing you up to your bed. You need your rest. You know I'm going to make you scrub that blood off the floor. And make me breakfast, too."

Lexus reached up, touching Henry's face with a hand already going cold. "Don't fool yourself. You have to be strong now. Stronger than you've ever been before. I know cooking eggs can be tough, but you'll find a way. Just make sure to take the pan off the heat when they're only half-cooked. The residual heat will be enough to—"

He interrupted himself with a ragged coughing fit. He tried to cover his mouth, but Henry still felt a spray of something warm against his face. He wanted to hope it wasn't blood, but he knew better.

Lexus recovered and went on. "It was only a matter of time, anyway. If it wasn't tonight, it might have been a week from now. Or a month. We knew I was dying, Henry.

At least now we know exactly when. You might even say that strange fellow did us a favor."

Henry began to climb the steps. At the moment, they looked like Everest. "I'm going to find the guy and make him pay. Whatever family he has…"

"Don't speak that way, Master Neumann. Revenge is what turns good men evil. Find him. Stop him. But only because he's a danger to the world. You have to understand that what he did here tonight has changed nothing. It has only accelerated what was already on its way."

In the bedroom, Henry laid his mentor out carefully and covered him up, so he would no longer see all the blood. He pulled a chair over and sat, refusing to leave until the moment came.

The old gnome was even tougher than Henry gave him credit for. It was hours before he died. But eventually, at around four in the morning, he took his last breath and spoke his final words.

"I love you, my son…"

Henry didn't have time to say it back, but Lexus already knew.

CHAPTER ELEVEN

As soon as he felt the old man's hand go limp, Henry stood and stomped out of the room. Tears clouded his vision as he rushed down the steps, slipping and nearly falling several times. He continued his mad dash into the basement. He ran into the garage area, grabbed the essentials off the rack, and hopped on the nearest bike that wasn't bent or broken in some way.

It was the new Ducati. It carried him out of the cave and into the open. The gate reared up before him, and he almost felt like smashing through it. Good sense won out, and he stopped to punch in the code. As soon as the gap was wide enough, he surged through it, gritting his teeth as he reached up to press the button on his necklace. His face became a blur. He didn't want the world to see him. Not right now. He felt like a monster, a beast of the night, and he wasn't even in wolf form.

A dark certainty came to him. Someone else was going to die this early morning. Whether it was him or the stranger…that would be up to fate.

He cruised through the dark, up and down side streets, through alleyways past glowing neon signs. The pavement was slick, and there was a smell of ozone in the air. No one was around. The streets were empty. The traffic lights were blinking. There were no cops, no other cars, which was a good thing. Tonight, the speed limit was more like the minimum.

He imagined people stumbling out of bed, confused, hurrying to the window to see what was happening and why it sounded like a jet was taking off outside. By then he would be long gone, three or four blocks away.

His reflexes worked overtime as he flew around corners like a speed demon. If he crashed, it wouldn't be the first time, but he couldn't afford to let the stranger get away. He needed to find the guy, not only because he'd killed Lexus.

The stranger had almost bested Henry in a fair fight. Mostly fair, anyway. Pulling out the sword had been a bitch move, but Henry could understand why he'd done it. He hadn't come to the house only to peek at the antique furniture. He was after something. If he was who Henry thought he was, he was after more items like the stone Ellie had stolen.

He had come looking for something his hired gang of miscreants might have missed.

Whoever this guy was, he was dangerous in every sense of the word.

He was also damn good at making a getaway. Henry searched the streets systematically, hoping to get a glimpse. There was nothing.

Now that he was miles from home, in the heart of Bremerton, the search was starting to feel hopeless. Henry thought of Lexus, the pain and weakness in the old gnome's voice. What would it be like, waking up every morning without his old friend there to pour his coffee? No more late-night talks, no more friendly voice in his ear when he was on missions.

His vision clouded again, and an almost suicidal rage filled his soul. Henry screamed inside his helmet and pushed the Ducati even faster.

The front wheel hit a divot in the road and left the ground. The back wheel sliced into a shallow puddle and lost traction. Henry tried to correct himself, but it was already a done deal. The motorcycle was toppling.

Henry ditched to avoid having his leg caught beneath its weight. He slammed to the ground, skidding along it, rolling and tumbling over. As the world spun crazily around him, he caught snapshot glimpses of the Ducati slamming into a guardrail, smashing itself to smithereens.

He finally rolled to a stop and lay there in pain, wondering how many of his bones he'd broken. The bike's dying engine echoed over to him, a pathetic splutter that faded into silence.

Henry stared at the sky, watching as faint morning light spread through the clouds. Suddenly he realized it would be pretty embarrassing for someone to find him like this, and at any rate, he had no time for the hubbub. He got up slowly, groaning in discomfort. By some miracle, he was able to stand. A quick check of his body revealed no catastrophic injuries.

It was odd to say he was lucky after all the shit that had happened tonight, but somehow he was walking away from this one.

Hobbling a little, Henry rushed over to the guardrail and peeked over. The bike's wreckage was scattered across a gully far below, out of anyone's way. It could stay there for now.

Moisture covered his face. That was when he remembered the cut above his eyebrow. It seemed like no action-packed night was complete without getting his face smeared with blood. He pulled his helmet off and felt something drop out of it, falling to pieces.

It was his necklace. The one Lexus had built for him. A one-of-a-kind tool, and the most useful one in his arsenal...other than his ability to turn into a wolf. Now it lay broken on the blacktop. Not only that, but the man who created it was dead.

Henry fell to his knees and mourned all over again. Tears joined the blood on his face, stinging his skin.

Eventually, he gained enough composure to walk away, pulling out one of his cellphones. He dialed a number, held the phone to his ear, and prayed the person would answer the call.

"Neumann?" The voice sounded sleepy and concerned. "What the hell is it? Why are you calling me? You almost never call me."

Henry sighed, glancing back at the scene of the accident. Other than a dent and a scuff mark on the guardrail, it looked like nothing had happened. "Hey, Hatch. I called because..." He drew a deep breath. The only thing trickier than giving good news was giving bad news. Maybe it was better to do it in person. "I need you to come get me. I'm at..." He looked around for landmarks. "Well, I'm on

Kitsap. I'll meet you outside that tattoo shop on the corner of Wycoff."

"Why? You finally decide to get some ink?" Hatch started laughing but quickly realized Henry wasn't in the mood for jokes. "I'll be there in a few minutes. Hang tight, old friend."

Henry hung up and limped the rest of the way to the tattoo parlor. He collapsed on the curb and let his head hang, feeling truly defeated. Dark thoughts flashed through his mind. He had left Lexus lying in bed, dead and alone. He had left the house completely undefended. For all he knew, the stranger had circled and come right back inside. He could be rampaging through the house right now, having whatever fun he came for.

Henry balled up his fists, the transformation trying to come over him. He was already in nothing but his underwear and his riding jacket with road rash all over his legs. He didn't need any more attention on him. He pushed his emotions down and forced himself to breathe.

Headlights came around the bend up ahead, and Hatch's pickup truck pulled up a few feet away. Henry stood, wincing, and made his way over as the driver's side window rolled down.

"Shit, Neumann, you look like you got in a fight with a weedwhacker!" Hatch shook his head and leaned over to pop the passenger door open. "Did you at least win?"

"Nope." Henry slid inside and slammed the door harder than he intended. Hatch didn't seem to notice or care. "Got my weeds whacked. Completely hacked to bits." He sucked in his lips and squinted, trying to hold back the tears. "Lexus is dead."

Hatch had already started driving, but he slammed on his brakes, staring at Henry. "He... What? Holy shit. What happened? I assume he didn't slip away peacefully in his sleep, going off how you're looking."

How much was too much to reveal? Hatch was already involved, in a way. He'd been involved ever since the dark families had transformed them together. Still, he didn't need to get involved any deeper. After Lexus, Hatch and Aspen were the only family he had left. No way he'd let anything happen to them.

"Just drive," he said.

Hatch nodded and drove forward again. "Where to?"

"I want to say your place, but..." Henry rolled his window down to feel the cool morning air. "You can take me back home. There's some shit I need to do."

"No rest for the wicked, huh?" Hatch gestured at Henry's legs. "Looks like road rash. Did you crash one of those million-dollar bikes again?"

"Ducatis aren't nearly that expensive. To answer your question, yes. I didn't just crash it, either. I pretty much turned it back into individual molecules. No, I don't know how I'm alive either. I guess we have mixed fortunes tonight."

It was clear that Hatch wanted to talk and ask more. He kept starting sentences but stopping himself. Finally, he threw up his hands and drove in silence.

"At the gate fine?" he asked as the truck stopped.

Henry nodded and started to get out, but Hatch locked the door.

"You've got power locks over there?" Henry grunted. "Thought this piece of shit was too old for that. Am I about to get a lecture? Remember, Hatch. You aren't that much older than me."

"But I'm worldly. Nah, Neumann, no lecture. I know you'd probably kick my ass right now if I tried launching into one. Just wanted to extend an invitation. How about a run tonight? I can meet you back here after dark. We can head out, just the two of us, maybe check out some new spots. What do you think?"

"I think I'll think about it. Can you let me out now?"

"Not so fast." Hatch reached into the back seat, grabbed a brown paper bag, and handed it to Henry. "Check that out."

Henry opened the back. There was a bottle of Johnnie Walker Blue Label inside. "Damn. So fancy it comes in a box. You didn't have to, Hatch. I thought you said this stuff was expensive?"

Hatch grinned and jabbed a finger into Henry's chest. "It is. You're gonna pay me back for it. Go see that guy I told you about."

Henry didn't know what else to say, so he got out and headed home.

CHAPTER TWELVE

He checked the time on his phone. It was almost ten in the morning, and the house felt as silent and empty as it ever had. Henry rubbed his hands together, feeling the dirt and grit under his nails. The shovel he had used to dig Lexus's grave was still leaning against the wall nearby. He kicked it over angrily on his way down into the basement.

It was time to leave. He didn't want to take a car, though. He wanted to feel the wind. The Ninja was still banged up, and the Ducati was still lying in a ditch off Kitsap Way. The only other bike was the Buell Firebolt XB9R. It was ancient, but it was new to him. He'd bought it off Hatch a couple of years back and never really rode it.

Today was the day.

He hopped on and kicked the old steed into life. His earpiece, synced to his phone now rather than Lexus' microphone in the command center, gave him directions. He sped out of town and headed south, the same direction he used to reach Seattle when taking the ferry wasn't an option. He took the exit for Mullenix Road south of the town of Bethel, then headed east past the elementary school. For a while, he coasted up and down gentle rises. Dense forest grew on either side of him, full of shadows and the song of birds.

The voice of the GPS in his ear took him as far as the quiet town of Olalla, and that was when he switched it off. The Wilderness Heights Sanitarium wasn't on the map anymore. He had to go off intelligence texted to him by Hatch.

He eventually found it, though. It was right where Hatch said it would be, off Orchard Ave. However, there was no longer a driveway leading to it. Henry stopped and wheeled the Buell down into a shallow gully. He pulled a camo tarp out of his backpack and tossed it over the bike, hoping that would be enough.

Hatch had warned him not to get caught trespassing. The history of this place was a sore spot in Olalla, and some of the more superstitious locals had made it their job to keep an eye on things. Letting himself get spotted would be a wrench in his plans.

Picking his way carefully, Henry moved through the woods. The glimpse he had gotten of the house from the road grew into a full view. The structure must have looked like something mighty back in the day, but now it seemed to be sagging in on itself, shrinking slowly.

Just looking at the place gave him the creeps. Wilderness Heights Sanitarium was often called by its other, more accurate name, Starvation Heights.

It would have been nice if he could tell himself he didn't believe in ghosts and curses. That would make him feel a whole lot better about going into a place where people had died miserable deaths. He knew too much about the world to fool himself.

Henry stepped up onto the spongy front porch and climbed in through a window. He entered a dark, damp place that smelled of rot and mildew. The floor was on the verge of collapse, buckling toward the center.

Maybe there were ghosts here. But there was also a crazy hermit who, according to Hatch, might blow his head off if he wasn't careful. Sneaking around was probably a good way to get shot, so he decided to call out.

"Charlie Brumfield! Are you here? I'm not the cops. I'm a friend of Hatch Latham's."

There was no answer. Maybe the guy wasn't here. Henry hoped he wasn't deaf because that would lead to a whole slew of problems.

He headed deeper into the building, coming out into a large room whose main feature was a brick fireplace. A rusty old pot hung from a hook. On either side of the fireplace, open doorways led away into deep, ominous shadows.

Henry stopped, biting his lip as he tried to decide what to do. Should he venture further and risk the hermit's wrath? Should he try calling out again?

He looked between the two doors. Both were creepy, but when he peered into the one on the left, the hairs on his arms and neck stood on end. He felt a shiver. His wolf sense was telling him something.

With a deep breath, he stepped toward the door. There was a clicking sound, easy to miss or misinterpret, but

Henry knew it. It was the sound of a shotgun being pumped and primed to shoot.

He took off his backpack and pulled out the bottle of Johnnie Walker. Holding it out in front of him, he slowly stepped into the room.

Charlie was sitting on a rickety rocking chair to the left, wearing a faded t-shirt from an old grunge band and jeans. The shirt was way too big on him. Henry took these details in over a couple of seconds, but the first thing he noticed was the hair. It looked like a bright white cotton ball on top of the guy's head, sticking out in several directions. His face bristled with stubble that was the same snow-white color.

The most important detail was the shotgun in his hands. He kept it aimed at Henry as he reached for the whisky.

"Scotch, huh?" Charlie spat on the floor. "Should have brought me some of that Westland American. Single malt. That's the stuff I like."

"Shit. Is there a liquor store around here? I can get you whatever you want."

Charlie looked him up and down. "Yeah, I bet you can. Hatch told me about you. Rich kid. So what? You come here to judge my living conditions? Anyway, scotch will do fine for now. Do I seem picky?"

Henry shrugged. "You asked me two different questions."

"They were both rhetorical. Which is my way of saying I don't care about you or any opinion you might have." His finger was still on the shotgun's trigger, squeezing it a little more tightly than Henry was comfortable with. He seemed ready to fire at a moment's notice. With his other hand, he grabbed hold of the whisky and tried to take it, but Henry tugged it away.

"You shoot me, and I drop the bottle. Nobody wins."

"I might not look like much, but I'm quick." Charlie gestured at the bottle with the end of the shotgun. "Maybe I shoot you, catch the bottle in midair, and drink up while I laugh at your corpse. How's that sound? Or maybe you tell me why you're here, then I can decide what to do."

"I need some information."

"Of course you do." Charlie finally took the shotgun away, laying it across his lap. "It's always the curious ones. Why else would anyone come here? Most of the time, I scare away any visitors I get. Mostly dumb kids. I have this technique. Got it down pat. I can whisper in a way that carries around corners. It'll send just about anyone running away in terror. It helps that they're already on edge before they even step foot inside."

Charlie grunted and stood, stepping past Henry into the main room. Henry followed the older man.

"You feel it, don't you?" Charlie put his hands on his hips and looked slowly around the place. "Bad things happened here. That taint still clings to everything."

Henry felt it. It took a lot of his willpower not to rush toward the exit. "Why are you even living here? I'm sure you could find a slightly nicer abandoned building to hunker down in. Why Starvation Heights?"

"Easy answer. I used to live here as a boy. A lot of bad memories, but it's still home. Plus, there's a kind of safety here. People with, you know, *sensitivities* can feel the bad energy here. Keeps them away."

Henry chuckled. "I don't think you need to have magical sensitivity to be creeped out by this place."

"No, but it helps."

"It would also help if you'd answer the questions I have."

Charlie sighed. "Fine, kid, you've got a deal. Come on back."

He led the way into the room on the other side of the fireplace. Charlie switched on a battery-powered lamp, revealing a decrepit old place that he'd made as clean and tidy as possible. There were two old Flintstones drinking glasses on a counter, dusty and grimy. Charlie gestured at them, and Henry poured the whisky. He raised the glass to his lips, staring down at the filth caked to the bottom.

Oh, well, he thought. *Alcohol kills germs, right?*

"Thank you kindly." Charlie took his glass and sat at a metal table. The table was like a shallow trough with a drain hole at one end. Henry took his seat, trying not to imagine what it was once used for.

"You know," Charlie said, "the history of this place is pretty interesting once you get past the ugly details of enemas and starvation. Here's a fun fact for you. Back in the early 1900s, there was a woman who died here. Norwegian immigrant. She had a son named Ivar. Name ring a bell? Yup, that's the same Ivar who started the restaurant chain. You ever been there? Best fish and chips in Seattle."

"That's like asking if I've ever been to the Space Needle. The answer is yes."

The mention of Ivar's made Henry think of Lexus again. In the interest of changing the subject and getting the hell out ASAP, he decided to launch right into it. He told Charlie about the stone, the carvings on it, the strange properties, and the loose history he knew about it. Before he finished, Charlie was nodding.

"Has to be Pictish," the old man said. "Bunch of crazy bastards, those Picts. They used to fight naked. Shaved their body hair off so their crazy tattoos were more visible. And they pretty much invented the man bun, way back then. There used to be this guy, a warrior… I can't tell you his name, but he was a good…" Charlie cleared his throat, taking a quick sip of whisky. "Longest, wildest mustache you ever saw. I'm talking right down to his nipples. Really wild."

"Strange." Henry pretended to take a drink and slid the dirty glass away. "I've read all about the Picts, but I never heard about some guy with a mustache like that. Where'd you find that anecdote?"

Charlie took another drink, averting his eyes. "Don't remember."

Henry shook his head in wonder. There was something about the way Charlie talked about these ancient people. Maybe he was a history buff. Or maybe he had been alive back then. But that was crazy, right? Way too long ago. Anyway, Charlie had already talked about spending his childhood here at the sanitarium.

Charlie eventually went on. "They were fierce people, the Picts. Nothing could destroy them, definitely not on their home turf. I'm talking about a group of people who fought naked, with rudimentary weaponry, who were still able to hold off the Romans. The fucking Romans! The

Picts were some gnarly sons of bitches for sure. But then, something happened. Something ended their history."

"Did it have something to do with the stone?"

"Keep your pants on, Johnnie Boy. I'm getting to it. Legend has it that the Romans had an ally. A dark entity that helped them win all their conquests. When the Picts turned away their northward expansion, the Romans called on their evil friend. Centurions with superior tactics and state-of-the-art weaponry couldn't defeat the Picts, but they knew an unstoppable wave of dark magic would succeed where they had failed. The stone was not what caused the downfall of the Picts. It was one of their weapons."

Charlie brought both hands up, rotating them around like he was forming a dough ball. Or energy. "The Picts were a magical people. The way they used magic was by way of these carved stones. We see a big, heavy lump of solid matter, but to the Picts, these stones were like open channels. They could pull energy through them like water through a pipe.

"They didn't only use the stones to channel energy. They used them to transform that energy completely and put it to new uses. The Romans only thought they were going after primitive people with spears. They were going after a rather sophisticated mystical race with plenty of magical energy at its disposal. But that magic eventually came back to bite them on the ass. You drinking that?"

Charlie grabbed Henry's neglected glass and poured its contents into his. He took another long drink, then wiped his lips on his sleeve.

Henry leaned closer, his curiosity overshadowing the

dread that came from being in this building. "Their magic got used against them?"

"Oh yeah. Big time." Charlie poured himself more whisky. "Some of the stones got into the hands of the enemy, and they were used to essentially steal the life force from the Picts, leaving them as empty shells. Broken and fragile. Sometimes they died outright. So the legend says."

"So the legend says."

"Yeah, that's what I said."

The ideas were already surging through Henry's mind. "If the legend is true, where did the energy go?"

"The essence of all those Picts?" Charlie shrugged. "No one knows. Maybe it floated away. Lost to entropy and all that. Why do you want to know, anyway? I assume you're not the only one out there who's looking for this information."

"I don't think so, no. If anyone else comes by..."

"Don't worry. I got a nose like a bloodhound. Well, figuratively. Point is, I can smell trouble. But you... Be careful, kid. Nothing good ever seems to come from playing around with this kind of energy. I might know a lot more about it than most other people, but there are still holes in the story the size of the Grand Canyon. No one knows what these stones can really do. Think of them like amped-up batteries, full of unstable energy."

That made Henry's inspiration turn into a full-on brainwave. He knew a thing or two about batteries. Energy could pass into them. Energy could pass out of them. Or it could stay locked inside, waiting to be released.

Charlie narrowed his eyes. "You have one, don't you? A Pictish stone."

"I did. Let's just say it's no longer in my possession and leave it at that."

"Suit yourself. But do us all a favor and get it back sooner rather than later. These things are dangerous, especially in the hands of modern people who have no idea what they do. In the right circumstances, they can still become active."

Henry took his glass back, poured a little more whisky, and bolted it down. He coughed, wiping a bit of drippage off his chin. "Like a Drow holding it? Could that be the right circumstance?"

"Maybe. Maybe…" Charlie leaned back in his chair, running a hand over his brow as he stared into space. "It's been a long time, kid, and the story's been retold a thousand times. There's no way to know for sure. But you can decide now.

"What do you want to do? Do you want to wait and see, or do you want to go after the truth and force it into the light? Either way, it's a dangerous game. A few people might die in the process."

Henry grinned. "Oh, I'm counting on a bit of death. There's one person in particular I'd like to see take a dirt nap."

It seemed his business here was concluded. He bade Charlie farewell and left.

Henry headed back toward Bremerton on the Firebolt. It was broad daylight with plenty of traffic, so he couldn't go nearly as fast as he wanted to. He was looking forward to going on a run with Hatch later.

CHAPTER THIRTEEN

Henry and Hatch stepped off the bus at Admiral Way. They pretended to be checking their phones, waiting for the bus to leave. Once it was gone, the squeal of air brakes fading into the night, they looked around.

Hatch sniffed the air. "There's rain coming. The good news is, it seems like we're alone. Hell, my fur coat could use a wash anyway."

They headed down the street. To their right, over the roofs of darkened houses, they could see the water of Puget Sound and a few lights twinkling on the distant shores of Bainbridge Island.

Henry stuffed his hands in his pockets, making fists. A nervous habit of his. "Are you sure this is a good idea?"

"Hell no. I'm pretty sure it's a *bad* idea. Which makes it fun. Think about it. What's the worst that could happen?"

"I dunno. We might get spotted and spawn a wolf hysteria that eventually leads to helicopters circling Seattle and shooting everything that runs on four legs."

"You've got quite an imagination, Neumann. For the

sake of our furry friends, we'll have to make sure no one sees us." Hatch pulled out his phone and checked the shifter app. "No one else active in the area. Big shock there."

They reached the Schmitz Preserve trailhead, stepping onto the trail between two stone pylons. The path went immediately uphill and curved soon after that. Combined with the dense trees and the many low-hanging branches, it was easy to become lost. Henry listened closely, letting his wolf senses engage. They didn't give him any information. There didn't seem to be anyone around.

"Right here looks good." Hatch lifted the bag off his shoulder and strode into the trees. "I'll go first. You have no choice but to see me naked in wolf form, but in human form? That's another story. You might get jealous."

Hatch winked as he vanished into the foliage. Henry heard the sound of a zipper, followed shortly thereafter by a low growl. He felt his hair raise as Hatch transformed. He trotted out of the trees a moment later, a magnificent beast with charcoal fur. Hatch cocked his wolf's head toward the trees, a signal for Henry to go ahead.

Henry walked past his old friend, running a hand down Hatch's furry flank. "Good doggie. Keep an eye out for me, would you?"

Hatch growled and snapped, nipping at Henry's hand. There was a glint in his amber eyes. Henry knew that glint well. If Hatch had been in human form, he'd be about to piss himself laughing.

"Fine, asshole." Henry pulled his hand away. "Don't even think about asking me to scratch your ears."

Hatch let out a fake whine. Henry flapped a hand to mimic a talking mouth as he disappeared into the trees.

It was the same ritual as always. Take off your clothes, and feel the cool night air on your skin. Good thing it was still summer. Running in winter was the worst. All the fur protected you in wolf form, but on your way in and out you had to suffer the chill on your fragile human skin.

The charcoal wolf was joined on the trail by the wolf with the silver-striped back. They trotted down the path a little way, moving cautiously and constantly sniffing the air. With their senses now much sharper, they soon confirmed that they were alone. That was when they ran.

They took it slower than usual, savoring the air and the feeling of freedom. It was dangerous here to open up and go at top speed. The Schmitz Preserve Park was a much tinier area than the Hoh Rain Forest, and it was smack in the middle of civilization.

Not that it was very easy to tell once you got into the middle of the place. In the daytime, the hustle and bustle of the nearby streets would give away your true location. At night, though, there was none of that external noise. Henry let his imagination take over. For everything his eyes, ears, and nose were telling him, he might as well be in the middle of nowhere.

He'd had his doubts, but it turned out that Hatch was right. A run was just what he needed. He thought he felt Lexus' spirit there with him. The old gnome could watch over him no matter where he went, freed from his flesh's infirmities.

It was a nice thing to think about, anyway.

He didn't think about Lexus for long. The point of

going on a run was to let yourself be free, not only from the physical confines of modern life but also from the psychological ones. Henry tried to forget who he was, to put himself fully in the mindset of a wolf. An animal like that wouldn't be worried about revenge, magic stones, or bills and taxes.

It was all about the moment you found yourself in.

Just when he was starting to attain that beautiful mindset, his senses warned him of something that broke him out of it. He caught a scent in the air—people nearby. There was something vaguely familiar about the smell, but he couldn't place it.

Hatch had caught the scent too. They went low to the ground, prowling toward the source. Leaving one trail behind, they carefully crossed through the trees until they approached a separate trail segment. That was where they saw the teenagers. Five of them walked through the dark forest. They moved with purpose, like they were on their way to or from an important errand.

Or maybe they were just afraid of being caught, too.

Henry looked at Hatch. Hatch looked at Henry, then tilted his head in a way that seemed to say *Fine. Have it your way.*

Hatch turned and slinked back into the trees. Henry watched the teenagers, waited until they were a hundred or so yards away, then leaped out onto the trail and followed them.

He moved like a shadow, silent and unobserved and always at the same distance. The teenagers were talking, but he couldn't make out any words. Henry knew who they were now. The scent had finally registered in his brain.

These were some of the same kids who had broken into his house.

One of them was eating something. A chocolate bar. Henry could smell it. A minute later, he came across the empty wrapper on the ground and growled. A reflex. He hated littering. He cut the sound short as soon as he heard it coming out of his throat, but the teenagers had already turned, looking in his direction.

Henry flattened himself against the trail, letting his mostly dark fur blend into the shadows.

One of the teenagers cracked a joke, and pretty soon they were all laughing as they continued their walk through the park.

Henry picked up the chocolate wrapper with his mouth and nudged it into the first garbage can he came across.

The teenagers didn't stop at the edge of the park. They kept going out onto Manning Street, then down Fifty-Third. Henry got nervous as motion sensor lights triggered on all the houses. A dog in someone's window spotted him and went wild, screaming like it had seen a monster.

Technically, it had.

Henry stayed hidden whenever possible, weaving in and out of parked cars. If he had to cross the pool of light from a street lamp, he did it quickly. Thankfully, this was a quiet section of Seattle. All family homes. Anyone still awake inside them was probably zoning out in front of the TV, oblivious to anything happening outside.

The teenagers led him on an odyssey, walking another couple of miles beyond the park. They stopped for a little while at an elementary school and messed around on the playground equipment. Henry hunkered down in the shadows and watched them, baring his teeth in anger and impatience.

First, they threw trash on the ground. Now they were making him wait. Not to mention the fact that they had broken into his house and failed to the point where their boss had to return and...

No. Don't think about Lexus. Focus.

The teenagers eventually moved on. One of them started to smoke but put it out as soon as they saw a cop car driving through the intersection ahead of them.

Finally, they reached a sports pitch and climbed over the chain-link fence. Henry found a spot where he could crawl beneath it without making too much noise and followed them. The teenagers approached the bleachers and looked around, then quickly ducked underneath them.

"Oh, shit!" one of them cried out, pointing directly at Henry. The little bastard was wearing something on his eyes. Henry thought they were sunglasses at first, a lame attempt at looking cool, but he saw now that they were goggles, probably enhanced to give better night vision.

The other kids came back out at a dead run, scattering in every direction. Henry looked between them all, growling as he tried to decide which one to chase. Only two of them were girls, but neither looked like Ellie.

He ran toward the boy with the goggles, but the kid was fast. He went up and over the fence in a flash and sprinted away on the other side. Henry clawed at the fence and growled, laughing internally as the kid let out a high-pitched scream and almost fell.

So much for the element of surprise. The kids were

long gone. They were separated, but Henry knew they must have someplace where they could regroup.

However, the night was not yet lost.

Henry padded over to the bleachers and squeezed underneath. He found himself inside a little cavern. It was almost cozy, especially with all the amenities the kids had brought inside.

One of their bases. Not a major one, and not where they were living or spending much time. It was something… but not nearly enough.

Henry sniffed around, looking for one scent in particular. Ellie's. He caught it in a couple of places, but it was much too faint. She hadn't been here in several days, maybe longer.

The kids were probably smart enough to avoid this spot for a while, so Henry knew it was a dead end. He would have to keep looking.

Sniffing the air one last time, he turned and left the alcove. With no need for sneaking now, he reached the sanctuary of Schmitz Preserve very quickly, howling to find his friend.

CHAPTER FOURTEEN

The run was a fun time, but it was soon back to work. However, Henry knew he couldn't do much until he fixed his arsenal. Especially the necklace that hid his face. He spent the next few days at home, trying everything he could think of. His tricks failed until he was down to the most rudimentary means.

The timer on his phone went off. Henry quickly racked his weight and ran over to the command center. If his calculations were correct, the glue should be completely dry now. However, all the calculations in the world wouldn't make him feel less like a third-grader in art class.

He picked up the necklace and delicately draped it around his neck. If his theories were correct, and a few loose connections were the only remaining issue, it should now turn on.

He hit the button. It sank into its socket but didn't bounce back when he lifted his finger. He frowned, pushing down again and wiggling the button around to try and free it. There was a *crack*, and the delicate balance of the glue failed. The necklace fell apart again, the pieces clattering to the floor.

Henry slammed both fists on the table, then pounded them against his head. "Damn it! You're a big smart scientist aren't you, Neumann? Well, why can't you figure this shit out? Some old guy from a different world was able to build it out of scrap parts, and your dumb ass can't even put it back together!"

He spun in his chair, looking around at the mess that filled the command center. There were scattered bits and pieces of a dozen different projects. Some were weapons or other gadgets that would help Henry on his missions. Others were toys, little knick-knacks Lexus put together to make himself laugh. All were either unfinished or broken. Henry had possessed a foolish dream that he would complete the work Lexus had started, but he'd begun to doubt he had the capability.

Most of this stuff was magitech, and it wasn't like he could get on the magical dark web to order a manual on how to fix them.

Henry stood, tearing his hair and letting out a ferocious growl. It echoed around the cave and bounced back to him, picking up desolate notes along the way. He could make all the noise he wanted, but it would only ever accentuate how empty this place was and how alone Henry had become.

This realization caused a dam to break inside him. He could almost always stop the change when his emotions caused it to start, but this time he almost didn't want to. He felt powerless against it. His limbs stretched and bent into new configurations. His muscles swelled. His gym shorts stretched to accommodate the change, but his tank top immediately split right up the back.

Henry screamed again, a wordless and distorted howl halfway between the anguish of a human and the fury of a wolf.

Something shifted in the cave's shadows, stepping forward and revealing itself. It was Aspen, clutching a Starbucks cup. She waved and plopped into a chair, taking a sip and wincing.

"Tastes like burned ass. Man, I miss Tully's."

Henry was shocked by her nonchalance. He changed back into human form almost without trying and fell to his knees, gasping.

Aspen stared down at him with raised eyebrows. "Is this how you get when you're alone? I guess I never realized what a social animal you are. It makes sense. The wolf thing and all. You know, you can call me whenever you want."

Henry fell to the floor, laying himself out. "I was going to."

"Yeah, I figured. When you finished moping. You're different than other men in a couple of key ways, Henry, but in every other way you're the same. You never seem to realize that you don't have to suffer alone. I'm here for you. I am right now, at least. If I didn't have such a busy schedule, I'd be here every day. Why don't you come stay with me in Seattle for a while?"

Henry shook his head. "Got work to do."

"On that new battery of yours?"

"Maybe. Maybe not. Got lots of irons in lots of fires. You know how it is."

"Oh, I know." Aspen entered the command center area, her eyes traveling across the screens. Most of them were off. Four were still on, showing security feeds that swapped between cameras throughout the house and grounds. "Are you keeping your eye out for someone?"

Henry got up with a grunt. His head swam, and he almost toppled over. A reminder that he hadn't eaten all day. "Yeah, I sure am. The Publishers Clearing House prize patrol. I heard they're giving away five grand a week forever, and I could use the money."

"Hah, hah." Aspen reached out, switching all four monitors off one at a time. Henry almost lunged forward to yank her hand away, but he'd have to explain why he was keeping an eye out. She was too smart for excuses and lies to work.

"I'm calling it, Henry. You've spent too much time alone. Look, I know how you feel. I lose people all the time. Well, maybe not all the time, but it happens. And it never gets easier. You do what you can to get yourself ready, but in reality, there's no way to truly prepare yourself."

Henry nodded, tears coming to his eyes. "How do you deal with it?"

"You don't. Not really. You just keep going. Everything fades away eventually. The fondest memories, along with the darkest ones. The best thing we can do is get on with living. It would help out a lot if we found you a new best friend."

"It's a bit soon for that."

"Yeah, I guess so. Sorry. In my profession, you eventually learn to look at death in a more lighthearted way. Let's see here…" She strode past him into the area where all the vehicles were parked. He followed. "I see there's nothing new here."

"There was." Henry gestured at an empty spot. "I keep wrecking them. The Ducati was the latest casualty."

"Maybe you need to go back to driver's ed, bro. These are some nice toys, but a man cannot keep company with machines alone. What's over here?"

She strode further into the cave and entered the gym area. To Henry, it was sacred ground, a temple of sorts. A cloud of stench surrounded the place. The sweat of every workout he had done. It soaked into the equipment no matter how much Lexus had tried to scrub everything clean.

That was yet another duty Henry would have to take over now. The old saying of "you don't know what you have until it's gone" was proving itself shockingly right.

Aspen looked around, her lip curled up. "This place is disgusting. Look at this!" She ran her finger along a barbell. It came away almost black. "What is that? Do I even want to know?"

Henry folded his arms defensively. "That's just rust. We've got some industrial dehumidifiers, but it's still a cave. In the Pacific Northwest. Shit gets damp."

"I'll bet. Is that why there's a wet spot on this bench in the shape of someone's back?"

"Hey, I was just doing a few sets before you got here."

"Fair enough. I'll also point out that you used the word 'we.' When you were talking about the dehumidifiers."

"Yeah, so?" Henry thought about it for a second, then frowned. "Just shut up about it, all right? I know he's gone.

I know I shouldn't sulk around in the dark and give into misery. Yeah, yeah. Save it."

Aspen turned in a circle, craning her head back to stare at the ceiling that glowed with constellations. "Are the stars your only companion now, Henry? You have to admit, this mausoleum you have here is way too big for one lone wolf."

Henry tossed himself down on the bench and busted out a few more reps. His muscles had gone cold by now, and the weight was more of a struggle than it should have been. He racked it and sat back up, shaking his head. "Are we making wolf jokes now? Really?"

"Come on. You thought it was funny." Aspen nudged him. "I saw the start of a smile. Besides, we have a deal. I get one a year. Feel free to fire back with any surgeon-related jokes you might have."

Henry nudged her back. "You're such a comedian, sis. You always leave me in stitches."

"See? That was funny. Right? Come on. You can laugh." She bent to the side, checking out the weight plates loaded on the bar. "Holy shit, how much is that?"

Henry finally smiled. "Three plates."

"Sorry, I don't speak meathead. Care to try again?" She cupped a hand to her ear.

"What, you want it in CCs? Yeah, I know that's a measurement of volume, not weight. Save your breath, Ms. Know-it-all. It's three-fifteen."

Her eyes almost bugged out. "As in three hundred and fifteen pounds? And you just lifted it like it was nothing?"

"Hell no. But I'm glad I made it look that way." He shook his arms and stood, grabbing a sweat towel and mopping his face. It turned out he had left his fresh towel in the command center, and this one was an old towel from some workout in the past. Could have been a week ago. Or a month. All he knew was it smelled like ass. He tossed it over his shoulder.

"Done?" she asked. "Good. Feel free to offer your sister a drink. I know I'm a lightweight, but I took public transport to get here. And I walked to the ferry in Seattle. So if I leave a little wobbly, it's no big deal."

They went upstairs, where more reminders of Lexus lurked. Henry put his head down and led the way into the drawing room, where he poured a glass of cognac and handed it to Aspen.

She took a sip and smiled. "I don't know what this is, but it's as smooth as a baby's ass. Actually, it's smoother."

Henry sat on an armchair, waving away the dust that came out of it. "Damn, I guess I need to sit up here more often. Anyway, you're drinking a glass of Louis the Thirteenth cognac."

"Huh." Aspen held the glass to the light, twirling it around. "Is it expensive?"

"You could say that. It's all good. I've had the same bottle up here for years. I don't use it for anything except to impress guests. What do you think? Are you impressed?" He snorted, shaking his head.

Aspen sat next to him, lowering herself gingerly to prevent a similar puff of dust. "I don't think it's about impressing anyone, Henry. I think it's about making people happy.

"Remember when we were kids? You'd always give me all your best stuff. All your toys, all your games. When there was only one slice of cake left you'd let me have it, even if it was from your birthday. You were the sweetest kid and the best big brother anyone could have."

He nodded and turned his head away so she wouldn't see the fresh tears in his eyes.

Aspen went on. "I thought, after all that…bad stuff happened, it might have killed what was good inside you. I worried about it for a long time. But then, the first time you came to see me at work, there was that little boy."

Henry nodded. "Adam Leary. I remember him."

"He was scared. His dad was at work, and his mom had to leave to let the dog out. She was only going to be gone for half an hour, and I know you were busy that day. You still sat with him. I have no idea what you talked about, but by the end of it he was laughing his head off. I had to pull you away because I didn't want him getting too worked up. That was when I realized you were still the same person. You were still my big brother."

"How is Adam, by the way?" he asked, changing the subject.

"Good. Last thing I heard, he had a girlfriend, and he had gotten into sailing. Damn, they grow up fast, don't they? When you're a kid, it seems like it takes forever to become a grownup. Then you have to spend an actual forever as a stressed-out old fart. Life's funny." She swallowed the rest of her drink and stood. "I can tell you're never going to say yes to my offer to stay at my place. I can also tell that you'd rather be alone right now, even though it's the worst thing for you. But I'll leave."

He almost protested, but he knew she'd see right through it. She was right about everything. He didn't want anyone else around right now. If he couldn't have Lexus, the silence and the isolation were the next best things.

Before she left, Aspen turned to deliver some parting words. "I said earlier that I knew how you were feeling, Henry. But I lied. I can't even imagine the strain and the pressure you're under. But life can still be beautiful again. Maybe you should start taking it easy. The job of saving the planet shouldn't fall on one man. If you don't want another best friend, at least get an assistant to move in with you or something."

She set her glass down and left. Henry didn't move for a long time as he mulled over her words.

Could life be better? He shook an imaginary magic eight-ball in his mind, and the response came up, *answer unclear*.

CHAPTER FIFTEEN

Henry was still mulling that question over, but he knew one thing. Aspen was right about him needing a new assistant. He had no idea what he was doing with any of the magitech crap in his arsenal, at least not when it came to maintenance.

That was how he ended up in Seattle a few days later, knocking on the door of a brick townhouse on Sixteenth Street. There was no answer and no hint of movement inside.

"Dirk, I know you're in there. It's Henry Neumann."

He heard the creaking floor now. Probably Dirk looking out through the peephole. The door opened, and the scrawny, suit-wearing wizard stared at him expressionlessly.

"Forgive me for being slow to answer, Henry. These days you can never be too careful about who comes to your door. There are Jehovah's Witnesses and debt collectors, not to mention Girl Scouts peddling their baked confections. I have been looking forward to your visit."

"Um, yeah. Sounds like it. So, can I come in?"

Dirk stepped aside. "Do remember to remove your footwear. I recently steam-cleaned the carpets."

Henry nodded. He knew the rules of visiting the peculiar wizard's home, and he'd come prepared with a comfy pair of loafers. Easy to slip on and off. He picked up his shoes and carried them as they entered the living room.

"I like what you've done with the place," said Henry. "Looks like my dorm room when I was in college. Is that a poster of Jennifer Love Hewitt? I kind of forgot she existed."

Dirk's lip twitch. "She's a timeless beauty. You'd do well to remember that. But I'm forgetting myself. To what do I owe the pleasure of your company?"

"Oh, yeah." Henry smiled, raising a finger. "Remember that time I saved your bacon?"

"No, I don't recall that. I wasn't aware that my bacon had ever needed saving. I generally prefer sausage as a breakfast meat."

"You idiot, I'm talking about when I saved your life. You remember?"

Dirk nodded. "Of course. How could I ever forget the moment? I was staring down the barrel of a twelve-gauge shotgun, already preparing my speech for when I met my maker. I was thinking of how I might introduce myself and begin the ingratiation process so I might carve out the most desirable afterlife for myself."

Henry spun his arm in the air, trying to hurry the wizard along. "Then I showed up. You remember what you said? You pledged a life debt to me."

Dirk let out a long sigh and sat heavily on his couch.

"Have you come to cash in the debt, Henry? I was hoping I might have more time."

"Nah. I just need to get to Oriceran. The Dark Market, specifically."

Dirk shot to his feet, smiling awkwardly. "That I can do very easily. Just step back."

"Why? I want to get through. If the portal opens right in front of me, doesn't that mean I can get through that much faster?"

"Possibly." Dirk held out both hands, his arms starting to shake as magical energy passed over Henry like a cool breeze. "Or you could simply fall between the cracks and end up in the World In Between, where you'll be doomed to walk among lost souls and malevolent entities in a gray, lifeless world where nothing ever happens, and no joy can ever exist. Forever."

"Hm." Henry took a few steps back. "I guess I'll wait over here. Hey, is that a poster of Denise Richards? I kind of forgot she—"

The portal burst open, and that was Henry's cue. He knew these openings could be unstable. When you saw a way through, it was best to take it as soon as possible.

Without another word, he ran and dove through the opening, rolling up onto his feet in lush grass with the sounds and scents of a gloomy and foreboding forest around him.

The portal was already starting to shrink, but Dirk approached it on the other side.

"I'll meet you back here in six hours," the wizard shouted.

Henry gave him the thumbs-up. The portal shrank to

nothing, sealing itself, and Henry turned to survey his surroundings. At first, it seemed he was in a clearing in the middle of nowhere, but then he picked out faint crowd noises. He headed toward them, taking narrow pathways through the trees.

High in the sky, far off to his left, he caught sight of a brief glimmer. A long, dark thread suddenly shot down to the ground. Barely visible was the distant shape of a person hurrying down this ethereal stairway. Not just a person, a Light Elf. From what little he knew off the top of his head, this was the very edge of their kingdom, where it blended in with the no man's land called the Dark Forest. The outermost trees of which he was walking through now.

Henry shook his head. "This place is wild."

He soon joined up with a broader thoroughfare and a stream of foot traffic. He followed the main flow and found the Dark Market. Nearby, standing at the mouth of a trail that led deeper into the trees, was a Wood Elf weaving some sort of magical barrier. It seemed the forest itself was closed at the moment.

For a while Henry wandered the tents aimlessly, taking in the sights. He was overwhelmed by everything he saw but eventually found a table full of items he could recognize. They were MP3 players, iPods, Zunes, and other brands. A sign claimed that they were pre-loaded with all the latest hits and timeless classics.

He turned away from the MP3 players and spotted a tent selling magitech parts. This was where Lexus had procured most of the pieces used in crafting his various gadgets. Henry walked over, stepping up behind a couple of magicals drooling over all the shiny toys.

"You know," Henry said casually, "I could get you all the stuff you could ever want. If you're looking for work outside of Oriceran. I need someone good at inventing and maintaining instruments that assist someone on a mission or a job."

One of the magicals, a dwarf, turned and regarded Henry with narrowed eyes. "Criminal missions?"

Henry nodded but said nothing. Best not to give anything away yet. These guys could think whatever they wanted.

"Criminal." The dwarf nodded slowly, running his fingers through his beard. "You know, that would be a grand way to stick it to my brother. I may be interested, tall man. How's the pay?"

"I'd rather discuss that when we're not surrounded by dangerous, seedy people. If you don't mind. You don't have to call me tall man. The name's Henry Neumann." He offered his hand.

The dwarf shook with his. "Winter Snow. Pleased to meet you."

Henry laughed. "Winter Snow? Your mother must have been creative. What's your brother's name? Green Leaf, or something like that?"

The dwarf growled. "Funny jokes from a funny man. His name is Johnny Walker."

"Huh. What a coincidence. I just bought a bottle of the blue label for someone."

Winter reached up and tapped him lightly on the cheek, shocking Henry into silence. "Not the whisky, you dope. I'm talking about Johnny Walker, my brother. Not that I care about defending his honor. We don't talk much these days. He's too busy playing with Feds, and he never visits."

Winter walked away without another word, but he didn't go far. He stopped at the next tent over and positioned himself behind the table.

Henry followed him over, gazing down at all the wares. He picked up what looked like an ordinary pencil. "Did you make these?"

Winter slapped his hand, deftly catching the pencil as it fell and placing it back down carefully. "Careful, you big oaf. One touch of pencil lead against your skin is enough to inject a hundred microscopic spybots into your skin, and I don't care nearly that much about your personal life. Although I am curious how you got those monstrous pecs." He cupped his hands in front of his chest. "They remind me of the twin mountain peaks near where I grew up. You must make a lot of ladies jealous with those mammaries."

Henry pulled the two halves of his jacket together, blushing. "It's all muscle, man. Anyway, my job offer's only good until I leave Oriceran. Unless you want to sit around here and peddle your wares."

Winter frowned, scanning all the instruments on the table. "I've been here all day, Hank. And I haven't made a single sale. Everyone at this market is too stupid to know a genius piece of work when they see it."

"That's too bad. And it's Henry."

"Is that what you said? Hm." Winter bent down, grabbing a large bag. He proceeded to shove everything on the table into it. "Fine. I'll come to see about your offer. I reserve the right to throw it in your face if it isn't to my liking."

"Of course. You're coming to America. Telling people to shove their offer up their ass is a way of life." Henry tried to take the bag from him, but Winter pulled it away.

"I can manage, pretty boy. You worry about carrying those huge balls of yours out of here. You must have huge ones if you're coming to the Dark Market to poach talent."

Henry shrugged and laughed, trying to play along even though he had no idea what the dwarf was talking about. His curiosity eventually won out though. "What do you mean? Is it dangerous, what I'm doing?"

"Could be." Winter stepped easily between the legs of a towering Kilomea. "For all you know, I'll kill you as soon as we're alone and take all of your crap. But I won't do that. On my honor."

Henry had no idea about the dwarf's honor. As long as he could fix the necklace and maybe finish some of the things Lexus had started, Henry thought he could handle whatever else Winter Snow threw at him.

CHAPTER SIXTEEN

Now that he'd found a potential new assistant, it was
time for Henry to start moving things forward. As
much as he didn't want to, the show must always go on.

The day after returning from Oriceran, he bought a
bunch of moving boxes and walked through the house,
packing away all of the old gnome's most prized posses-
sions and anything that would only serve as a sad
reminder. The latter group included a set of reading
glasses on an end table in the living room, along with the
sudoku puzzle book Lexus had been working his way
through.

It was hard to seal all of this stuff up in a box, but he
forced himself to do it. He muttered to himself as he
worked. "Shit, it feels like I'm already trying to forget. I
promise I won't, Lexus. I don't think I could even if I
wanted to."

At the eastern wall of the library, he came to what
Lexus liked to call his "fun wall." These were all the objects
he had procured that were unique and interesting but

served no practical purpose. They included various puzzle boxes and other mind teasers.

The one that drew Henry's eye was a strange-looking object Lexus had built, powered by one of the prototype batteries constructed by Neumann Corp. It was a shadow box, about three inches deep, filled with fluid.

Immersed in the fluid was a metal sphere. It floated lazily, following predictable routes as it bounced from corner to corner, driven by magnetic forces. But every ten seconds it would suddenly start spinning rapidly, then its course through the liquid would take on strange properties. It seemed to defy physics, but of course, like anything else in the universe, it simply followed rules that weren't immediately obvious.

"The Magnus effect." Henry frowned, grabbed the frame, and placed it in the box. He paused for a moment, then took it back out and set it back where it had been before. "Not everything has to go, right? Christ, now I'm talking to myself. Lexus, why did you have to leave?"

The doorbell rang, echoing through all the rooms. Henry set the box down and hurried to the front of the house to open the door. Winter Snow was standing outside with an improbable number of suitcases and bags hanging off him.

Henry forced a smile onto his face. It wasn't as hard to do as he expected. "You look like an armored turtle."

"So? Is that supposed to be an insult, comparing me with the unique and wondrous wildlife of your planet?" Winter cursed as he nearly dropped one of his bags. "All right, Henry, either help me with all this junk or get out of my way. Preferably both."

Henry grabbed two suitcases and was almost pulled to the ground by the weight. "Jesus H. Christ, what the hell did you bring with you? Fort Knox?"

Winter laughed and stepped easily past him into the house. "I thought you were supposed to be strong, laddy. A big tough guy, and all that. I guess looks can be deceiving. Are you coming or what?"

Henry shook his head and followed the dwarf. Winter made it as far as the bottom of the stairs and let all his bags tumble unceremoniously to the floor as he looked around.

"What a house! Almost as huge as the post office on Oriceran, I'd say. Is there some kind of magic at play here? Because I'd swear it was bigger in here than it looks from outside."

"Watch the floors," Henry grunted. He carefully set his burden down. He set to picking up and stacking the bags in an orderly fashion. "Like you said, looks can be deceiving. For instance, you look like a complete idiot, but you're apparently a great tinkerer. Unless you were lying when I interviewed you yesterday."

"No, I only lie to my girlfriends, not the guys paying me." Winter sighed, patting his belly.

"That's cold." Henry grinned. "You like to lead women on? Not me. With women, I'm always frank and earnest."

"In Chicago you're Frank, and in New York you're Ernest." Winter rolled his eyes. "I know all the best Earth jokes already. You'll have to try harder."

Henry scowled, shoving the last of the bags out of the way. "I was going to say Seattle and Bremerton, but whatever."

Winter smacked both hands together with a thunderous noise. "I need to see the rest of this glorious sanctum, Henry. Care to give me the tour? For the record, I was lying to you before. I don't have a girlfriend. There have been some in the past, but only one at a time, and I always tell the solemn truth. I am an honest dwarf, after all."

Winter picked up the two heaviest suitcases. Despite having asked Henry to give him the tour, it was he who led the way. Henry had to rush to keep up. The small man was quick, despite the load he was carrying.

"Oh, now this is a nice place! You weren't kidding when you said you were well off. If I was this well off, I really would have girlfriends. Plural. You must be some kind of ladies man, Henry."

He shrugged. "Not really. I'm too busy for all that."

"Really? You, too busy? I thought when guys got rich they stopped doing anything useful."

"That does seem to be the trend." The corner of Winter's suitcase bumped a pedestal, and Henry had to lunge to catch the bust of Nikola Tesla before it fell. "Watch it! This is like chasing a two-year-old through the house. You've got to be more careful."

"Roger that, boss." Winter tossed off a lazy salute. "What's this? Some kind of library? Are you one of those guys who buys a billion books but never reads them?"

Henry opened his mouth to make a retort, but after thinking about it, he could only shrug. "Like I said, I don't have time. Any spare moment I have usually gets taken up immediately by something else."

They finished touring the downstairs. Winter spent a particularly long time surveying the kitchen and had many good things to say about it. Finally, there was nowhere else to go but down.

"Let's see it," Winter said. "Where the magic happens. I can't wait for this!"

Henry opened the secret door, and they went down into the cool shadows of the underground tunnel, which took them into the cave. Winter's eyes lit up like a kid in a candy shop as he took in the space.

"Just when I thought this place couldn't get any more impressive. You've got everything down here. Let me see…"

Winter dropped his suitcases and moved from area to area, touching and asking about everything. Henry had to explain what a Ferrari was, as well as a GHD machine.

"What is this, some kind of torture rack?" Winter thumped the cushions with his fist.

"No. You get on it like this." Henry jumped on the machine and pumped out a few reps. "It's for hitting the glutes and the hamstrings."

"Oh, is that why yours are so luscious? You might as well be dripping with gravy, Henry. But I admit, a torture rack would serve a more practical function. Now get off there. You're embarrassing yourself."

They eventually came to the command center, the space full of screens and computers. It doubled as a tinkering area. A huge U-shaped worktable dominated the floor space, still overflowing with gadgetry. Winter grabbed his suitcases and heaved them up on the table. When he opened them, Henry saw that they were full of tools, spare parts, and other objects whose purpose he didn't know.

Winter started shoving things aside carelessly. A few

things fell to the floor, and he didn't bother picking them up. He went right on unpacking his tools, slamming them down on the table, shoving more things out of the way to make room.

Henry bit his tongue, trying to avoid an outbreak of anger as he watched the dwarf tossing Lexus' projects around like they were junk. He knew that if Lexus were here, he'd look up at Henry with a smile and say something like, "It *is* all junk, Henry."

You're right Lexus, he thought. *It is all junk. But it was yours.*

"There we are." Winter started sorting through his tools, laying them out in order. "I think I brought everything I need. It seems there were some fairly wild projects getting worked on here. What sort of things are you looking for, anyway? What does a superhero vigilante like you need while running around spooking bad guys in the dark?" He turned suddenly, narrowing his eyes. "Don't tell me a bat bit you."

Henry sat on an office chair and spun slowly around. He knew that if this partnership would stand a snowball's chance in hell of working out, he would need to let Winter in on the full truth.

"I'm a shifter. I wasn't always, though. I started as a normal human."

Winter nodded. "That's a tough break. It's always hard to get forced into something rather than being born into it. So, you turn into a beast at every full moon and start rampaging through town."

Henry let his shoes skid against the floor, making him stop spinning. "That's a werewolf, dude. I'm a shifter. We can change whenever we want. Into a wolf, not a *were*wolf. It's completely different."

Winter tossed a random bolt at him. "I know that, genius. I was making a joke. You're going to hear a lot of jokes from me, and they won't all be funny, so get ready for it. Anyway…" He turned back to his tools. "I already knew you were a shifter. I felt it as soon as we met. That's one of my many gifts, you see. I always know who I'm dealing with. Not that I had to try very hard with you. Wolves are easy to sniff out. Mostly because they stink."

Henry grabbed the bolt off the floor and threw it back. Winter dodged without looking, ducking his head to the side. The bolt ricocheted off the table and flew off into the cave.

Winter laughed. "I meant no offense, of course. As you can tell by my tactful choice of words. Anyway, I wanted to see if you would tell me the truth about yourself on your own. Job interviews work both ways, you know. The employer has to learn who he's hiring, and the employee also has to learn who he's being hired by."

Henry started spinning again. "What if I didn't tell you?"

"Well, then, Morty's holding my table at the market for a month. I paid him upfront. I can always go back."

Henry pulled his legs in and spun faster. "Good to know. I guess maybe you are smart after all."

"Of course I am. Dwarves are the most intelligent race in either world. Of course, we pay for our intelligence by being the ugliest race. Or maybe it's me." Winter dropped the empty suitcases to the floor and kicked them under the table. "You're a shifter, then. Affected by magic but unable to harness it yourself. That explains why you need so many mechanical tricks. Again, I mean no offense. You certainly have the brains and the brawn, but none of the oomph that magic can give us."

Henry stuck out his legs again, letting himself slow down. He stood and balanced himself by grabbing the edge of the table. "Yeah, magic can help. So can a well-calibrated weapon. When it comes to fighting the average thug, a solid punch usually does the trick anyway."

"Truth." Winter reached out to squeeze Henry's bicep. "I imagine a punch from you wouldn't feel too good. But if that was all you needed, I wouldn't be here. So, what do you want from me? I can fit the power of a tornado in your pocket, Henry. I can build a device that'll enhance your punches and make them twice as powerful. Except maybe that's a bad idea unless you want someone to have to scrape your enemies off the ground with a shovel. Oh, here's an idea. How about—"

Henry held up a hand, stopping Winter in his tracks. "I didn't bring you here to do what I say, Winter. I brought you here to do what I can't. To *think* in a way I'm not capable of. My friend…Lexus, the gnome I was telling you about…"

"Yeah, what about him?" Winter set his tools down and drummed on the table with his knuckles. "I assume I have him to thank for this nice short work surface. Perfect for a man of my stature. But…" He took a closer look at Henry, and his eyes softened. "Take all the time you need, Henry. I'm not going anywhere, not until I get my first paycheck at least."

Henry laughed, blinking fast a few times to clear away

the tears that started to form. "Lexus worked on all these projects because they were his passion. He built whatever he felt like, and most of the time it ended up being useful to me somehow. He had a funny way of doing that, come to think of it. He would come up with some random thing, and it was almost always what I needed."

Winter nodded. "Perhaps he was paying closer attention to your needs than you thought. So, you want me to decide what I build. Even better. Now tell me something. What do you do out there in the city at night? Are you always in wolfie form, or what?"

Henry took a seat again, answering all the questions Winter threw at him. It was a much more intense grilling session than he had subjected the dwarf to the day before when they first returned from Oriceran. But Henry put his impatience away and got through it, entertained by Winter's colorful epithets as he toiled away.

Finally, the dwarf picked something up from the table and showed it off. "What does it look like to you, Henry?"

"Um..." Henry rubbed his chin, leaning forward for a closer peek. "It looks like a pencil."

Winter grinned, pressing a spot on the pencil's shaft. A bright red light shot out of it, landing in the center of Henry's chest. "The first thing I saw when I came into this cave was that arsenal you have hanging on the wall. That hidden umbrella gun is genius, but I wondered how you were able to aim it. Now you have a nice inconspicuous laser light. No one will be the wiser."

Henry took the pencil and tossed it back and forth from hand to hand. "Huh. Feels like a pencil, too. Not bad, Winter. Not bad at all."

CHAPTER SEVENTEEN

Getting back on the horse was always hard, but Henry knew it was time to get out and save the world. Or at least save a few stupid kids from themselves.

He parked his brand-new Suzuki Hayabusa on the lower ferry deck to begin the long, boring ride across the Sound. Boring wasn't always bad, though. It gave him a chance to head up to the passenger deck and walk a few laps, getting his thoughts and plan in perfect order.

"So, you're sure this thing is going to work?" Henry lifted the face shield on his helmet and let the sea breeze hit him in the face.

Winter's voice came through his earpiece. "No, not completely. That depends on the prevailing conditions over the past few days. Scents are funny. Depending on the weather, they can either stick around for months or disappear in a few hours. It's worth a try, though. What I'm confused about is why you didn't sniff them out that night when you had a chance."

Henry came upon an older couple leaning on the railing, soaking in the breeze. He waited until he was well past them before answering. "I was in the middle of the city, so I didn't want to expose myself. I also had to get back to Hatch. It'll be much easier if I can find them in human form."

The ferry approached the city, and Henry made his way back to the lower deck. He was first in line disembarking and was off into the city as soon as the boat docked.

It was a quick drive back to Schmitz Reserve Park. He retraced his steps from the night he went running with Hatch and found his way to the sports field. There were a bunch of teenagers around, kicking soccer balls and throwing footballs back and forth, but thankfully no one was using the bleachers except for a couple of kids doing their homework.

He ducked under the bleachers and made his way into the hideout. He felt at ease. No wolf sense caused the hairs on his arms to raise. It was safe to assume the hideout was currently empty, which turned out to be the case.

Everything was as it had been the night he first found the place. It seemed that no one had dared to come back, probably for fear of encountering the big bad wolf.

"Well, I'm here knocking at your door." Henry reached into his satchel and pulled out a device that looked a bit like an electrician's multimeter. "I'll huff, and I'll puff, and I'll blow your asses out of the water. Okay, Winter, how does this thing work?"

"It couldn't be simpler. Turn it on and let it do its thing. Hey, you might want to put on those glasses. They make you look smarter."

"Oh yeah." Henry reached back into the satchel and found a glasses case. He pulled the glasses out and put them on. "How's that?"

"Perfect signal. That is, if you are currently standing in a shadowy place that seems to be littered with filthy rags."

"Sounds about right." Henry hit the power button on the scentmeter. It beeped once, and the tiny LCD screen displayed a message. **Calibrating... Detecting scent profiles...**

It flashed with a series of readouts of various compounds in the air. It stopped after a moment, showing traces of urea and something called methylhexanoic acid. Henry remembered from some casual science reading that these were compounds found in human sweat.

"We've got something here, Winter."

"I see that, genius. Now let it work for a moment. Hold it very still. It's working on a profile. Pretty much all the same substances are found in the sweat of every human on Earth, especially among individual ethnicities, but the proportions and amounts are unique to everyone."

Henry had already been keeping his arm still, but it suddenly became a lot harder now that Winter had told him to do so. "You're from Oriceran. How do you know all this?"

"Because I build things that get traded between worlds. Because in my profession, knowledge pays. Okay, we should be good any second now." The scentmeter beeped again, showing one green light. It then switched to all red. "Good. It's got that specific scent profile saved in memory. All you have to do is start moving around. Follow the lights."

Henry nodded, stepping out of the hideout. He emerged into the sunlight and checked the scentmeter again. Only five of the lights were red now. The sixth had gone orange. Henry left the park and started walking in a random direction. The sixth light went red again. He turned the other way and walked a bit further, and watched the light go from orange to green.

"We're in business. This thing's pretty handy, Winter."

"Yeah, you'd better get used to saying that. I'm a genius, you know."

"If this works, I guess I'll have to start believing you." Henry had only gone a block, but the sixth light had already died, and the fifth one was green now. "Damn, I guess we're pretty close to them."

Winter laughed. "Correction. We're pretty close to wherever this scent trail ends. For all we know, it'll take us to a gym where this kid took a shower and washed the stink off. Hopefully, we get lucky and end up somewhere more useful."

Henry now had the right direction, so he returned to the Suzuki motorcycle and strapped the scentmeter down between the handlebars. "Keep an eye on it for me, Winter."

"Will do. I'll guide you from here." Henry started to drive, and Winter fed him directions. "Take a right. Okay, go straight… Keep going straight… take a left, maybe? Never mind. Turn around."

By fits and starts, Henry finally wound up outside the last place he expected. It was a bakery, the window display filled with cakes and pies.

"Quit staring. You'll make me hungry," Winter growled at him.

"What do I do?"

"You're the smart guy. Figure it out. Might I suggest going inside?"

Henry went in, smiling at the cute chime of the bell above the door. A kindly older woman greeted him from behind the counter, her smile widening when Henry pulled up the face shield on his helmet.

"She thinks you're cute," Winter told him. "Probably wants to pinch your cheeks and set you up on a date with her daughter, who finally had the guts to divorce her deadbeat husband who was having an affair with her childhood best friend. Or something like that. Come on now, Henry. Put on the charm."

"Good morning." Henry put on his best smile, the one he used for presentations and press conferences. "I wish I was here to buy some of these delicious-looking pastries, but actually, I was looking for someone. Maybe you can help me out. A friend of mine…he's afraid his teenage son might be involved with a gang. He told me he saw his son coming in here. I'm kind of like the cool uncle, in a way, so he sent me. You know how it is."

"I don't know if she does," Winter replied nervously.

The old lady suddenly smiled and nodded her head. "I don't know which one of them your friend's son might be, but I've been feeding a group of kids lately. I hardly ever see them because they come here late at night. Instead of throwing away whatever pastries I have that are on the stale side, I've been leaving them outside the back door in a box."

Winter piped in. "Okay, Henry, I think we have what we need. If not, we can always come back."

Henry thanked the woman and left. He drove the bike around to the back, where the scentmeter beeped once to show it had picked up a recently saved scent.

Henry shook his head in wonder. "Damn. I wish I had this thing a long time ago."

They followed the same plan as before, Henry driving and Winter routing. This time, the journey wasn't nearly so meandering. In less than fifteen minutes Henry was rolling into a nearby neighborhood, a sleepy street lined with small houses with junky cars parked out front. A lower-income area.

The scentmeter indicated one house in particular. It didn't look strange at first, but as soon as Henry got off the bike and walked up the driveway, the hairs on his arms and neck stood straight up. He kept his face shield down as he approached. As he came near the door, he noticed that someone had boarded up all the windows on the inside, completely sealed from prying eyes.

Talking to Winter aloud would give away the fact that he was here to whoever might be lurking inside, so Henry knew he had to go this one alone. Use his wolf senses and find his way through it.

Or maybe he was thinking too hard. After all, they were a bunch of kids, not supervillains. He already knew from his encounter with Ellie in his office that they were fairly approachable, maybe even reasonable.

He cleared his throat and knocked on the door.

"What the hell are you doing?" Winter demanded. "They're probably already halfway out through the back windows. You'd better circle around to cut them off."

"We don't even know if they're here right now. They probably have bases all around the city. Besides, I know how to deal with rebellious teenagers. I used to be one." He knocked again and waited.

There was no answer, even after several minutes. Henry leaned against the outside wall, sticking his hands in his pockets to appear casual, even though the shield over his face ruined that illusion. The day was warm and breezy. Nothing was going on except a battle in the trees between a few rambunctious birds.

Apparently, no one was home.

So why were his senses telling him otherwise?

He was starting to plan out a different course of action when he suddenly heard a humming, ratcheting sound from the front of the house. It was the garage door opening.

Winter's shaky voice sounded in his ear. "I don't like this, Henry."

"So it's not only me getting weird vibes. Good to know."

Henry sidled along the wall and peeked around the corner, trying to see into the open garage. It was too dark and shadowy inside due to the overcast sky and the prevalence of trees around the property.

However, he knew someone was in there. "Ellie? Are you there? It's me, Henry Neumann. The guy whose house you broke into, if you don't remember. I know, you break into tons of houses. Pretty dumb of me to expect you to remember a specific one."

Silence held sway for another few moments. Henry's eyes began to adjust to the shadows, and he concluded that the garage was empty. The thought occurred to him that it was a trap, the sound of the door opening a ruse to get him into this position. The idea came too late.

Pain exploded at the back of his skull below the edge of the helmet. Henry lurched forward, turning and trying to find his adversary through his spinning vision. He saw a familiar man standing there. It was the guy who had attacked him at home that night—the same guy who killed Lexus. He had clobbered Henry in the head with his obnoxious walking stick.

The guy looked surprised. "I put most of my force behind that blow. I had hoped to incapacitate you with it. You're even more resilient than I feared. No matter…"

He twisted the shaft of the walking stick, pulled the shell away, and revealed the deadly blade beneath.

"I think I shall kill you in the same manner as that freakish creature I skewered in your home. His death may have been a loss in its own right, but yours will not be. You are a parasite, Henry Neuman. You are a parasite who is hoarding so much power for yourself. I have made it my mission to liberate that power."

Henry knew he had a concussion. He fought the dizziness and nausea, stumbling back and forth to try and keep himself upright. His vision was still split and fuzzy, and he watched as two of the men charged toward him.

In his present state, it was all Henry could do to dodge. He was vaguely aware of Winter shouting in his ear, but the words escaped him. He dove to the side and rolled clumsily to his feet, watching as the other man corrected his course and charged again.

This time, Henry rolled onto his back and caught the man in the chest with both feet. He heaved the guy up and over, sending him into a wild flip that there was no way he could recover from.

Somehow he did, landing on his feet. At least the blade was gone, having fallen out of his grip and bounced away across the driveway.

"A clever move." He rolled up his sleeves and pulled his leather gloves on tighter. "I give you some credit, Neumann. I knew you'd be smart enough to find this place but a bit too dumb to realize it was a trap. The name's Stryker, by the way. Bechtel Stryker. You're no honorable man, but I am, and I believe it's good for a person to at least know the name of who kills them."

Some of the fuzz cleared from Henry's mind, and he finally heard Winter's words. *"Get up! Get out of there!"*

As soon as he got to his feet and tried to run, he knew that was impossible. He felt like he was moving in quick-sand. Stryker easily intercepted him, doubling him over with a vicious kick to the stomach.

Henry keeled over. It hurt, but he played it up. Trying to lull Stryker in for the death blow. At the last second, Henry shot upward, aiming an uppercut directly at the underside of Stryker's chin.

Instead, he hit nothing but air. He didn't even see Stryker anywhere. Turning in a circle, he tried and failed to reacquire his enemy. "I don't know where he went, Winter. Did you see? Where the hell is he?"

"No idea, but now's your chance to get out of there. No dying for you today. Who would pay all my bills?"

Henry fished his keys out of his pocket and stumbled out into the road. He flung himself onto the seat of the Suzuki and started the engine.

There was a roaring sound back at the house, and Henry looked up to see Stryker rolling out of the garage in the saddle of his own motorcycle.

"*Shit.*" Henry pulled up the kickstand and twisted the throttle. The Suzuki showed its power, lurching forward. Henry used one hand to yank his helmet off, tucking it under his arm. He pulled his glasses off and put them on backward, draping them over the back of his head. "Can you see him, Winter?"

"He's closing in on you. Thirty feet back. Twenty. Ten."

Henry twisted the throttle again, pulling even more speed out of the bike. He clipped a curb and went airborne for a second, crashing back down to earth as he left the neighborhood and joined traffic flow on the main road.

"Still coming. Not slowing down. Who the hell is this guy?"

"No idea." Henry gritted his teeth, squeezing the brakes a little as he wove in and out of traffic. Kids stared at him through back windows, and adults yelled at him to slow down. "Whoever he is, he's got some magical mojo that I don't have. I should have torn him apart when he broke into my house."

"Aye, you should have. You'd be wise not to miss another chance like that."

"I can't shift right now, Winter. Not in broad daylight. I've got to get away from this guy."

"Well, you aren't having much luck with that. He's right behind you."

Henry caught a glimpse in someone's side mirror. Stryker was less than a car length back and closing in. Whatever aftermarket gear he had on the ratty old motorcycle he was riding, it was faster than Henry's stock Suzuki.

"Watch out! He's trying to hook you!" Winter shouted.

Henry gave the engine another blast, but Stryker's walking stick was already hooked into the back collar of his jacket. The increase in speed only served to yank him out of his seat. Henry seemed to hang still in the air for a second, watching as the brand-new motorcycle ghost-rode itself straight through the intersection up ahead.

That was all he had time to see. In midair, he quickly stuffed the helmet back over his head in preparation for a rough landing.

He was on his back a fraction of a second later, skidding along the asphalt, but heard the telltale crash. He just hoped the bike hadn't hit someone else's car.

"Well, that didn't go very well," Winter remarked.

"No shit." Henry sat up, looking around. He figured he was safe now, being in the middle of public, but that was a false hope.

Stryker's foot hit him in the side of the face, spinning his helmet around and cutting off half of his vision. Henry rolled to the side, reaching out for anything that could help him get to his feet. Another kick landed on his ribs, driving every last bit of air out of his lungs. He collapsed, wheezing and breathless.

There was a single blare of a siren, followed by a shouting voice. *"Stop right there! Don't move or I'll shoot!"*

Henry had never been quite so thankful for the Seattle

Police Department. He fixed his helmet and saw Stryker quickly ripping a side mirror off a car and chucking it at the cop. The cop ducked to avoid having his nose busted, and by the time he stood back up, Stryker was gone. The sound of his motorcycle engine faded into the distance.

CHAPTER EIGHTEEN

If Henry could say one good thing about this disaster of a day, it was that the Suzuki was in better shape than he expected. Its speed had been arrested a bit by a few bushes, and by the time it hit the telephone pole, it was going fairly slowly.

Even so, the bike was squealing miserably and begging for mercy by the time he wheeled it back inside the cave. Henry wasn't doing much better, fighting for each breath through the massive bruise on his side.

Winter was waiting for him, his powerful arms folded across his chest. He regarded the broken Suzuki with a frown. "Quite a nice piece of machinery to die so young. Automotive technology is its own kind of magic. Unfortunately, your vehicles are quite sensitive to sudden stops. Especially when they involve a collision with a solid and unmovable object."

Henry shrugged, then grunted in pain when the motion tugged at his bruised flesh. "You'll get used to it, Winter. It happens. A lot."

Winter followed Henry as he limped toward the medical bay. "You're telling me, Henry, that you continuously throw your money at high-end motorcycles only to crash them one after the other?"

"That's exactly what I'm telling you." Henry heaved himself onto an examination table and started cutting off his shirt with a pair of shears. "Some guys blow their money on travel and nights out at clubs. I blow mine so I can at least have something nice to crash on. Better than doing it on whatever piece of shit that Stryker guy was on."

"That piece of shit gave your little steed a run for its money, I'd say." Winter stole the shears and slapped Henry's hands away. "Put your clumsy fingers somewhere else. Let me do this."

Henry winced, preparing for a dwarven walloping, but it didn't come. Winter was surprisingly gentle as he touched Henry's bruise.

"Must be a cracked rib or two. And a hell of a bruise. You won't be able to take a full breath for a while, laddy, but I think you'll make it. Now let's see about this bleeding." He sat Henry up and used a gauze pad to clean a gash on the back of his head. "Yep, he hit you hard. I'm as surprised as he was that you didn't go out for the count."

"I guess when my sister told me I had a hard head, she was right." Henry hissed in pain as Winter pulled the wound together. "Speaking of Aspen, I was worried I might have to call her in, and I'd have to deal with her lecturing. Where'd you learn to do all this?"

Winter grunted. "Me? Oh, I have siblings of my own, Henry. A lot of them. Don't even get me started on cousins. The whole lot of them are clumsy or involved in dangerous business. Or both. Knowing a little about how to stitch someone up…the knowledge always comes in handy eventually. Plus it's good to do favors for family. Keeps the scarier cousins from looking at me funny, you know. I reckon I can stitch this up quick."

Henry winced, feeling the first stab of the needle. "Sounds like you have a close-knit family."

"Aye. The closest. Hold still, you dope. Unless you want this to take five times longer than it needs to. That's what I always tell my girlfriends, too. Maybe one day I'll learn how to make love to a woman properly."

Henry laughed, causing his whole body to shake.

"I said hold still!" Winter flicked the back of his head. "You humans and your big bodies. So clumsy and unstable. It's a wonder you can move around at all. There, that ought to do it. Only three stitches. No big deal."

Henry reached back to feel at the wound. "Thanks, Winter. I had no idea I was even bleeding."

"That's probably the concussion, making you stupid." Winter kicked himself toward the command center on his rolling chair. "By the way, I got a bit bored waiting for you to get back, so I decided to work on something special. I think it'll come in handy now."

He came back holding a contraption that looked like a heavy-duty potato masher attached to two thick leather straps. "Give me your arm."

Henry stuck out his arm, and Winter strapped the thing to him, snugging it tight. "What is it?"

"It's what I talked about before." Winter beamed proudly. "A punch enhancer. Go and try it out." Henry tried to get up but immediately wobbled around. "On second thought, it can wait. It's a simple device. It detects a punching motion and explodes out just before the moment of impact, effectively doubling the delivered force. If I've done my math right, it probably won't cause the bones in your arm to shatter."

"That's good to know." Henry lifted his arm, testing the weight of the thing. "The ferry from Seattle only takes an hour. How'd you have time to make this?"

Winter waved expansively. "I'm just that clever. Here, I'll take that off before you get confused and try to scratch your balls or something. Wouldn't want any unfortunate accidents."

He took the device back to the command center and returned with a bag of beef jerky. "Pilfered this from the kitchen. Care for a bite?"

Henry grabbed a few pieces and laid back on the table, chewing slowly.

"You know, Henry, I think I understand some of what you do and why you do it." Winter tossed a piece of jerky into the air and caught it in his mouth. "But I still don't know you. The man you are beneath all this. I don't expect you to let me in on that secret. Not yet, anyway. Even so, I feel like I know more about you than most people in your life."

Henry sighed. "Shut up and give me some more jerky."

"Here you go. Take some more. I'm good at sharing. Not so good at shutting up. So think about this for a moment. Sometimes when we have one big secret, Henry, we get so caught up in maintaining it that we lock away every last thing about ourselves. Makes it impossible to build a tribe." Winter held up a hand. "I know. You have a pack you run with. But they aren't a tribe, not if they don't know your real name."

Henry sighed and sat up, looking toward the broken Suzuki. Past it, he saw the workbench he sometimes used to fix up his bike parts. There was another knick-knack sitting on it, a wire sculpture of a bird that Lexus had fashioned one day. He laid back again.

"Hatch knows who I am," he said.

"Because you told him?"

"Not exactly. We were there together, at the start. We were both turned into shifters together. We had our entire lives taken from us. The dark families completely disrupted our futures. So we bonded. We kept each other sane during that initial period."

Winter crumpled up the empty jerky bag and threw it onto the floor. "Okay. I get it. But you aren't only a shifter, are you? You aren't only a vigilante billionaire, and you aren't just an angry guy trying to get his magic rock back."

Henry stared at him. "What do you mean?"

"I mean, laddy, you're a man. Aren't you?"

"Last time I checked." Henry glanced down at the hem of his pants. "I guess I can make sure…"

Winter waved both hands urgently. "No go, Henry. The last thing I need to see is your tallywhacker. I'll trust you when you say it's there. What I'm talking about is that you're a person. You were somebody before all this happened to you."

Henry nodded. "I was a normal kid. Kind of a cocky little shithead who thought he was the best at everything, but I also cared about the people around me. I took care of them however I could. There's always been something in me, Winter."

The dwarf nodded. "A drive to make the world a better place."

Henry shook his head. "No. More like guilt. For as long as I can remember, I felt like I had to prove to myself and the world that I deserved to exist. I don't know where that feeling came from, but I figured out that doing things for other people made it go away for a little while.

"Other than that, I was normal. I went to school, I had friends, and I mostly got along with my baby sister. When the time came, I went to college. I was studying for a chemical engineering degree. But all that got kinda derailed."

"Aye, that tends to happen when the dark families scoop you up and turn you into their latest test subject." Winter went back into the command center and returned with a package of cookies, which he had already eaten half of. "It wasn't a good start to your adult life, but you've turned it around. You should be proud of yourself for that. Cookie? Chocolate chunk. My favorite."

He offered the package. Henry shook his head. "You're still hungry?"

Winter shrugged, munching his cookies. A bunch of crumbs fell into his beard. "Sure. And you're not? After all that work trying to keep that weird bastard from killing you, I thought you would have worked up an appetite."

Henry laid back, throwing an arm over his eyes. "I feel kind of sick. Probably the concussion. Don't worry. I know you're not supposed to fall asleep."

"Actually, that's a myth. It's fine to sleep when you have

a concussion. Your sister could probably have told you that." Winter brushed the crumbs away and set the cookies aside. "Gotta watch my figure. What's she like, by the way?"

"She's not into short, round bearded dudes if that's what you're asking. She's a badass who saves kids for a living. I always tell her she's got a way more important job than I do. Of course, she always tells me right back that she wouldn't be able to do her job without lights and electricity."

Henry smiled as his thoughts drifted to better days. "When we were kids, she was always so bossy. I let her have her way. My dad always used to say I shouldn't do that. She'd grow up to be a stuck-up woman who couldn't handle being told no. I guess we proved the old man wrong."

"She sounds like a treat, all right." Winter sighed wistfully. Then he came back to attention. "Not like that, I mean. So, um, you were kidnapped and all. What was that like?"

Henry frowned as his mind shifted into a much darker place. He lifted his arm off his eyes and looked at the dwarf. "I don't really talk about that. Not with anyone other than Lexus. Even Aspen doesn't know all the details."

"Oh, um..." Winter looked around desperately. "Oh! Here, I wanted to show you this. I noticed when I was checking your ribs that you have a good deal of scars. Check this one out." Winter pulled up his sleeve, revealing a huge, rough-edged scar that covered half of his forearm. "Ever seen a Kilomea up close, Henry? I have, in the middle of a land skirmish I took part in."

Henry sat up, getting a closer look at the scar. "You survived a fight with a Kilomea?"

"Aye." Winter's expression went sober. He pressed his lips tightly together. "I was the only one who did. It was me and fifteen others in my group. All hale and hearty dwarves, ready to split skulls and make new songs of victory. I remember it was an eerie day, silent and full of fog. The kind of day that makes you want to huddle up inside and lock the doors. But nothing was going to get our spirits down. Until…"

He swallowed, his eyes sweeping through the room as though he were back there, scanning the vista of the battlefield.

"We were on our way to the front lines to offer our aid. Ahead of us, we saw what we thought were hillocks. Little tufts of grass. At least, that's what I saw. When we came closer, we realized they were bodies. The dead, scattered all across this broad field. We realized the skirmish was already over, and our side had lost. But not all of the enemy forces had departed. Suddenly, out of the fog, we heard this great bellowing roar. The Kilomea came, dashing toward us. We had little time to react, but as one we all charged into battle. Brave, noble dwarves that we were. Not one of us came away but old Winter Snow."

He reached for the cookies again. This time, when offered, Henry took one.

"At this point, though, the story takes a more positive turn. My group was not the only reinforcement headed to the front that morning. Others arrived as we were dying at the hands of the Kilomea. They struck the beast down. Then we realized it was the sole remaining enemy and that many of the dead on the ground belonged to the other side. We won the battle.

"In the end, I had the land and no one to share it with. It figures. I would rather have it the other way, my friends but no land. The regret still lives right here, fresh as can be."

Winter pounded a fist against his chest, then quickly wiped a tear from his eye.

"You see, Henry," he went on, "you're not the only one who lives with shadows at the back of your mind. It can help to let them out, once in a while."

Henry got up slowly, holding a hand to his side, and headed for the stairs. "There's only so much weight one man can bear, Winter. The looks. The questions. It's too much."

Winter rushed to catch up with him. "Try me, Henry. I can listen and work at the same time. We don't even need to make eye contact. It'll be like you're talking to an empty room."

The dwarf took a step away, keeping his eyes on Henry. When he saw that Henry wasn't going anywhere, he made his way back to the command center and started tinkering with something.

Henry had to speak up to be audible in the large space. "It started as a normal day. I spent most of the morning in classes. I remember wanting to bang my head against the wall. Chemical engineering is hard. I thought it would be the hardest thing I ever had to do. It's funny to think back to now."

He found himself slowly crossing the space, getting closer to Winter.

"There was this weird spot on campus, an out-of-the-way little pathway between a couple of lesser-used buildings. Even during the busiest part of the day, it was always deserted. I liked walking through there. It gave me a chance to recharge a bit between classes. That's where I was, walking along and minding my own business when they got me."

Winter didn't stop what he was doing. He didn't slow down or show any other sign that he was listening. It helped give Henry the courage to go on.

"I didn't see much. They put this bag over my head, and I assume they must have used magic on me because I couldn't hear anything. It was like I was lost in the dark, completely cut off from the world. But I could still feel. They put me in a van, and we drove for a long, long time. I was scared, but I had no idea what horrors were waiting for me."

Henry had reached the worktable now, resting his hand on the edge of it and feeling the vibrations of Winter's work. They stopped for a moment as the dwarf finally looked at him. The look only lasted a second before he returned to work.

"I don't remember all the details myself." Henry took a few steps closer, curious about what Winter was doing. "That kind of suffering will do it to you. It screws up your mind pretty bad. You repress a lot of it. But there's no way anyone could forget the pain they put me through. I wouldn't wish it on my worst enemy."

Winter nodded. "Not even Bechtel Stryker, huh?"

"No, not even him. The experiments were only the start of it. It was almost better when I didn't know what they were for. Eventually, though, I felt that something was different about me. The first time I transformed, it was the most terrifying moment of my life, even to this day. Words can't describe the confusion and shock. Eventually, though, I came to find a bit of solace in transforming. They let me outside when I was in wolf form. I was watched, of course, and I would never make it very far. But they let me hunt. Mostly small animals at first, as I learned the ropes."

"Very kind of them to let you get some fresh air." Winter kept working as though he were listening to a radio play. "I take it they weren't all that kind, in actual fact."

"No. Mostly they tortured me. One of their favorite things to do was to hang me upside-down under this broken water pipe. Nothing quite like having all your blood pooling in your head while a constant torrent of filthy water blasts up your nostrils. It was almost impossible to breathe. They'd leave me like that for hours. I assume if I didn't have the resilience of a shifter, it would have killed me. They were experimenting, is what they liked to say. Trying to find out my limits, and why some of us healed faster or slower than others."

"Sounds like torture to me, Henry. How the hell did you ever get away?"

Henry shrugged, tapping nervously on the table. "They kept us at this estate in the middle of nowhere in Kentucky. It was pretty secure, but there were some holes. One night I saw a sliver of an opportunity. I decided to take it, because why the hell not, and I got lucky. I shifted, and I ran my ass off as soon as I was clear. I didn't even care what direction I was going.

"I remember there was this woman… I had no idea who

she was. Sort of a tough-looking chick. I could feel that she was someone powerful, and I half-expected her to stop me. But she let me keep on going."

Winter laughed, hammering away at something that looked far too delicate to be hammered on. "Who would try to stop a huge wolf running at them in the middle of the night?"

"I guess you have a point there. But I still remember her face. I could be wrong, but I really think it was a woman named Leira Berens. What are you working on?" Henry gestured at the delicate doodad.

"I'm working on listening to your sob story and looking like I'm doing something useful." Winter put his tools down. "It's no use, though. I know of Leira Berens. Not many people from my world don't. Tell me the rest."

The dwarf hooked his ankle around the legs of a stool and kicked it over. Henry sat and concluded his tale.

"I changed back to human form somewhere in the woods of Kentucky. Naked and alone, completely unsure what to do next or who to turn to. I eventually found a house and snatched some old clothes from their tool shed. Hitchhiked home. It took a few days, and I was terrified that they'd catch up to me.

"When I got there, only Aspen was home. At first, she just held me. We were silent for a long time. I finally told her, knowing she'd probably think I was insane. She didn't. She never questioned my story even once."

Henry lapsed into silence, feeling completely drained. He stared at the floor for a long time and didn't see Winter coming over until the dwarf set a hand on his shoulder.

Winter held out his other hand. Resting in it was the fragile-looking doodad.

Winter smiled. "I lied. I *was* working on something. You can take it. It's safe until you throw it at something with enough velocity."

Henry grabbed the little spherical object, giving it a gentle squeeze. He felt how dense it was. "What is it? Some kind of grenade?"

"Pretty much. Using hammer blows, I transferred a good amount of kinetic energy into it. It'll hold that energy until a large enough force breaks it open. It's not going to shred things quite like your normal hand grenade. Think of it more like a very strong wind."

"A wind grenade." Henry smiled. "Come on, Winter, you expect me to believe you made a damn wind grenade?"

Winter took the object back. With the end of a screwdriver, he broke a tiny piece off the sphere. He chucked the piece at the floor, and it made a sharp snapping sound. Henry felt a force against his legs, like a strong gust of wind or a shockwave.

"Holy shit!" Henry stood, pointing at the spot on the floor where the piece had landed. "A wind grenade!"

"Never doubt me, muscles. Now, how about we go find ourselves a proper meal?"

CHAPTER NINETEEN

Time passed, and Henry made no further progress on the Bechtel Stryker problem. Winter Snow settled in at the base and life went on mostly as normal.

Henry worked from home for an entire month, reluctant to have to explain his injuries if he were to go into the office. He stayed in Bremerton, recuperating from his disastrous run-in with Stryker.

He spent days ruminating at his desk, thinking of what he could have done differently. He spent nights being pestered by Winter to try his newest gadget. But something about this new villain was bothering him.

Stryker was more dangerous than he was used to, far from a street thug he could take down in an evening. The consequences of what the man was doing could be worse than anything Henry had ever faced. He felt it in his shifter bones.

By Friday, he felt the edge of a new idea, but it was still eluding him. He was about ready to bang his head against the wall when his phone suddenly rang. It was Aspen. He answered it with a smile. "How's it going? Got some downtime at the hospital?"

Aspen yawned. "Not really. I'm calling you while waiting for the ADM to dispense some amoxicillin."

"Hey, I knew one of those words. I had to take amoxicillin for pneumonia when I was a kid. You remember that?"

"I remember saying to Mom that it sounded like wet rocks when you breathed. She told me I was destined to become a doctor and I said, no, ew, I don't like touching sick people. I guess she was right and I was wrong. Anyway, onto the reason I called so I can get back to work…"

Henry sighed, staring at his bank of monitors. "Tell me about it. It's been a long week, but hey, only two hundred and nineteen emails to go."

Aspen chuckled. There was a faint clattering sound. "Got the goods! Emails, huh? Shouldn't you be focused on solving the energy crisis? We can talk more some other time. Gotta be quick now. Basically, I called to tell you that I'm getting an award."

"Oh! Nice little pizza party in the breakroom? You deserve it."

"Yeah, something like that, but at fancy digs and with everyone wearing tuxes. I'd like you to come. I'll text you the details. Gotta go."

She hung up, and Henry tried to get back to work. He got the text a moment later, and his eyes went wide when he read it. "The Aerlume, huh? Eight o'clock tomorrow night. Damn, sis, what kind of award are they giving you?"

Henry asked Winter to hold down the fort and headed out in a car this time. He didn't want to risk crashing into anything while on his way to Aspen's big night.

The Aerlume was close to the ferry dock on the Seattle side, so he parked his car at the Bremerton terminal and walked onboard. A little over an hour later he was jogging up to the Aerlume from the eastern side. It was a low, unassuming building surrounded by glass to give the best view of the water and the setting sun.

As soon as he came inside, he noticed two things at once. There were a lot of people here. And his sister's face was plastered all over, on signboards and banners. Henry grabbed a champagne glass from a passing tray and carefully looked over the crowd for familiar faces. Friends and foes. It was second nature to him, no matter where he was. Always be aware of your surroundings.

Mostly he saw strangers, but one person stood out to him. Henry gazed at the familiar woman standing near the back windows. A smile crept across his face at the sight of the long, graceful legs barely covered by the short black dress and dark hair cascading down a curvy back. He waited for another waiter to pass and quickly snatched another glass from the tray. "Excuse me."

He weaved through the crowd to the woman by the window and gently touched her elbow.

"Nicole Thomas, bounty hunter," he whispered. He walked up next to her and stared at the view through the glass. "Beautiful, isn't it? You should see the Sound during the sunset. The way it lights up. It can catch you by surprise." He looked over at her, arching an eyebrow. "Didn't expect to spot you here tonight. Is there someone in the crowd I should be watching?"

Nicole glanced over with a knowing smile. "I don't work *all* the time, Henry." She took the second glass of champagne and gently swirled it. "Can't say I'm surprised to see *you* here."

Henry let the question drop but casually scanned the crowd again. Nothing off-center, for now.

"I saw Aspen's name at the top of the invitation and cleared my schedule." The bounty hunter lifted her glass. "Not often I can find a free night. I'm always up for a reunion. Besides, I've never been here before. Nice place, isn't it?"

Henry stopped watching the people and looked around at the décor. "Very nice. Understated. You might be surprised to hear it's my first time here, too."

"Not really. The rest of the world sees you as some aloof billionaire inventor, but we know better." Nicole turned her back to the window, taking a sip of champagne.

"Not very discerning with who they let in, though," Henry teased, gently nudging her smooth shoulder. "Tell me, who here at the party had the bad taste to invite the likes of you?"

"Is that any way to pick up a lady? I assume that's what you were going for. Bold of you to assume that you're close to my type, though."

Henry grinned and grabbed a chicken skewer from a passing tray. "I'm rich, and I haven't started going bald yet. I assumed I was every woman's type."

It was their usual banter, always laced with a hint of danger.

She batted her eyelashes at him. "My mistake. Oh, please, Henry, sweep me off my feet. I'm a poor damsel who needs someone to put her name on a joint checking account. Oh, wait, I just got paid a hundred grand for bringing in a psycho drug baron."

"Still in the game, huh? How's that going?" Henry took a filled puff pastry from a waiter working through the crowd.

"Like I said, Henry. A hundred grand. That kind of speaks for itself. Hey, give me one of those." She snatched one of the appetizers from Henry and took a bite. "Nuh-uh. That's goat cheese. Never mind."

She looked around, casually wrapping the pastry in a cocktail napkin, setting it down on the windowsill a few feet from where she was standing. She swallowed what was left of her champagne and reached for Henry's glass. He gave it to her, grinning.

She grimaced, finishing his glass. "I *hate* goat cheese."

"I can tell." A band that had been setting up by the wall finally started to play. Henry offered Nicole his hand. "Care to dance?"

She set the glass down and took his hand. "Just as long as you promise not to step on my feet like you did last time. If you bruise any of my toes, I'll bruise the rest by kicking your ass."

"Don't worry. I've been practicing."

The song was energetic, and all eyes were on Henry and Nicole as they twirled through the room. What they lacked in finesse they met up for with sheer panache, tossing each other back and forth, performing dips and twirls. When the song ended, the crowd cheered for them.

The next song was a quieter one. Henry and Nicole slow-danced, their heads close together so they could talk quietly. The sound crept up Henry's back, stirring the shifter inside him. He moved gracefully around the floor but to no particular style of dance.

"Did you growl? What the hell was that, Henry? Tango? Salsa? Fucking samba?"

"It wasn't anything. I learned a long time ago that I'm not really capable of remembering specific steps. So now I try to empty my brain and move to the music. That's how all these specific dances got invented, anyway."

"I'm not sure about that, but we'll go with it." Nicole suddenly hissed. "I said watch the toes, dingus!"

"Sorry." Henry shuffled his feet away from hers. "Gotta admit, it's been a while since I danced."

"I can see that. Been too busy with your big company, huh? What have you been up to?"

"Oh, a little of this and a little of that… By the way, you look stunning tonight."

She pushed him away, staring up into his eyes. "You're avoiding the question."

"All right, fine." He took her hand and led the way to a table, where they sat. "I could use a break. I've been working on some new energy technology that has to stay top secret. There are spies everywhere, with different intentions." Henry took another glance around the room. "You never did say exactly why you're here."

"No, I didn't." She tilted her head in the way he always

loved. "How about you tell me about your new technology, and I'll tell you about who I'm hunting."

Henry grinned, sneaking a long look over her shoulder. Was that a new waiter? "We've already played 'you show me yours, and I'll show you mine.'"

Nicole followed his eyes, glancing behind her as she leaned an elbow on the table. "Relax. This is only a reunion. I really did take the night off. Don't you trust me?"

"Fine. We'll both keep our secrets."

Nicole nodded, turning to a waiter. "Can we get some water, please? Thanks." She looked at Henry, letting out a long sigh. "Does the whole caped crusader thing ever get old for you? At least I get paid when I risk my life."

Henry took a long drink of water. He set his glass down and grimaced.

"Money will only take you so far. This is my city and the world has changed. The lines between good and evil are blurry at best. Right now, the line is here." He traced a line across Nicole's wrist.

"If we wait for someone else to clean things up and stop a monster or two in their tracks, the line moves here." He drew another line across the inside of her elbow. "Then along comes a new monster who has a bigger plan and no remorse, with the muscle to get somewhere. And the line is crossed." He gently dragged his finger across her throat. "People you care about get kicked out of the game."

Nicole drew in a short breath and sat back in her chair. "I'm going to need something stronger than water. Why do I feel like you've already seen your new monster, Henry?" She held up her hand and gave a gentle headshake. "You don't need to tell me now. I trust you. You'll let me in on the monster hunt when I'm needed. Unless I spot him first."

Henry smoothed out his tie and looked around the long, sleek dining room.

Nicole watched him, tapping her fingernails on the rim of her glass. "You were always good at multitasking. One of my favorite things about you."

Henry decided to take a chance. "You're needed now, Nicole. You're right. I have seen my monster. Or maybe I have. I'm not sure, but…"

"But they never look like monsters at first. Not the really smart ones. And by the time you realize it…"

"It's too late," Henry said in a low growl. "His name is Bechtel Stryker. I don't know much about him yet, other than he might have a connection to an ancient group of people from modern-day Scotland. They were known as the Picts."

"Yeah, I know who they were." Nicole used her straw to stir the ice in her glass, searching for the perfect piece. She fished one out and crunched it between her molars.

"I need to get a bead on him. A connection," Henry said.

"I might know a guy who knows a guy. A contact of mine here in Seattle. We're working together a bit on my current case. Kind of a weird guy, even by Seattle standards. Goes by Boris. He's an expert on anything weird and creepy, no matter how old or new it is."

"Great!" Henry pulled out his phone and opened the notes app. "How do I get hold of him?"

"You aren't going to be able to call him." Nicole sucked desperately at her straw, seeking out every last vestige of water. "He definitely won't answer. You can probably find him at Ye Olde Curiosity Shop. Here in town. You know where that is?"

Henry nodded. "It's on the pier, down by Ivar's."

"Perfect. I still know jack shit about Seattle."

"You're a bounty hunter, Nicole. Try the lie on someone else. You would have done your homework before you showed up on my turf."

"Fair enough. Go see this guy. It'll be worth it, I think, even if he is kind of a pain in the ass. Make sure to tell him I sent you, or he'll probably tell you to put an egg in your shoe and beat it. He doesn't like talking to people. I think he prefers interacting with dead things. Now that business is taken care of, how are things? How's Lexus? I haven't seen that little old bastard in forever."

She sat back with a contented sigh, waiting for Henry to start talking. But he said nothing for several moments. He couldn't find the right words.

"He's...gone," he finally muttered, twisting to look out at the darkening sky. "That's another reason I want Stryker."

"Shit, Henry." Nicole stood, coming around to hug him. "I didn't know. That's really hard. He was family for you."

Henry shrugged. "It's fine. Death's inevitable, right?"

"Yeah, but that doesn't make it fine. It's part of my job to read people's faces, Henry. I can tell you're hurting."

He leaned into her, feeling her warmth. She ran her fingers through his hair, screwing up the 'do he'd meticulously fashioned in front of the mirror. He didn't care one bit.

The music abruptly stopped, and someone spoke through a microphone. "Ladies and gentlemen, I'd like to introduce our honored guest of the evening. The medical profession is full of selfless people working tirelessly to save lives, which makes it even harder to pick out an MVP. This woman made our job easy for once. Please welcome the latest recipient of the SPS humanitarian of the year award, Dr. Aspen Neumann!"

Henry and Nicole headed for the stage, clapping as Aspen came out. She waved at the crowd, taking her spot at the microphone.

"Thanks, everyone!" She held her arms wide. "What I do takes a team of dedicated people. Many of them are here tonight, but most are back at the hospital, taking care of critically ill children." She lowered her head, her cheeks reddening. Henry smiled, the wrinkles deepening around his eyes.

Aspen went on, looking back out at the rows of faces. "I get to go to work every day and be reminded of the best parts of who we are and what we're capable of on any given day. Okay, okay!" She smiled, raising her hand to bat at the air. "I know we work long, *long* hours, but at least the coffee is pretty good."

A low chuckle passed across the room. Nicole nudged Henry, standing on her toes to talk into his ear. "Wow, Neumann. I know the two of us kick ass on a daily basis, but your sister is the real hero."

Henry nodded. "Always was."

The ceremony continued. Aspen soon accepted her award, a nice trophy and plaque with her name etched into it.

"I'd like to thank…well, too many people for me to say without wearing out my voice and putting you all to sleep.

First of all, thanks to the Seattle Pediatric Society for thinking of me. Thanks to the people at Seattle Children's Hospital for giving me a job. And thanks to my brother, Henry." She pointed at him, and all eyes in the crowd moved over. "You always had my back, big bro, and I always tried to have yours. So, thank you."

Henry smiled and nodded, bowing and thanking people as they clapped for him. He was too busy resisting the urge to flee from all the attention to see what was happening around him.

He didn't notice the man in the bespoke tux standing near the back of the crowd, holding a phone and aiming its camera at him. By the time Henry made his way through the well-wishers and handshakes, the man had already slipped out of the building and into the back seat of a waiting car.

CHAPTER TWENTY

enry looked up Ye Olde Curiosity Shop and discovered it closed at nine. If he wanted to get there tonight and save himself a trip to Seattle tomorrow, he had fifteen minutes to make it.

He found Aspen and quickly hugged her again. "I'm off, kid. Got work to do."

"This late?" She tilted her head, distracted by yet another well-wisher. "You're burning the midnight oil, huh? Just don't burn the candle at both ends like me."

He ruffled her hair and rushed out of the restaurant. The sounds of her protests followed him, but the sound of traffic quickly drowned them out as he dashed down the street.

He made it to Pier 54 at 8:55 and burst through the shop's doors. There were still some shoppers milling around. He breathed a sigh of relief and slowed down, looking around at the oddities. There were skulls every-where, totem poles, and some kind of a leathery mummy standing in a display case.

Henry stopped by another display case and frowned. Inside the case was a mermaid dangling from the top. Her claws were outstretched as if she was trying to break free.

"Who the hell is this prick Nicole sent me to? And what the hell is this?" He turned and barely registered surprise at a stuffed bird with a rabbit's head. "Whoever he is, he knows how to open a portal to Oriceran. Or he knows someone who does."

A young woman with a nametag—*Emily*—approached him. "Is there something I can help you find, sir?"

Her voice had an edge Henry recognized. Quit staring at the merchandise and buy something.

"Yeah, I'm looking for someone named Boris. I guess you're probably not him, huh?"

She smiled and gestured at the mummy case. "He's back there."

Henry thanked the girl and made his way among the curios. The only person in the vicinity of the mustachioed mummy was a guy hunched over a tray of glittery rings, wearing a tweed cap. Henry cleared his throat. "Boris?"

The guy gave him the stink eye. "Who's asking?"

"Nicole sent me." Henry gestured to the mummy. "Ugly son of a bitch, huh? I wonder how he died?"

"There's a debate for ya," Boris grunted. "The most popular story holds that old Sylvester here got caught cheating at cards back in the old west, and someone gave him a gutful of lead as a prize. That's why his arms are kind of folded near his stomach like that. But anyway, why the hell am I telling you that? Who are you?"

"I'm Henry Neumann."

Boris grunted again. "Boy, if we were outside right now

I would have hocked a loogie at your feet and told you to dance in it. In other words, pound sand. Who the hell is Henry Neumann supposed to be?"

Henry stuffed his hands in his pockets and looked meekly around the store. "Jesus Christ, man. I told you, I'm one of Nicole's friends."

"You didn't say that. You said that Nicole sent you. That doesn't mean you're friends."

"But we are. Do you...um..." Henry licked his lips, trying to think of an approach that might calm the beast. "Do you come here often?"

"No, you just happened to find me here by sheer coincidence. Yeah, I come here often. I wasn't planning on being here tonight, but Nicole texted me and said my presence was required. I thought she was coming, but instead, I see this pretty boy walking in."

"Thanks. I try." Henry narrowed his eyes, sizing up Boris. "An interesting place to hang out. But why here?"

"Because I prefer dead people to live ones. And because magicals don't like the place." He turned in a slow circle, indicating all the odd and macabre pieces Henry had seen before. "Too creepy for them. Bad energy, sort of."

Henry nodded. "Yeah. Kind of like Starvation Heights."

"I have no idea what that is." Boris's face wrinkled up like he tasted something sour, but he finally put out his hand. "If Nicole thinks you're all right, well, you might be. Nothing's certain yet so watch yourself. She said something about Bechtel Stryker."

Henry shook hands with the guy. It felt funny, doing it right before the dead gaze of a guy shot way before Henry was born. "Yeah. Stryker. Do you know him?"

"I know *of* him, is a more accurate way to put it." Boris put his hands in his pockets, shuddering. "If you know where to look and where to listen, you hear stories about the guy. He's a vampire. A monster wearing human skin.

"Some say he's an immortal warrior from long ago. I don't know if any of those legends are true, but one thing's for sure. He's a mean, crazy asshole who wouldn't think twice about ripping that cute face right off your skull. So be careful who you go looking for."

"Actually, I've already run into him. Twice."

Boris looked him up and down. "And you're alive. Either you're tough as hell, or you're the luckiest man ever to live. If the latter is true, you mind buying me a couple of scratch-offs?"

Boris didn't laugh at his joke or even smile. Henry began to doubt whether it was a joke at all. He looked around and realized that there were no other customers in the store and the employees were staring at him.

"I'd like to know more, Boris. Mind if we walked a little way?"

"I've got to walk back to my car anyway." Boris shrugged. "Where's the harm? Other than the fact that your presence is already beginning to annoy me."

Boris charged ahead, leading the way, and Henry followed. He still had no idea if Boris was joking or not, but for his sanity, he decided to believe that he was.

They headed back up the pier, moving slowly, watching the dark water rippling below.

Henry pulled a quarter out of his pocket and flicked it into the water for good luck. "I think we can rule out Bechtel Stryker being a vampire or a literal monster wearing a human meat suit. How about the immortal warrior angle?"

"How about it?" Boris made good on his words from earlier, clearing his throat and launching a wad of phlegm over the railing. "It's a legend, and there are a hundred different versions. He used to fight for Alaric the Visigoth, and the enemy cursed him to roam the Earth forever. Or he was a vagrant who tried to steal from a witch, and she's the one who put the curse on him. All the stories contain curses in some capacity. Is it because they're partially true, or because people aren't very creative? Who knows."

"Well, I think we can also rule out Visigoths and witches. They don't make sense. Are there any other versions? Maybe involving native people of the modern-day United Kingdom?"

Boris reached out for the railing and let his hand run along it. "Sounds like you're fishing for something, boy. What are you looking for? The Fir Bolg, maybe? Why don't you say it, and don't act like I'm stupid."

"Okay, you got me. I'm talking about the Picts."

Boris nodded. "Warrior people from ancient Scotland. Famous for fighting in the buff, wearing blue tattoos, and generally being scary and weird. But you have to give them some credit. They were an equal society. The women were just as good at ripping your head off as the men."

"I can imagine." Henry thought back to some images he had seen online of naked female warriors. "I've seen it."

Boris narrowed his eyes. "What, are you gonna tell me you're immortal too?"

"No, I'm saying that Pictish warrior-woman cosplay is

currently experiencing a renaissance. Are there any stories involving Bechtel and the Picts?"

"Maybe. But there are stories involving him and pretty much every other group of ancient people, too. If you ask me, the Pict angle checks out. Rumor has it that Stryker has attracted some fanboys over the years, and they all like to wear blue tattoos. Could be something to it."

"Fanboys? As in followers?"

"Sort of. Stryker likes to work alone, mostly. He'll take help whenever it offers itself, but he doesn't exactly invite an entourage to follow him everywhere."

They came off the pier and headed down Alaskan Way, past Ivar's and the fire station.

"It's too bad you didn't get to shop earlier," Boris went on. "It's a safe place where I know I can talk about guys like Bechtel and not lose my head over it. But we should also be safe in the immediate vicinity. Before we get too far, let me get to the good stuff. The reason you came to me, I assume."

"You know where I can find him?" Henry waited with bated breath.

"Not exactly. Just like everything with this guy, it's mostly rumors. Some say he lives underground like a sewer rat, and that's why people rarely see him. You know, the Seattle underground is a lot more expansive than people know. Others say he has a home in a group of abandoned warehouses at the city's edge. No definite indicators there, though."

Boris paused under the stairs that led up to the ferry terminal. He looked around, scanning his surroundings.

"I *have* heard one little nugget recently, Henry. But you know what they say. Information isn't cheap."

"Do they say that?" Henry took out his wallet and grabbed a few bills, handing them over. "I guess I'll take your word for it. So, what's the latest?"

Boris took a step closer and lowered his voice. "You didn't hear it from me, but Stryker's been spotted a few times recently. Always in the general area around Smith Tower. Maybe you'll find something there. Maybe not. Doesn't matter. No refunds."

"For the pleasure of your company? I'd never even think to ask." Henry pulled out his phone and punched in Smith Tower to get directions. Then again, he thought that just walking in might be a good way to get killed. "Thanks, Boris. Like you said, I didn't hear it from you. And the reverse is also true."

"I never saw you." Boris nodded. "This conversation never happened. Now if you'll excuse me, the *Golden Girls* reruns are about to start, and I need to get my ass home."

He shuffled away up the sidewalk, leaving Henry alone.

"I guess it's time to get my ass kicked by Bechtel Stryker." Henry sighed, looking northward. "Again. Or maybe not. It's a hell of a nice night, and I feel lucky."

He was going to need a vehicle. He called Hugh, his chauffeur, and walked into the ferry terminal parking lot to wait for him.

CHAPTER TWENTY-ONE

Hugh arrived less than twenty minutes later with a fresh set of wheels. A brand-new Honda Rebel. It wasn't top of the line, and it was a bit beefier and brutish looking than the style Henry preferred. But it would get the job done.

"Thanks, Hugh." Henry pulled the remaining cash out of his pocket and stuck it in the man's beefy hand. "For the ride home. Take a cab."

Hugh looked at the money like it was an alien object. "I usually just take the light rail."

"At this time of night? Take a cab." Henry hopped on the bike and let the engine growl. "If you're lucky, you'll see this bike sitting in the garage when you get to work in the morning. In one piece."

Hugh gave him a knowing smile. "If I'm lucky. And if I'm unlucky, which is a way higher possibility, I'll have to spend half the day at the dealer getting a new one."

Henry laughed. "I think I pay you enough to suffer. Just a little."

He twisted the throttle and let the back wheel slide around on the wet pavement. He gained traction and flew out of the parking lot onto the dark streets of Seattle.

Next stop, Smith Tower.

"Winter, are you getting this?"

There was an annoying crackling sound in Henry's ear as the connection established itself. The dwarf's voice followed. "Aye. Not very loud and clear. What is this place?"

Henry craned his neck to take in the entirety of Smith Tower. It was easy to forget how impressive a structure it was until you were right underneath it. It resembled a clock tower in shape, with a larger lower structure and a skinnier tower jutting from the top, all capped off by a unique pyramid-shaped roof.

"The oldest skyscraper in the city." Henry twisted the key, killing the engine. "Used to be the tallest building too, until the Space Needle came along. I almost bought the penthouse on the top floor a few years back when it was on the market. Kind of regret not going for it."

"I don't even want to know how much that would cost. Actually, I do." Clicking sounds came through as Winter typed on a keyboard. "Says here that you can still rent it. Seventeen grand a month. I don't know a lot about your world's money. Is that a lot?"

Henry whistled. "Yeah, you could say that. I could afford it, but a place like that deserves to be filled with party animals and champagne bottles. I don't think I'd do it justice."

"No, you wouldn't. Best to let me have it, Henry. Women love a guy with a penthouse. There's a whole magazine about it. That is what the magazine is about, isn't it? I saw one in your bedroom, but I didn't get a close look."

"What the hell were you doing in my bedroom? Henry tugged at his collar.

"I need to know the lay of the land. Anyway, what are we talking about? Do you have intel or what?"

Henry got off the bike and walked across the street, approaching the doors to Smith Tower. There were lights on inside, but when he pulled on the door handle it didn't budge.

"Shit." He glanced to the side, looking for buttons. "Maybe I have to be buzzed in."

More typing sounds came through. "Says here they close at ten."

Henry checked the time. "But that's ten minutes from now. The sneaky bastards closed up early."

"So what? You're a billionaire. It's not like you can get in trouble. Just go around back and break a window or something."

"Yeah, sure. You come up with all those gadgets so I have to resort to breaking a window and setting off an alarm. Great idea. Hold on…"

Henry stepped out to the sidewalk's edge and looked up at the tower again.

"What are you doing there, muscles?"

"Give me a minute." Henry sniffed the air, a narrow line of

fur briefly appearing along the back of his neck and disappearing again, just as quickly. "This isn't right. No way Stryker has anything to do with this building. It just doesn't fit."

"So your intel was wrong?"

"Not necessarily. The intel said he'd been seen in the vicinity, not at the tower specifically." Henry scanned for street signs, building a mental map of the surrounding area. "The intel also said Stryker might be living underground. But here's the first thing I learned out here, Winter. There's always more to learn. Never take the obvious as the last word. Isn't there some kind of tour place around here?"

"Let me check." More furious typing, along with a few curses. "Damn, I thought I had the finger dexterity of a surgeon until I tried using this keyboard. Guess it's not designed for strong, manly dwarf hands. More like your kind of hands. Thin. Delicate. Yes, there's a place nearby. Bill Spiders."

Henry laughed. "Bill Speidel's."

"Yes, that's the one. What kind of name is that?"

"Don't know, don't care." Henry was already running across the street, hopping onto his bike. "Right now it sounds like the kind of name I need. Going there now."

"Do you need directions?"

Henry shoved his helmet on and lowered the face shield. "I hope not. I'm in this city almost every day. My sense of direction better not be that pathetic."

He headed for Pioneer Square and breathed a sigh of relief when he saw the sign for Bill Speidel's. *Underground Tour* was painted in tall gold letters above an entrance painted black and shuttered by a metal gate. Notices of different bands and coupons for a nearby Chinese restaurant papered the window.

"They're closed, too," he told Winter. "Not that I would have gone inside anyway. I doubt Stryker's hanging out in there, waiting for me."

"That would be convenient, though. Just like this Hot Pocket I found in your freezer." A second later, Winter hissed and moaned. "They weren't lying, Henry. This thing is hot! But somehow the middle is cold? What magic is this?"

"The magic of the microwave, my friend. I didn't realize I had Hot Pockets. They must be pretty old." Henry parked the bike between two benches and headed around the back of the buildings.

In the alleyway behind Bill Speidel's was a staircase going down, with a door at the bottom. A single dim, orange bulb glowed on the wall above the door. It wasn't enough to dispel many shadows, but it *was* enough to give the place a generally creepy air. Henry drew a deep breath and headed down. He pulled the door open, staring into the blackness.

"No lock?"

"There used to be." Henry kicked at the remnants of a padlock on the ground. "Someone broke it off. Doesn't look like they used any precision instrument. Probably a hammer."

"Maybe Stryker *was* here, and he punched it off."

Henry shook his head. "Punched it? With his hand? Don't be ridiculous. This place must be part of the tour. Eerie times two."

"Yeah, and so are you. Some guy in leather with a

motorcycle helmet on, stalking the city." Winter let out a giddy laugh. "This is so much fun!"

"Of course, it is for you. You're sitting in a nice, warm… I mean, a nice, cold cave listening to this from a distance."

Henry pulled out a penlight and let it shine down the dark corridor ahead of him as he started walking. After taking a few steps inside, he already felt like he was a million miles away from the sane, normal world above. The feeling only intensified the farther he went.

"If Stryker's here, he'll see that flashlight," Winter warned him.

"And do what?" Henry aimed the light into a side room, checking for movement. "Run away? That's not his style. If he tries to fight me, I hope he's ready for a couple of surprises."

"Did you put it on? The punch enhancer?"

"I did. While I was waiting for Hugh."

"Hugh?" There came the sound of Winter scratching his beard. "I don't know a Hugh."

"Sure you do. You know Hugh. Last name Mungous."

"Hugh Mungous? Never heard of him. But what are we talking about Hugh Mungous for? Are you seeing anything?"

Henry kicked at some debris on the floor and stifled a laugh. "Just a lot of junk. Remnants of the past. A lot of it looks scorched. Leftovers from the fire in the late 1800s. Hey, maybe you know the other Hugh. He works for me, too. Hugh Jass."

"Nope, don't know him either. Hold on, let me look this up." Winter started typing again, and Henry thought the dwarf would realize he was pulling his leg. He was looking up the fire instead. "Wow, they rebuilt the whole damn city twenty feet above where it originally stood. I assume Seattle wasn't nearly as big back then, but…"

Henry nodded, turning in a circle and letting his light play. "That still gives us a significantly large underground area. Bechtel Stryker could be hiding in any nook or cranny. Let's hope he isn't feeling like a coward tonight. I want him to come out and play."

He knew it sometimes helped to get in the headspace of whoever you were trying to find, so he turned off his flashlight and let the darkness flood around him. He walked a little way like that, finding his way by faint light bleeding in through occasional overhead grates.

However, that wasn't the only light source down here.

"I'm seeing some kind of dim computer light, Winter. I'm going silent for now. Talk with you when I get topside again."

"Give him what for, Henry. Oh, one more thing before you enter stealth mode… I do remember a certain Hugh, now. I met him the other day. Maybe you know him."

Henry racked his brain, trying to remember any other Hughs. "I don't know, Winter."

"Oh, you have to know this guy. Hugh Jaynis. Really nice fellow."

"Come on! That's a bit too far."

"Is it? Or are you mad I got all sneaky and beat you at your own game? Now shut your trap and get to some sneaking of your own. I'll mute myself."

Henry winced, trying to get a certain mental image out of his head as he stalked down the corridor.

Henry's ears twitched. His shifter hearing picked up on

a distant sound of someone grunting in effort over and over again. A perfect pattern.

Henry closed his hands into fists, feeling the shift coming over him, his muscles rippling and growing. He sucked air between his teeth, biting down hard and willing himself to stop. "Not yet," he whispered. No need to run into a homeless person in fur and fangs, scaring them out of their warm hiding place.

It didn't take long before he was outside an open archway, where the light and sounds were coming from. He leaned out just far enough and saw a group of magicals, all teenagers, gathered around an older console television. They were playing *Street Fighter XI*, and Ryu was punching the hell out of Luke repeatedly.

"Hey, ease up," said a young Light Elf, frantically pushing the buttons on the controller in his hands.

A teenage wizard with a mohawk laughed, mashing his buttons. "Don't hate the player, Rami. Hate how much you suck at the game."

None of these people were Stryker. Henry almost backed away, but he suddenly recognized one of the girls. A Drow with hair that ended in silver tips.

Ellie.

Henry stepped confidently into the room, his boots falling heavily against the floor. The teens looked over at him in unison, their expressions curious at first. Then their mouths all dropped open.

A skinny boy with dirty blond hair stood and grabbed a baseball bat. "Who the hell are you?"

Henry put out his hands in a neutral stance. "I just need

to talk to Ellie. And I need to know if Bechtel Stryker is nearby."

A dark-haired Light Elf grabbed a crowbar as a fireball formed in his other hand. "How do you know that name?"

Henry sighed, reaching up to remove his helmet. Both armed teens lunged at him as soon as they saw him divert his attention. Henry twisted out of the way, and the kids crashed into each other, going down in a heap.

A young gnome who had an uncanny resemblance to Lexus flew over them, aiming a kick directly at Henry's chest. Henry stepped to the side, grabbed the kid's leg as he sailed past, and redirected him straight into the floor.

"Stay down. I just need to—"

A spray of small fireballs peppered him from behind. It was enough to send him stumbling back out into the hall. His back thudded against the wall on the other side, and he pushed off, turning to face his attackers. Five teens were on him all at once, clobbering him with whatever they had on hand.

"You idiots, I'm not here to hurt you!" Henry glimpsed silver-tipped hair. He grabbed a lock of it and yanked, pulling the Drow against his chest and pinning them. "I got your Drow! Stand down!" The captured Drow let out a deep growl, and Henry realized his mistake. *Not Ellie.* "Oh, shit. You have *two* Drow. Brother and sister?"

He let the boy go. His patience had run out, and he charged forward, knocking them out of his way as he lunged back into the TV room. He had to give the small band of magicals some credit. They went down fast and bounced around like bowling pins, but they got up even faster. By the time he turned back to face them, they were already jumping at him again.

"Enough!" Henry sent both fists flying, landing two punches in the middle of two bony chests. Both teens let out groans of misery as they landed hard on their backs. "Next kid that comes at me will need their jaw wired shut, so don't fucking try it. Would you let me talk for a second?"

The rest of them stood back and watched warily. Henry bent, picked both winded teens off the floor, and stood them up. "You two all right?"

"Just knocked the wind out of me," one of them wheezed.

"All right. Take it easy. Go sit or something." Henry shook his head in exasperation and finally pulled his helmet off. "You break into a guy's house, steal his dangerous magical shit, then you have the balls to try to beat him up when he finally finds you. You underage magicals are lucky I didn't bring the police with me. Or worse."

"Silver Griffins don't exist anymore," snarled the young gnome. Lexus would have liked this one, maybe.

There was a crackling sound in his ear as Winter unmuted himself. "Good speech. Just leave out the part where you weren't expecting to find them here."

Ellie stepped forward out of the group. "Are you looking for me?"

"I'm looking for my stone." He held out his hand. "I'll take it back now."

Ellie shook her head. "I already told you. I need it."

"Yeah, you did say that." Henry stepped toward them, hoping they would get scared and step back. But they didn't. "But you're just an ignorant child who has no idea what she's doing. I've learned some new things about that stone. Don't bother asking because I'm not telling you. All you need to know is it probably has the power to blow Bill Speidel's sky-high and reduce you and all your friends to little bits of charred meat. So how about I take it and put it somewhere safe?"

"It's that powerful? Good." Ellie folded her arms and stared at him. "I've learned some new things too, old man. I'm starting to figure the stone out. I know it can protect us. Especially if Bechtel ever decides we're a liability and he wants to get rid of us."

"Give me the stone, and I'll make sure that guy will never bother you again." Henry held out his hand again.

He didn't think she would hand it over. He was looking for a tell, and Ellie gave it to him. Her resolve cracked for a moment, and her eyes flicked to something behind him.

Henry looked over his shoulder and saw a door leading into another room. He walked inside, and the teens immediately ran for him again, letting out their battle cries. That was the second tell. If there wasn't something in this room they wanted to stay hidden, they wouldn't react so violently.

The same two kids he had punched in the chest came first. Henry dodged their tackle attempts, letting them hit the floor and slide away. He headed for a shelf in the corner, where a few metal canisters stood. The first one he yanked open had a bunch of canned food inside.

He was trying to reach for the second one when Ellie grappled onto his arm and tried twisting it out of its socket.

Henry grunted in pain and grabbed a fistful of her hair.

He pulled just enough to make tears well out of her eyes, and she let go. He shoved her away and grabbed the other canister.

There was something heavy inside, wrapped in a piece of cloth. He pulled it out and could already tell by the weight and the shape that it was the stone.

Ellie marched toward him, screeching. "*Give it back!*"

Henry smiled. "Try to make me if you want to get your asses kicked. If not, get out of the way. Please. I'm a lot like you, Ellie. I'll do what I have to do, but I don't want to hurt you or your friends."

"Family," Ellie corrected him. "They're all my family."

He stared Ellie down, waiting patiently. She finally cursed and waved at the others.

"Everyone step aside. Let him through. Don't worry. We'll get the stone back. Mark my words."

Henry shrugged as he sidestepped past, keeping his eyes on them. "I'm never letting you have this stone again. Mark *my* words. I can offer something else. Protection. You know I have the resources."

Ellie made a face like she was getting ready to spit venom at him. "Take your protection and shove it, rich boy."

"Suit yourselves. Maybe you can protect yourselves. You're a tough group of kids. Pretty smart too, but your magic is still spotty. Doesn't always work, does it? You're in over your heads here. I'd start trying to settle into a new lifestyle if I were you. Maybe stick to stealing jewelry or paintings, And I'd do it fast."

As soon as he was out in the hall, Henry ran. He didn't slow down until he was back at his motorcycle.

CHAPTER TWENTY-TWO

The next night, Henry stayed at the office late. He kept checking his security feeds and checkpoint data. He was watching for signs of Ellie. She knew where he worked, and she had already proven she could get in undetected. He was also watching his employees in the R&D department. The new project was too close to the finish line.

As soon as they all left, Henry turned the monitors off after redirecting the images to the bank of screens below his house. There, Winter could keep watch. He hopped out of his seat and headed down to R&D with the stone tucked under his arm, whistling as he passed the guards, exiting the elevator. He was still alert, listening for anything unusual in case Ellie decided to make a late appearance.

There was no sign of her, and Henry decided she was probably still licking her wounds at home. He had taken the wind out of her sails, and he felt kind of bad about it.

Better than letting her blow herself to bits, though.

Henry felt a hell of a lot better now, knowing where the stone was.

He held it out as he walked, admiring the etchings. "If Stryker wants to get his hands on you now, he'll have to face me on my home turf. This time, I'm ready for him. I think so, at least."

It still hurt to draw a deep breath, a harsh reminder of what Bechtel could do.

Once inside the Research and Development lab, Henry got to work readying his experiment. He brought out a prototype of his latest battery and hooked it up to a meter, checking the charge.

"Almost dead." He smiled. "Perfect. Let's see what we can do about that."

"About what?"

Henry jumped, turning to see who was talking. Then he realized the voice was inside his ear.

"Winter, don't scare me like that! Glad to see you're still awake."

"Of course. This is when all the best TV is on. I've got reruns of *Alf* playing next to the inner workings of your office. When did you get so jumpy? Hey, you should pick up some more cookie dough ice cream on your way home."

"Are we almost out?"

"Almost? No. Completely? Yes. What are you up to?"

"Too tired to describe everything. Wait a second." Henry took the glasses out of his pocket and put them on. "Better?"

"What's that? One of your fancy batteries?"

"It is." Henry pulled the meter leads off the battery and carried it to another table. "A prototype. Everyone who works in this lab is confused about where the power keeps coming from. I'm the only one who knows. I've been experimenting for years with magical relics. They're all old, almost dry on energy. But the magical energy I'm able to find is so potent that I can use even trace amounts to power a battery like this and it can keep an electric car running for hundreds of miles. For starters."

"That's a lot of kinetic energy, muscles."

"You're right. I'll take some credit here and admit that the design of these batteries is revolutionary. Even without magical power, they would still be the next big thing. We're talking about incredible efficiency. You can store them for years without them losing any juice. At least, that's how they should be when they're finished. You caught me at a good time, Winter. I was about to try something new."

"Yeah? So was I. Namely, I was going to find out if it tastes good when you melt peanut butter in the microwave and pour it over your ice cream." Winter went quiet for a moment. "The results are in. Yes, it is delicious. Who's the real genius inventor here, Henry? Me or you?"

"Why not both of us? Or are you not good at sharing the limelight?" Henry wrapped the stone in a special conductive material. Foreseeing Winter's question, he decided to answer it ahead of time.

"We call it a smart-sleeve. It can pull energy out of or into pretty much any substance you slip it over. It all depends on where you attach the leads. I tried using it to cook an egg once. That was how I learned how hard it is to scrape egg whites off ceiling tiles."

He attached the battery leads to the terminals on the

sleeve labeled OUT, then quickly jumped back, crouching behind a desk. Nothing seemed to happen.

Winter sighed. "Seems to be a dud of an experiment. I was thinking about getting some popcorn, but I guess I won't be needing it."

"Just give it a minute. This is a stone we're talking about." Henry stood and took a cautious step forward. "It's not like it's a conductive piece of metal or something. But I'm starting to think we might need to find Ellie. She's got some kind of special touch. Maybe she can…"

"Hold it!" Winter cried. "Something's happening!"

"I know. That's why I stopped talking." Henry narrowed his eyes, taking another step forward. "The etchings are starting to glow. It makes sense that they would glow first. They're closer to the core of the stone. A guy I talked to told me these stones were like conduits. The Picts used them to channel magical energy. Maybe they weren't the source of that energy, but they were a passageway for it. And maybe a means of storing it as well."

"Like a battery."

"Exactly. Let me see if I can get a read on this." Henry grabbed a multimeter from a nearby station and stuck its leads against the two OUT terminals. "Yup, the needle's spiking. We're getting a transfer here. The battery is charging up!"

"So what?" Winter grunted. "You're moving energy from one battery to another. What's so exciting about that?"

"I'm pulling magical energy from a damn *rock*, my friend. Isn't that super cool to you? Maybe not. I keep forgetting you're from Oriceran. You probably toss magical rocks around like they're nothing."

Suddenly, the multimeter leads started smoking. Henry tried to pull them away, but they wouldn't budge. He realized that the metal was melting, fusing itself to the terminals on the smart-sleeve.

"Uh-oh."

Winter was yelling at him to get away, but Henry was already doing it. He turned and dashed for the exit, reaching out to pull the handle that would turn on the fire suppression system.

He made it less than ten feet before there was an explosion. There was no huge fireball, only a burst of strange wavering light. The shockwave hit Henry and pushed him up off the floor. He did a full backflip and landed on his ass, his ears ringing and his tailbone screaming for mercy.

"Heavens to Betsy! Are you all right, Henry?"

"Yeah, I think so." Henry groaned, rocking back and forth and rubbing his sore spots. "Where did you ever hear *that* expression? I'm pretty sure even my grandparents thought that was outdated."

"It was in an old movie I watched. Don't you think it should make a comeback?"

Henry grabbed the edge of a table and pulled himself to his feet. He looked himself over. Other than a couple of bruised butt cheeks and some singe marks on his jacket, he seemed okay. "Here's a better question... When I turn around, am I going to see a melted crater where half of my building used to be?"

"Probably not. The lights are still on. The damage must not be too severe."

Henry turned. The battery he had been trying to supercharge was nowhere to be seen at first, but he eventually spotted it halfway across the room under a table. Dented but unruptured. The stone itself was sitting exactly where it had been before, surrounded by a huge circle of black char that spread up the walls and across the floor.

"I think we're good, Winter. It seems to have stabilized." Henry crossed the room and cautiously touched the stone with the back of his hand. "It's not even hot. And there isn't a mark on it. Whatever mojo those Picts had, they managed to beat out my modern technology. Those crafty bastards."

"You're lucky you didn't blow your pecker off, laddy."

Henry carried the stone back to his office and put it in his satchel for safekeeping. "I'll see you in the morning, Winter. I should probably stay and clean up my mess before I clock out."

He fell asleep at his desk after scrubbing soot for several hours. He woke around ten in the morning and hurried out of the building, anxious to get home and get the dwarven tinkerer's input.

When he finally reached home, it was well into lunchtime, and he found Winter half-buried in the refrigerator. He came out with an armload of items. Everything from tomatoes, lettuce, and pickles to salami, roast beef, and thinly sliced Emmental cheese. The gnome was wearing a pair of enhanced glasses, the glow of the screen reflecting on his face.

"I haven't bought cheese in months." Henry pointed at the Emmental. "You might want to check that for mold."

Winter shrugged, pulled open a bread bag, and dumped out a half-dozen slices. "Mold is a form of fungi, Henry. So am I. I'm a very fun guy. Get ready to see my latest and greatest creation."

Defying all expectations, Winter ducked back into the fridge and came out with another load of items. This time it was all about condiments. Mayonnaise, mustard of three different kinds, guacamole, and horseradish.

He fashioned a sandwich of incredible proportions, an edible tower of bread and toppings.

Henry marveled at it. "I haven't seen the likes of that sandwich outside of comic strips, Winter. How is it still standing?"

"By a careful application of toppings. It's a feat of engineering and a feat of the culinary arts, Henry. I'm not sharing, so don't even think about it."

"Don't worry. You can have that monstrosity all to yourself. I have something better. Take a look." He took the stone out and laid it on the counter.

Winter lifted the glasses and leaned down, studying the stone closely. "It's just as you described it to me. Two major etchings of a lion and a lamb. Smaller etchings around them…they look like symbols. Some sort of language."

"Can you read them?"

"This is an ancient language, Henry, and long since dead. But you're in luck because I know about half of the symbols."

Henry let out a breath. "Hey, I'll take it. Half is a lot better than the zero percent I know."

Winter pulled an errant pickle slice from the side of his sandwich and munched it as he scanned the symbols. "Something about death and darkness, here. Being reborn or remade, something along those lines. These symbols here, I have no idea about."

He ran his finger along the stone to the last set of markings. "These have to do with something being lost. A piece of the whole. Translated directly, they would say something like 'the part entire.' That's the best I can do."

Henry pulled the laptop out of his satchel and opened a text document, writing everything down. "Good. This is great, Winter. Do you know anything else about this stone?"

"Only that it's powerful and dangerous, which you already knew." Winter touched the lion etching and shook his head. "Who'd you hurt to get your hands on this, anyway? Whose head did you bite off with those big, ugly teeth of yours?"

Henry growled, and Winter quickly picked up his massive sandwich, using it as a shield. The glasses fell back into place over his nose. He took a bite out of the sandwich, wiping tomato juice out of his beard.

"Okay, okay, you didn't hurt anyone. You're a gentler, kinder shifter. Maybe."

Henry reached out, making Winter flinch, but he was only going for a piece of pastrami. "They're kids. Teenagers. They were going to get themselves killed if I didn't take it from them, so I did what I had to do."

"Fair enough." Winter held up his hands, covered in mustard. He went to the sink to rinse off his hands and returned with a gleam in his eye, reaching for the stone. "Let me have it. Come on, gimme, gimme!"

Henry slid the stone closer to the dwarf. Winter held it in one hand and stared at it, tilting his head from side to side, narrowing his eyes and shutting them one at a time.

"Nope, nothing." He took another bite of his sandwich, then noticed how Henry was staring at him and tapping his foot. "Getting restless, muscles? Calm down. I had to know. Maybe this was going to be my moment. I guess I don't have Ellie's special touch, but don't worry. I'll figure out something we can do with it. Hm…"

He rubbed his chin, his eyes distant. "An energy conduit that amplifies what passes through it. That seems to be what we have here. This is going to be a good afternoon."

While Winter was busy theory-crafting on the stone, Henry headed into his library, seeking a moment of peace. He sat among the towering bookshelves. Instead of reaching for a bit of reading material, he took out his phone and opened the shifter app.

A few shifters were broadcasting their location in the surrounding area, lurking around the outskirts of Bremerton. *Who are they?* Henry traced a dot that was moving swiftly through Illahee Preserve. A pack was on the move. That had to be the silver Luna wolf he had seen, sometimes outpacing him. *Have I walked past you on the street? Do you live nearby? Shit, maybe you even work at my company.*

He had always been curious about who these people

were in real life. What they did for a living. What kind of lives they led.

The opposite must also be true. *They must wonder about me. Someday, my friends.* He closed the app. *Someday. Maybe.*

"Maybe I *should* do it." He tapped the arm of his chair, absentmindedly drumming out the rhythm of one of Lexus' favorite songs. "Come doused in mud, soaked in bleach, as I want you to be…" He let out a deep breath, his head resting back against the chair. "Someday I'll let everyone know."

He thought back to a day he had spent driving with Lexus, shopping in Silverdale and Poulsbo.

"Men like you find it hard to make friends, Henry. After all, what do you have in common with anyone else?" Lexus had asked.

The gnome was right. The average billionaire already would have found it hard to relate to the average person. Add in all the secrets Henry had to keep, and he was destined to be a loner.

Maybe not. He reopened the app and watched the blips moving around at the edge of town, smiling as he imagined running out to meet them. His tribe. They shared the same violent hobbies, along with golf on the weekends and movies with friends.

The library was quiet. A cool breeze flowed through the open windows, carrying the sound of birdsong. Henry hadn't felt this relaxed in weeks.

It didn't last long. He felt a shudder through the floor, which quickly grew and propagated until books started toppling from shelves. Henry ran out of the room, hurrying down into the cave.

Everything seemed fine, but there was a putrid smell in the air. It wasn't until Henry reached the command center that he realized it was the odor of burned hair. The tip of Winter's beard had been melted away, and his shirt was charred all across the front. A thin haze of smoke filled the space.

"Not to worry, friend." Winter gave the thumbs-up. "All is well. Experiment number thirty-two ended with a bang, but I did get a few helpful notes out of it. What are you staring at? How is a man supposed to work when he feels scrutinized? Go on, go away. I have this all under control."

Henry stuck a finger through a hole in Winter's shirt. "Yes, this is what control looks like. Don't blow up my cave, Winter. And let me know when it's safe to come down. I need to get a workout in."

He reluctantly went back upstairs, saying a prayer. "At least let the house stay standing."

CHAPTER TWENTY-THREE

Henry was in the middle of a rare good dream when his cell phone rang. He sat up fast in his oversized bed, looking around in confusion as his sleepy brain made sense of the chirping noise. With a grunt, he rolled toward the nightstand. It took him a full rotation and a half to reach it, grabbing his phone and answering the call.

"Hello? Who is this?"

"Henry!" He barely recognized the panicked voice. It was Ellie. "I guess we might, you know, kind of need your help."

Henry flung the blanket aside and stood, flexing his muscles in the cold, trying to get some blood flowing through them. "Your choice of words is relatively calm. Or you might call it chagrined. You sound like either you're scared out of your mind, or you've been running for the past ten minutes."

"A bit of both, maybe. Listen… Stryker came back. To our hideout under the tour place."

Henry nodded, then tucked the phone between his cheek and shoulder. "What happened? Did he hurt you?"

"Not any worse than you did, but not for lack of trying. At first, I think he had another job for us, or he was there to check up on our progress. When he figured out we lost the stone, he blew up. Luckily, most of my peeps were already out in the city looking for food. It was just me, Wexell, and Benji down here. We got away. Bechtel chased us. He was on this motorcycle, but we lost him in the alleyways. I'm sure he's still looking for us."

Henry opened his closet and grabbed a pair of what he liked to call his tactical sweatpants. He slipped them on, then dug for a good pair of socks. "Where are you now? Somewhere safe?"

"Well, about that… We kind of have this rotation of meet-up spots. If we get separated, we can always go to one of these spots and reunite. We switch which one we use every three days, according to this plan Wexell wrote. The problem is, we think he knows some of those spots."

Henry grimaced. "So he'll start searching through the ones he knows until he finds you. Let's hope I can get to you first. So, where am I going?"

"We're still in Seattle. Terminal 86."

"The grain facility. I know where that is. You're lucky I like going for jogs on the Elliot Bay trail during my lunch hour. Otherwise, I might not. I'll be there as soon as I can."

"How long?" Ellie asked, her voice shaking.

"I don't know. As fast as I can. I can go pretty fast. Trust me. I'm going to hang up now. Call me if the situation changes."

He ended the call and shoved his phone into his pocket.

He quickly grabbed a pair of running shoes off the closet floor, already laced up, and pulled them on as he hopped toward the bedroom door. He crossed the hall and banged on a different door.

"Winter! We've got a problem!"

The dwarf opened up a moment later, rubbing his eyes. He had no shirt on, and the full, glorious expanse of his hairy chest and belly were on display.

"Have you been hitting the weights too?" Henry shook his head. "Never mind. It's Ellie and her gang. I need to get to Seattle pronto, but…"

"But you're looking for new toys." Winter wagged a finger at him. "Are we talking about a proper nocturnal operation here? Now, this is something worth waking up in the middle of the night for. Follow me."

Winter led him down into the cave, where he grabbed a new necklace and handed it over. This one looked like the dwarf had crafted it from wooden beads and pieces of shell.

Henry held it up to the light. "What's with the island look? I think my mom used to have one like this. She got it at a gift shop on our vacation to Maui."

"Don't like it? I thought it would be funny, but we can reskin it to look like anything you want."

"Does it work?"

Winter grinned, rubbing his hands together. "I don't know. You tell me."

Henry sighed. "I don't know if we have time for this, but all right. I can't resist."

He slipped the necklace on, feeling for the button as he walked into the gym. He positioned himself in front of a mirror and squeezed the button. All at once, he became the invisible man from the shoulders up.

"Holy shit."

Winter smiled proudly. "No blur here. More like total erasure. But that's not all. It has modes. Press the button again."

Henry did so. His face suddenly came back, but a second later he realized it wasn't *his* face. He was suddenly a completely different person with different features, including eye and hair color.

"Holy *shit!* This thing is for real, Winter. Great job. Does it have more modes?" He pressed the button again and faced the familiar ghostlike blur, like his face seen in a reflection of a steamy mirror. "Wow, you even included the original mode. You outdid yourself."

"Thanks. Now give me a raise. Just kidding. Or am I?"

Henry ignored him. "How do I turn it off?"

"Press and hold."

"Nice and simple." Henry smiled at himself in the mirror as his normal visage returned. "Cool. Lexus would love this."

Winter nodded. "He would be glad another genius has come along to take care of you, Henry. I hope I'll live up to him. You should finish getting geared up."

Henry moved toward the garage area, where his current arsenal sat lined up on a series of shelves. He removed his hoodie, attached the punch enhancer to his arm, and put the garment back on. He also grabbed his umbrella gun, along with the new pencil laser sight Winter had made for him. The glasses that would allow Winter to see everything Henry saw were there as well, and Henry put them on.

"Don't forget your wind grenade!" Winter handed it over. "I'll have to make more of those if it works well."

Henry grabbed the grenade and shoved it into a pouch on his utility belt. It was time now to pick a set of wheels. He settled on the faithful Mazda Miata, a new procurement.

Winter handed him the keys. "I looked up the price of that thing. It's quite a bit cheaper than what you usually go for."

"Exactly." Henry grabbed the keys and popped open the backseat, tossing his umbrella gun inside. "If it gets shot full of holes, blown up, or somehow flung into the Sound, I won't feel quite as bad about it. It still has a nice top speed of around 140 miles per hour, but it might be able to go even faster than that under the right conditions."

"You're going to get yourself a speeding ticket worth more than the car, Henry!"

"We'll see about that." Henry grabbed a socket wrench from the workbench and used it to take the license plates off. "I'll be going too fast for them to catch me. If I get caught on camera, so what? I'll have no plates. And no face either." He tapped the new necklace.

"You seem to have all the angles covered." Winter gave a satisfied grunt. "I'll be here, watching from a safe distance. Now go out and save those kids. If you need any extra motivation to not die...wait until you see what I've come up with regarding the stone."

Henry hopped in behind the wheel and cruised out of the cave. He left the windows down, letting the night air whip through his hair to shock the last remnants of sleepiness out of him. This would be a mad dash to make it to Seattle in time, and he needed to be fully alert.

Winter's voice came through his ear. "Steady as she goes, muscles. Drive like the wind, not like the hurricane."

"I'll try to keep myself under control. Maybe." Henry reached a long, fairly straight section of road and pushed the gas pedal to the floor. The familiar thrill passed through him as the car lurched forward, chewing up pavement like a starved beast. "I've got you in my ear, Winter. I know Ellie's a scrapper. She'll put up a fight alongside me. But I feel like we might need an extra set of hands on this."

"Are you thinking what I'm thinking?"

"If you think we should give Nicole Thomas a call, then yes. Get hold of her. Let her know I need her help at the Terminal 86 grain facility as soon as possible. Tell her my monster will be there."

"Got it. What if Stryker never shows up?"

"Then I'll have to give her the sad news myself. Nicole loves a good fight." Henry forced the car to go faster, speeding across the night. "Something tells me she won't be disappointed, though."

CHAPTER TWENTY-FOUR

Henry had no choice but to drop his speed once he got into the city. That was fine because Stryker was probably operating under the same constraint. Seattle traffic, even at this late hour of the night, made it too dangerous.

He headed up Elliot Ave, through the underpass beneath the wings of the Olympic Sculpture Park. He kept trying to spot his destination, but there was too much in the way.

"I'm not seeing this grain facility, Winter. I was pretty sure I was going the right way."

"You are. I'm looking at it right now. Following your little blip on this map thingy. You're just about alongside it now. You're going to want to take a left turn onto a little nubbin called Roy Street."

Henry saw it and turned left. He found that it was indeed a nubbin, a short stretch of road leading to a dead end complete with dumpsters and a graffiti-covered wooden fence. Henry got out, grabbed his special umbrella out of the back, and hoofed it toward the huge silo structures that loomed over him.

Beyond the wooden fence was a chain-link one collapsing in several spots. Henry hopped over it and crossed a set of train tracks, his feet crunching through gravel. Then he was on the grounds of the grain facility, jogging across smooth asphalt.

He reached one of the silos and put his back to it, feeling the cool metal against his sweaty back. He lifted the umbrella, attaching the pencil laser sight to it.

"Hope you brought yours, Stryker. It's going to rain bullets tonight."

It suddenly occurred to Henry that he didn't know exactly where Ellie and the others were hiding. She hadn't told him that fact. It wasn't a huge area, but there were plenty of nooks.

"Any sign of them?" Winter asked.

"No." Henry glanced around, trying to see through the shadows. "Maybe I should text them. Might be risky. If Stryker's already here and a buzzing phone gives them away…"

"Psst! Hey, rich boy!"

He looked over and saw a girl with tousled hair gesturing to him from between two of the tall, skinny silos. Henry jogged over to her, sidestepping into the hiding spot. Ellie was standing just behind her, keeping watch.

They were all huddled together in the middle of the silo superstructure in a cramped, shadowy place. There was a sweet, grassy smell of grain, but Henry could barely detect it over the sour scent of sweat. There was fear in the air, and he didn't need to be in wolf form to detect it.

Henry looked around, quickly counting heads. Twelve kids. "Is this everyone?"

Ellie nodded. "Minus Wexell. He's close by, though. Keeping an eye out. We think Bechtel will probably come through the main gate."

"Sounds about right. That seems to fit his supervillain aesthetic." Henry nodded, sheathing the umbrella on his utility belt. "I guess that means he isn't here yet. Let's hope this isn't one of the hiding spots he knows, and he doesn't show up. Either way, I hope you start reconsidering my offer of protection. If you're running wild all over the city, there isn't any way I can keep you safe."

Ellie shook her head. "What makes you think you're responsible for keeping us safe?"

Henry smiled at her. "I don't know. Why did you call me asking for my help?"

"Okay, you got me there." Ellie stared at the ground in embarrassment, grinding the toe of her boot through a pile of hard corn kernels.

"So," said the girl who had spotted Henry. "What do we do now?"

Henry lowered himself to the ground. "We sit. We wait. We hope the sun comes up before Stryker shows his face. Then I buy all of you a ferry ticket to Bremerton, where we can sit at my home and talk about your future. That is, if you find the terms agreeable."

The teens looked back and forth between each other. Ellie was the only one still standing; the rest were squatting in the shadows, hanging their heads miserably.

She was their leader. They trusted her to speak for them.

Ellie shrugged. "We'll see. I called you because I'm about fifty percent sure we can trust you. I'll need to be more certain before I agree to anything."

"Hey, that's fair." Henry tilted his head back, looking up at the faint view of stars between the silos. "You don't know me very well. I don't know you. I still hope he never comes, but if he does…there's nothing like a battle to bring people together."

Winter sighed in his ear. "You don't want a battle, Henry. They're no good for bringing anyone together. All they can do is tear people apart. Remember that."

"We don't always have a choice, Winter." Henry stood, focusing on the sudden roar of a motorcycle engine close at hand. "We might have company."

Wexell ran in a moment later, looking terrified. "He's here!"

The teens all looked at Henry simultaneously. Even Ellie, who had seemed so strong and defiant a moment ago, now turned to him with hope in her eyes.

"Don't worry." Henry laid a hand on her shoulder. "I've fought this guy before. And I've got some new tricks for him."

Ellie grimaced. "He probably has some new tricks for you, too."

"We'll see about that." Henry sidestepped between the silos and headed for the compound's interior. Above him, arcing high over the grounds of the facility and the waters of Elliot Bay, the grain elevator formed a stark line across the night sky.

"*Ellieeee!*" a voice called across the darkness. "I know

you're here. I saw your little sentry. There's nowhere you can run, nowhere you can hide, where I won't find you."

Henry stepped into the open, facing the facility's front gate. Stryker was there, a silhouette standing motionless in front of a shipping container. There were other dark shapes around him, huddled low against the ground. They almost seemed to be moving, but Henry figured it was a trick of the light.

Stryker raised both hands toward the sky. "Henry Neumann! I'm pleased to see that you survived our previous encounter. I had my doubts. I've killed much stronger men with a lesser application of force. Your constitution is strong."

Henry took a few steps forward. "Yeah, I drank plenty of milk as a kid. I even ate my vegetables. How about you? What were you eating back in the day?"

Stryker took a few steps of his own, bringing him into the moonlight where Henry could see the twisted grin on his face. "The souls of my enemies. It's a diet I've kept to over the years. Nothing nourishes the body of a warrior quite like it. Maybe you should give it a try."

"Henry," came Winter's voice. "Nicole is closing in. Just a few minutes out. We've formulated a plan for her entrance. It probably won't be as stylish and cool as stepping out and announcing what you liked to eat when you were a child…although Stryker did kind of outshine you with that line about eating souls."

Henry grunted and kept walking toward Stryker. He had an idea of where Nicole would enter, and now he had to keep the enemy distracted.

"You're alone, Stryker. I have Ellie and her group with me. This isn't going to go the same way as last time."

Stryker shook his head. "You're right. This is going to go much worse. For you. Because I'm not alone. Far from it."

He swept his hands forward. The dark objects near the ground behind him suddenly rose and shambled into the light. They were men and women, dressed in modern clothing with blue ink tattoos covering their leathery, tattered skin. Their jaws hung loose and their eyes, sunken deep into their sockets, still held something like the glimmer of life.

"What the hell are those things, Winter?" Henry demanded as the creatures shuffled toward him. "They look like Sylvester the card-cheating mummy!"

"I would reckon they're undead Pictish warriors. Hm."

"You make it sound like that's something you see every day!"

"You make it sound like it's something to worry about. Relax. They move like sloths, and they'll probably collapse into dust as soon as you breathe on them."

The opposite proved itself to be true. Their movements were stiff at first, but it soon seemed like their joints were loosening, moving more smoothly. All at once, the warriors drew weapons—swords and spears, a mace, a battle-ax. They charged, their bones clattering as they ran across the grain facility's vast lot.

Henry pulled his umbrella out and aimed.

Stryker's laughter echoed through the night. "What are you going to do, Henry? Fly away like Mary Poppins?"

Henry flicked on the laser sight, aiming it at the forehead of one of the warriors. He squeezed the handle, already celebrating in his mind. He expected the zombie's head to explode, but instead, the bullet passed clean through like it was going through a hollow gourd. It threw the warrior off-balance for a second, but he kept coming.

"Well, that's not going to work. Ellie!"

The teenagers flooded out of their hiding place and positioned themselves on either side of them. Henry turned to Ellie.

"Have you ever seen a zombie movie?" he asked.

She nodded. "A few, yeah."

"Well, throw away the whole 'shoot them in the head' idea. Doesn't work. I think the only way is to tear them apart. Completely. Got it?"

Ellie was shaking. "I think so. But they have weapons. Big ones."

Henry nudged her arm. "Don't worry. I've got something else up my sleeve. This might make it easier."

The warriors had closed more than half the distance, and they were only getting faster. Henry pulled the wind grenade out of his pocket and held it up, waiting for them to get a little closer. He threw it hard.

The grenade landed a few feet in front of the warriors and exploded, filling the air with a violently swirling cloud of dust. The warriors flipped and cartwheeled in every direction, thrown around like laundry in a spin cycle. They crashed down one after another. Weapons scattered. Someone's jaw bone broke away and tumbled across the ground.

"Clever!" came Stryker's voice through the dust cloud. "It's clear that you must never underestimate a billionaire with all the resources of two worlds at his disposal. But by the end of this night, Henry, we will also learn never to underestimate a man with nothing left to lose."

The dust settled. The warriors hauled themselves to their feet, grabbing their weapons. Some were missing legs. Others were missing arms. But they still kept coming, moving as fast as they could.

Henry gritted his teeth, assuming a fighting stance. "Get ready, all of you. If you can dodge their first attacks, you'll probably be okay. Stay close. Don't give them space to swing again."

That was the last word he got out before the warriors arrived. Henry surged forward at the last second, narrowly avoiding the chopping motion of a battle-ax. He got close to the offending undead warrior and delivered an enhanced punch straight to his withered ribcage. The warrior's spine completely snapped, and he folded over like a paper toward Henry, bringing his face in range for an uppercut.

Henry delivered the blow and watched as the warrior's head flew toward the sky.

"One down!" he cried.

His was the only triumphant voice. The teenagers were all either grunting with effort or screaming in pain. Henry didn't want to look over and see what any of those sounds meant, so he turned toward the next warrior in line.

The zombie tried to crush him with a clumsy overhead swing with her mace. Henry dodged to the side but ran straight into the flank of another warrior. This killed his movement, and the mace glanced off his right shoulder, causing an explosion of pain and a spatter of blood that spread through his shirt.

He used the pain to fuel his anger, letting out a deep growl as he charged straight for the one with the mace. He punched her so hard his hand went right through and out her back. The warrior kept flailing around, landing weak blows against Henry's ribs. He used the leverage of his arm through her torso to lift her, spin her around, and slam her headfirst into the ground.

The warrior's body crumpled, and she stopped moving. Two down, at least.

Henry turned to find Stryker. He was closer now but still thirty or forty feet away, watching the battle from the shadows beneath the grain elevator. Henry spotted movement over Stryker's shoulder.

It was Nicole, arriving through the front gate on foot. She was wearing all-black, including a mask that covered her face. But Henry would know the curves of that body anywhere.

He quickly looked away from her so he didn't give her arrival away to Stryker. He had no choice but to turn toward the teens…and was pleasantly surprised to see that they mostly held their own. They were gaining no ground, however, stuck in a stalemate with their undead foes.

Henry stepped into the middle of the battle to do whatever he could. He started punching arms, trying to sever them so the warriors would no longer be able to use their weapons. He managed to succeed a couple of times, but the warriors grew privy to his plan, and all turned to assault him at once.

Henry looked back and forth at the line of swords and

spears, ready to run him through. He tried not to show his fear, taking a defensive stance and getting ready to fight.

The teenagers came in, jumping onto warriors' backs, sticking their fingers in eye sockets and yanking on jawbones. The warriors went down under the weight of the assault, falling first to their knees, then onto their backs as the teenagers stomped and pummeled them into the ground.

Henry charged in to help, but he suddenly realized they didn't need it. The weapons were all tossed aside.

"Damn." Henry stopped, watching them with a smile. "Is this what a proud father feels like?"

"Aye. They're a tough group of ragamuffins. I'll give them that."

Henry left them to their dirty work and headed toward Stryker. The man was still in the same spot, watching casually with his hands hanging at his sides. Nicole was coming up behind him, barely visible in the shadows.

"Is that all you had for us, Stryker?" Henry called out. "Care to hop in so we can beat you down like we did to your warriors?"

Stryker didn't move. He said nothing. Henry wondered why Nicole was so hard to see, lost in the shadows, while Stryker was easily illuminated. It didn't sit right, but he didn't have time to dwell on it.

Nicole was only a few feet behind Stryker now, drawing her knife. Henry had to keep distracting him. "You think you're smart. Like you've got everything figured out. You're not afraid of me, are you? Come on, Stryker...why bring your warriors along if you aren't going to fight with them? Especially when you know you can beat me all on your own. I'm right here. Let's have a rematch."

Stryker still did nothing, and now he had run out of time. Nicole dashed across the rest of the distance, ramming her knife straight through the back of his neck.

It went straight through. And so did Nicole, stumbling through Stryker like he was made out of air. Henry ran over just in time to watch the form of Bechtel Stryker collapsing into a small projector on the ground.

"It's a damn hologram." Nicole shook her head, kicking at the thing. "Sorry, Henry. I got caught up in the hunt. I couldn't tell."

"Me neither. But if he isn't here, where the hell is he?"

A frightening thought passed through Henry's mind, and he looked back at the teens. They were still stomping away at the undead warriors, completely oblivious to the tall, dark figure striding out from between the silos.

Henry sprinted toward them. "Look out!"

Stryker pulled the needle-thin blade out of his walking stick and ran it straight through a girl's back. She let out a choking sound and fell to her knees. The other teens saw and began scattering in every direction, but Stryker reached out and grabbed hold of one of them. It was Wexell. The young Drow kicked and struggled, but Stryker's grip was firm. He pulled his sword from the girl and laid its blade against Wexell's throat.

"All of you, stop where you are!"

The teens stopped, slowly turning to face him.

"You too, Henry," Stryker called. "Throw that fancy gun of yours down."

Henry stopped, taking a glance over his shoulder.

Nicole was already gone. He dropped the umbrella to the ground. "Come on, Stryker. Leave them alone. They're only kids."

"These children have proven themselves to be unreliable. I left the stone with them as a test, and they failed it miserably." Stryker dug the blade in, making Wexell scream in pain. "We both have our codes, Henry. You try to protect the weak and the worthless while I exterminate them. We could stand around and argue about the merits of our viewpoints all night, but why bother? This could only end in one way."

Henry chanced a step forward, slowly closing the distance. "Yeah? What ending did you have in mind? If it has something to do with me punching your teeth down your throat, we can probably arrange something."

Stryker laughed. "An amusing mental image. It's not what I had in mind. I want all of these cretins dead, but I also want my stone. When I weigh the two desires in my mind, I come out in favor of the stone. If you give it to me, Henry, I will make you a promise. I'll only kill you. The children can go free."

Henry took one more step, keeping his hands up. "Done. I don't have the stone with me, but it's close by."

Winter grunted in his ear. "If by 'close by' you mean over here in Bremerton. What are you doing, Henry? You're alone out there now. Nicole abandoned you. You can't win. Maybe the best idea is to..." Winter sighed. "I can't think of anything. I guess just keep stalling."

Henry spoke under his breath. "That's exactly what I'm doing, numbnuts."

"Oh." A realization hit Winter. "Oh!"

A knife flew out from the shadows between two silos, burying itself in Stryker's back. He let out a sound that was more from surprise than pain and released Wexell. The young Drow ran for safety, and Stryker immediately forgot about him.

Instead, he turned to face Nicole Thomas. The bounty hunter marched boldly into the open, pulling a second knife from her belt. "You might be an immortal son of a bitch, but no one's too old to get stabbed. Come over here and try me."

Stryker smiled. "Gladly."

He met the swing of Nicole's knife with a parry from his sword. The sound of metal on metal echoed across the yard.

Henry ran again, with no thought in his mind except to get involved in the fight as soon as possible. Two against one were favorable odds.

Stryker saw him coming. The immortal warrior dove to the side, simultaneously ducking Nicole's next strike and dodging the freight train known as Henry Neumann. Stryker got to his feet, defying Henry's expectation, and immediately went on the offensive.

Nicole was quickly overwhelmed. It was all she could do to dodge Stryker's onslaught. Henry redirected his momentum, grabbing the back of Stryker's suit jacket and yanking him away.

Stryker fell, tucking into a backward roll that carried him between Henry's legs. Henry turned just in time to catch Stryker's wrist and prevent the sword from sliding between his ribs. He sent an enhanced punch at Stryker's chest and connected, sending the enemy tumbling backward.

Ellie was there, aiming a kick at Stryker's head. He rolled out of the way and got back to his feet, his eyes dancing between his attackers.

Henry laughed. "Three against one. I like those odds even better."

Stryker smiled, then turned and ran.

"Kill him!" Winter shouted. "Don't let him get away!"

Henry gave chase. "Wasn't planning on it."

"Why don't you shift, Henry? You can catch up to him better on four feet than two."

Henry shook his head. "I'm not getting naked in front of a bunch of kids, Winter. Besides, I don't need to shift. I can take him out in human form. It's time for some redemption."

Stryker wasn't interested in continuing the fight. Henry expected him to keep on running, get back on his motorcycle and hightail it out of here. Instead, Stryker jumped and grabbed the lower structure of the grain elevator. He climbed on top, gave Henry the finger, and ran up the slope toward the river.

"Hope you've been doing your pullups, muscles."

Henry used the same piece of structure Stryker had used and climbed after him. The elevator was enclosed, forming a nice flat roof of corrugated metal. Henry's feet drummed loudly on it as he sprinted up toward the sky, closing in on the silhouette of Bechtel Stryker.

Near the top, the elevator made a forty-five-degree turn and flattened out, jutting over Elliot Bay. Henry tried not to look down as he ran. There were no safety rails up here. Nothing to keep you from falling off and hitting water that would feel as hard as concrete. No barge was parked underneath, ready to receive a load of grain.

Stryker stopped at the end of the line, his feet a few inches from the edge. He turned to face Henry, his shoulders rising and falling from his labored breaths.

Henry slowed down. "You can't go any farther. No choice now but to fight. I think you know I can beat you."

Stryker laughed and crouched, removing his fancy boots and setting them aside. "Maybe you can. But you won't find out. Not tonight."

"Why are you taking your shoes off?"

Stryker stood, bending his neck side to side. "They'll just fill with water and drag me down. This isn't the first time I've made a dramatic escape."

Henry shook his head. "If you jump into that water, you'll die."

"Will I?" Stryker leaned out over the edge, studying the drop. "And that would suit you just fine. According to you, I only have two options. I can stay up here, fight you, and possibly lose, or make a leap of faith and swim away. I think I've made up my mind."

With no further ado, Stryker took a swan dive off the edge of the grain elevator.

Henry rushed to the edge and watched as the man plummeted out of sight. The darkness swallowed him, making him invisible, but the splash of water came a moment later.

"No way I'm following that." Henry sighed. "If the fall didn't kill him, I guess we'll have to deal with him another time."

He made his way back down to the ground, where Nicole was helping a few of the teens with their wounds. Henry found Ellie crouched by the side of the girl Stryker had stabbed. She was dead, but Ellie still held her hand, whispering to her.

Henry kept a respectful distance. "I'm sorry, kid."

Ellie nodded slowly. "If I had listened to you before…"

"Well, there are two good times to make the right choice. The first was then. The second is now. So, how about it?"

Ellie heaved a sigh that carried a weight of suffering beyond her years. "Fine. We'll do it. We'll come under your protection."

CHAPTER TWENTY-FIVE

As the teens recuperated at his home, Henry took Winter's new information and set out in the Lamborghini. He headed for Starvation Heights, the lost institution swallowed up by the forests of Olalla.

He parked in the overgrown lot and carefully looked around at the perimeter. It was a bright and beautiful day, but the sunshine did almost nothing to dispel the aura of fear and desolation that surrounded the place.

Henry picked his way through the overgrown ferns and found the older man sitting on a rotten old windowsill, kicking his legs.

"I don't know how you handle living here, Charlie." Henry set his satchel down and dug inside it. You must possess some freaky kind of mental toughness."

Charlie smiled, looking around at his home. "This is the safest place on Earth for me. Besides, you get used to it. You can get used to anything. I knew it was you by the sound of your engine. Fancy car. It's why I didn't greet you with a shotgun like last time." He leaned back through the windowsill and touched something inside. "Got it right here, though. Leaning up against the wall. Can never be too careful."

"Well, don't shoot me. At least not until I give you this." Henry pulled the paper bag out of his satchel and handed it over. "Stopped on my way down. A gift for you."

Charlie unwrapped it, revealing a bottle of Westland American single malt. "Well, I'll be… You shouldn't have. I'm glad you did. Care for a drink?"

He performed a surprisingly graceful backward somersault, landing on his feet inside the building. Henry climbed through and followed him into the back, where Charlie broke out the familiar Flintstones drinking glasses. This time, they appeared to be somewhat clean. Henry accepted his glass and took a sip.

"Good stuff, ain't it?" Charlie grinned.

Henry nodded, suppressing a cough. "Yeah. Smoothest American whisky I've ever tasted."

Charlie snorted. "Makes Jack Daniels taste like the nasty old cough medicine. Not that it needs any help tasting like that. Anyway, I assume you probably didn't come here to drink whisky and listen to an old man ramble on and start insulting American institutions like old JD. What's on your mind?"

"It's about the stone." Henry set his glass down. This time, he intended to finish it. "I've got this new assistant. A very smart guy."

Charlie raised his eyebrows. "He from Oriceran?"

"Yeah. A dwarf."

"You have to be careful with dwarves." Charlie sat with a groan. "They'll eat you out of house and home. Other than that, they're good people. Mostly. So, did your new friend figure something out?"

"He did." Henry pulled a chair over and sat. "He was in the middle of a bunch of experiments, trying to make something happen. Of course, the thing that ended up happening was a complete accident."

Charlie poured himself some more whiskey. "That's usually how invention goes. Our best attempts will never surpass fate's sense of humor."

"It was a bat. I get them in the cave sometimes. The thing was flying around all confused. Winter was trying to work on the stone, and he said the thing kept distracting him. He was getting ready to grab one of my weapons and shoot it when it ran straight into some metal scaffolding and broke its neck."

"Quite an anecdote, Henry, but what does it have to do with the stone?"

"Maybe everything. Winter was making some headway getting the thing to activate, for lack of a better word. He was consistently getting it to glow a little and let off a small amount of heat. I guess you could say it was 'open.' Winter cleaned up the dead bat and kept working. But he kept on hearing the high-pitched screech like it was still alive. He thought he was going crazy, but..."

Charlie leaned forward subtly, his eyes opening wide. "But?"

"The sound faded away after a while, but Winter formed a theory. I agree that it could be possible because I was already thinking about something along the same lines. What if the legends you told me about last time I was here were true? That the stone is capable of pulling out and storing the life force of a living thing? When the bat died, some of its essence was pulled in and stored. Winter accidentally let it all out, which is why he kept hearing the sound, and why it stopped after a while."

Charlie sat back, smiling. "I think you're on the right track. That's my feeling, anyway. The way I interpreted the legends, I thought they used the stones to sap the energy from the Picts. A weapon. Maybe they were more like a repository for life. If your friend hadn't kept on messing with the stone, who's to say the bat's essence wouldn't have lasted forever inside, waiting?"

Henry frowned. "Waiting for what?"

"I don't know, Henry. Here's another thought. If this theory is true, is there more essence stored in that stone? If so, how do we find out? How do we release it?"

"Do we *want* to release it?" Henry sighed and reached for his glass. "I spend most of my time thinking about difficult things, Charlie, but this is a new kind of mind twister."

"Well, hold on tight because the ride isn't over yet. I might have something to help, though..." Charlie stood and shuffled away into the dark recesses of the asylum.

Henry sat and waited in silence, trying to think of nice things. Puppies. Butterflies. The way Nicole looked in that tight black outfit.

Charlie finally returned, sitting back down with an old book in his lap. He opened it to the middle and rifled through the pages until he found what he was looking for. "Here we are. Not a lot of knowledge remains about the runes and incantations used by the Picts, but I have a few things here.

"It's possible that the stones never were used to store

essence but were instead temporary holders. Their main use could have been to pull the essence out, not hold onto it. When the stone remains 'open,' as you said, the stored essence might leak away. The way the bat's did. The essence would need to be transferred to a more permanent vessel."

Henry leaned over to look at the book. "Like what?"

"Like anything holding one or more of these symbols." Charlie tapped a line of three runes on the page. The first looked like an upside-down question mark without the dot. The second was a backward C with three dots in the middle. The third was an X with two lines running through it, left to right and top to bottom.

Henry took out his phone. "Can I get a picture of those?"

Charlie held out the book so Henry could get a good shot. "A vessel could be anything. If it was scribed with the proper runes, any old container would work to hold onto any amount of life essence."

"Are we talking like…Tupperware?"

Charlie cackled. "Hell, why not? Could be a whisky bottle, too. Or maybe that only holds a different kind of essence." He looked longingly at his bottle of single malt.

Henry stared at the older man. "Why do I get the feeling you know way more than you're letting on? If this thing about runes and vessels is true… I feel like you were letting me think something that was incorrect, but you had second thoughts and are trickle-truthing me."

"You're paranoid, kid. If I seem a bit flaky-brained, you can blame one of two things. Age, and whiskey. Speaking of, do you need a refill?"

"No, I still need to drive." Henry shifted in his chair, looking around the creepy place. "Tell me something, Charlie. And be honest with me. Do you like living here?"

Charlie shrugged. "Keeps me safe."

"That's not what I asked. Living in a jail cell would also keep you safe. I asked if you *like* it."

"As opposed to where?" Charlie shook his head and drank more whisky. "I've got nowhere else."

"But what if you did? You're here because it's somewhere familiar and keeps dangerous people away. What if I could offer somewhere just as safe while also being an actual home? Somewhere comfortable and bright."

Charlie grinned. "I'd assume you were offering to let me stay at your house."

"Not exactly. More like someplace on my property. You can stay in the house if you really want, but I think a guy like you values his privacy."

Charlie laughed, gesturing around him. "What gave you that idea? If this offer's for real, Henry…"

"It is. Come on. I'll help you pack."

Charlie got up and rushed ahead of Henry, gathering things up. His enthusiasm lasted until they reached the spot where he'd been sleeping. He turned glum, sniffling as he poked through his things.

Henry put a hand on his shoulder. "It can be hard, leaving behind familiar territory. I promise it'll be worth it. If it isn't, Starvation Heights will always be waiting for you. Not like anyone else is itching to move in."

"This place is a damp and drafty hellhole, but it's home." Charlie picked his bedroll up off the floor. "Or it was. Time for a change."

Henry followed Charlie through the rest of the place, letting the older man load him up with stuff. There wasn't much, and Henry could hold it all in one arm. They came to a large, antique wooden chest against the wall. Henry thought it was original to the asylum until Charlie set his hand on it.

"Don't worry about this beast, Henry. I'll get it."

Henry shook his head. "That thing looks like it weighs a ton. What's in it?"

"Clothes."

"Charlie, you're wearing the same grunge t-shirt and pants as last time I was here. How much clothing do you really have? Come on, what's in there? Is it empty?"

"How about you mind your own business," Charlie suddenly snapped. "I'm sure you've got plenty of it. If you're going to be nosy, I might as well stay right where I am."

"Okay, okay." Henry turned away. "You can have your secrets."

"Don't go prying."

"I won't." Henry headed for the exit. He couldn't help but keep wondering what was in that chest. If Charlie hadn't been so defensive, he would have assumed it was empty.

Somehow, the old man was able to drag the chest all the way out to the road. It took some doing, but they managed to cram it into the Lamborghini without scratching anything.

From there, it was a short drive back to Bremerton.

"Don't take this the wrong way, Charlie." Henry rolled the windows down. "But you reek."

Back at home, Winter was out in front of the house ready to greet them. He ran over, all smiles, and tried to grab the chest out of the back. But Charlie slapped at his hands.

"No touching!"

Winter stepped away, looking wounded. He grabbed Henry and pulled him to a safe distance. "Did you really have to bring the feral old man here, laddy?"

"He's not feral." Henry glanced at Charlie. "Not completely, anyway. He's actually a scholar of sorts, and he knows a lot about the Picts. Now we can consult him without me having to drive down to Olalla every time, and he gets to live in a real place. It's a win-win."

Winter raised an eyebrow. "Did no one ever tell you that you don't need to house everyone you make friends with?"

The teens were playing frisbee near the back of the lot, in an open grassy area. They came running over, greeting Henry and the new arrival. Wexell moved toward the car to try and help Charlie with the chest, but both Henry and Winter hollered at him.

"I wouldn't do that if I were you!"

Ellie wandered over to the two of them, sweaty from chasing the frisbee around. "What's the matter with you two? Why are you making that poor old man carry that heavy thing on his own?"

Winter shrugged. "I tried helping. He almost bit my face off."

Charlie did allow the teens to help with his other belongings, and the whole group headed across the lot toward a shaded, overgrown spot near the trees. It was difficult to make out the structure lurking in the under-growth until you were right up on it.

"The groundskeeper's house," Henry announced. "Don't worry. I didn't take you out of one rotten old shell and bring you to a new one. No one's lived in there for a long time, but I have people come by and take care of the inside on a regular basis. It's all good. Here, this is for you."

He pulled a keyring out of his pocket and handed it to Charlie. "There's one for the guest house and one for the main house. There's also a paging system inside that goes to a speaker in the kitchen in case you need help with anything."

Charlie took the key with tears in his eyes. He looked around at the group in disbelief. "Could it be...I have a family?"

Henry looked at Winter. Winter looked at Ellie. Ellie looked at Wexell, and so on. Finally, Henry shrugged. "I guess you could call us a family. Why not?"

As Charlie settled in, the teens returned to their game of frisbee, and Henry and Winter took a little walk around the property, soaking in the sunshine.

The dwarf pulled the branch of a tree down to his nose and sniffed the delicate pink flowers that blossomed there. "It's funny how things can change. One moment, you're fighting for your life against an immortal warrior and his undead friends, and the next..."

"You're taking a nice walk on a quiet day, surrounded

by new friends." Henry smiled and stuck his hands in his pockets as he idly kicked a few overgrown tufts of grass.

"Have you heard back from Nicole?"

Henry nodded. "She texted me a few hours ago. She's fine. Stryker never managed to touch her. He got a knife in his back, so I guess you could say we won the fight. Sort of."

Winter patted Henry on the back. "I try not to tell people how to live their lives, but I'll make an exception right now. You should ask that lovely lady out on a date. I'm sure she'll say yes, and I think you've earned a good time like that. Just don't go moving her in. At least not yet."

Henry laughed. "Hungry? Let's go get a sandwich."

CHAPTER TWENTY-SIX

After lunch, Henry sat alone on the front porch, staring down at his phone. He drew a deep breath to soothe his nerves and hit the call button.

As soon as he heard her voice, the nerves melted away.

"What's up?" Nicole said. "Did you catch wind of any Pictish pricks washing up dead on the shore? I've been keeping an eye out, but so far, nothing."

Henry sat back with a sigh. "If only. I'm not calling about Bechtel Stryker, though. I wanted to ask how you were doing."

"Oh. Well..." There was a clicking sound like Nicole was typing. "I'm free all this afternoon if you can believe it."

"I guess you didn't hear me."

"Yeah, I did. But in my profession, you learn pretty fast to hear between the lines. You're asking me out. Maybe you were pressured into it by one of those adolescent magicals you're housing, but my money's on Winter. Did I get it right?"

"Dead on. That's impressive, Nicole. I guess the cat's

out of the bag now, so I'll tell you what I was thinking. How about a little ice skating?"

"Sounds cliched and awesome all at once." He heard the smile in her voice. "I couldn't help but notice it's a warm, beautiful day outside. I assume you know an inside place? When I did my Seattle research before coming here, I didn't exactly focus on leisure-time activities."

"As a matter of fact, I do know a place." Henry stood, performing a little dance on the porch. "How about we meet at the ferry dock in an hour?"

They didn't talk much on the drive toward the north end of Seattle. Henry focused on weaving through the midday traffic, and Nicole was busy sticking her head out the window, smiling as the sun beat down on her face.

"It's been a long time since I *did* something on a day off." She pulled her head back into the car, smiling as she fixed her hair. "Usually I sit around under the pretense of recharging my batteries. Honestly, I'm a lazy girl at heart."

"Well, you came through for me when I needed you." Henry smiled at her. "If you keep being a hero like that, you can do whatever the hell you want on your days off. However, I must insist that you spend this one with me. Afterward, you can give me a rating out of ten."

"Hm. Sounds good. I guess we'll have to see what you have planned."

A minute later he pulled into the parking lot of the Kraken Community Iceplex, a modern glass building covered in a façade of wooden slats that gave it a Scandinavian feel. Nicole started getting giddy as they went inside and rented their skates. Henry couldn't help but keep smiling.

She looked up from lacing her skates. "What are you grinning at, Henry?"

He shrugged. "Seeing you happy. It's nice. I'm mostly used to seeing you in business mode."

"Well, you're about to see me in Nancy Kerrigan mode in a second. Don't let your jaw hit the floor when you see my skills."

"I can agree to that, as long as you watch out for hired thugs with police batons. Ready to hit the ice, or what?"

She took his hand and let him help her up. They timed their entry onto the ice, slotting in between a few other couples. It wasn't long before they were sailing along, pumping their legs and holding hands so they wouldn't drift apart.

"Like sleeping sea otters," Nicole observed, squeezing his hand tighter.

Henry let his eyes wander up and down her body. "Very graceful stride, Nicole. But the way you were talking up your 'skills' I expected something more."

"Well, watch and be amazed."

Nicole separated from him, pumping her legs harder to gather some speed. She suddenly hopped off the ice, doing a clean turn and a half, landing on one foot and sliding along the ice backward. She wobbled a bit and almost fell, but managed to recover. She brought her other foot down and bowed.

Henry gave her a round of applause. "I had no idea you had tricks like that up your sleeve, Nicole."

She grinned proudly as she skated back to him and took his hand. "Maybe there's a lot you don't know about me. I'm a bottomless well of surprises."

They skated around for a solid hour, taking their turns pulling increasingly ridiculous stunts. Doing knee-slides and jump-kicks and anything else they could think of. They finally made their way off the ice, covered in a sheen of sweat and a few new bruises.

"That was a blast, Henry." Nicole patted his shoulder, then used him as a prop to hold herself up as she pulled her skates off. "We should do it again sometime."

Henry waited until she was sitting and squatted to unlace his skates. "I agree."

"If you want, you can drop me right back off at the dock. I can catch the light rail."

"I guess I could do that." Henry picked up both pairs of skates and set them on the counter. "Or we could get lunch. I don't know about you, but ice skating always revs my appetite."

"Oh." Nicole started fussing with her hair again. "I guess I could probably eat."

"Then it's settled. Come on. There's a place nearby I want to try out."

They left the Iceplex and headed for Bongos, a Caribbean restaurant on the shore of nearby Green Lake. The place's exterior had a splash of bright colors, and the inside was pleasantly low-key. There was outside seating, the tables and chairs set right down in the sand.

They sat, ordered drinks, and looked at their menus. When the waitress came by to take their orders, Henry was ready.

"Citrus braised pork? Sounds tasty to me. I'll take the Desi plate."

Nicole stared at her menu, biting her lip. "Um...so much to choose from. I have no idea what most of it is. Oh, hey, jerk chicken. I like the name, and I've heard of it, so I'll go with that."

The waitress took their menus and walked away in no real rush, dancing a little to the music coming from inside the restaurant.

"Very chill place," Nicole observed, looking at the beach décor and bright murals. "I think I'll move to some Caribbean Island when I retire. Assuming I survive that long."

Henry sat back with his frosty bottle of beer. "You're the best bounty hunter I know, Nicole. I'm sure you'll be fine."

"Oh, thank you. Am I also the *only* bounty hunter you know?"

He smirked. "Not telling. How's work, anyway? Did you solve whatever case you were working with Boris?"

Nicole blew a raspberry. "Not yet. The guy's proving to be very elusive. If we're talking jobs… There was this warlock a few months back. He built up a hellacious reputation. Supposed to be real nasty.

"I took the job on a whim. I guess I was feeling kind of cocky. Anyway, when I found the guy, he was piss-drunk. He thought I was his girlfriend and tried to kiss me. All it took was a knee to the crotch, and he was done."

Henry laughed and swigged some beer. "That's the best kind of job. Easy and smooth. Not like this guy Stryker." He sighed and sat forward. "No. I told myself I wasn't going to talk about him. This is our day off. The weather is lovely, and I'm sitting here with you. Nicole Thomas, international woman of mystery."

She shrugged. "Mostly national these days. Plenty of creeps right here on my native soil."

Henry frowned. "It just occurred to me that I don't even know where you're from."

"I probably left that out intentionally. Why, is that something you're dying to know?"

The waitress danced back out. Henry looked her way, his stomach grumbling, but it was far too soon for their food to be ready. She was bringing appetizers to another table.

"I would be lying if I said you didn't tickle my curiosity, Nicole. We've done plenty of talking…"

"Bantering, I'd call it," she returned with a smile and a raised eyebrow.

"Fine. We've done plenty of bantering. I've probably told you some things about myself, but I don't think you've ever told me about you. So, how about it?"

"Nuh-uh." She shook her head, taking a sip of her iced tea. "I don't do that. In my business, wanting a regular life too much gets you distracted. Maybe it gets someone hurt. It might be my day off, but that doesn't mean I'm not keeping vigilant."

Henry opened his mouth, ready to tell her how trust-worthy he was. Then he realized that trust wasn't something you gave because someone said the magic words. It was something you earned through mutual experience.

Maybe, after they made it through a couple more scraps together, she'd start to open up more.

Henry closed his mouth, smiled, and vowed that he would crack this particular nut one day.

CHAPTER TWENTY-SEVEN

With so many new people around the house, Henry decided it was a good idea to work from home for a while and keep an eye on things. The day after his date with Nicole, still feeling in high spirits after the successful outing, he sat in his home office on the ground floor, intending to get some serious work done.

After sipping coffee and staring into space for a while, Henry finally opened his emails and started reading. "Hm... More shareholder meetings. Looking forward to that...*not.*" He grinned and typed out a quick reply.

"Oh, Susie needs some time off next month. She's finally getting that carpal tunnel surgery! Nice." He went to his calendar and put in a note for the fifteenth of next month—*Buy Susie a get-well-soon gift.*

That was as far as he got. The teenagers were awake, and it sounded like a herd of cattle was stampeding down the hall outside. He went over to his door and opened it, afraid of what he might see. Benji and a young witch named Lauren were racing down the hall. They stopped at the end, turned, and came back.

"Hey, Mr. Neumann!" Lauren waved as she went by.

"Good morning." Henry sipped his coffee. "Looks fun, but I can't help but wonder…what exactly are you doing?"

"Oh!" Benji skidded to a stop, breathing hard. "Just getting some sprints in. Gotta stay in shape, Mr. Neumann. Just in case any big, ugly wolves decide to chase us again."

He and Lauren high-fived.

Henry shrugged. "Good idea. But I will call into question your decision to do your exercises right outside my office door. I'm sure you can find somewhere else."

They smiled, nodding like it was the most brilliant idea they had ever heard. They moved away, disappearing around a corner.

"At least they aren't stealing anything." Henry shook his head. "Or breaking anything. Theoretically."

He put his headphones on and cranked up the volume. "Pour some sugar on me," he muttered. He closed his eyes and was mentally transported to the forest at night, running in wolf form.

Of course, his mind kept coming back to the teens who were running rampant in his house, and not being able to hear them was making him worry even more. He finally took off his headphones and stood with a sigh, resigning himself to not getting anything done.

Not at work, at least. There were still some things he could do, like making the rounds and checking if everyone was settling in all right.

He stepped out into the hall and immediately had to dodge a basketball flying past his face.

"Whoa! Sorry, Mr. Neumann." The young gnome ran by, catching the ball and dribbling it with both hands. "Won't happen again."

"You're right about that, Shia." Henry jerked a thumb over his shoulder. "If you want to play around with that ball, it has to be outside." He grimaced, muttering to himself. "Fuck, when did I get to be the old man around here?"

He continued into the library, where he found Ellie and Wexell draped over sofas in extremely uncomfortable-looking positions, reading intently.

Henry approached Ellie and peeked at the book she was reading. "*The Dust Bowl*. Cool." He went to Wexell. "*The Rise and Fall of the Third Reich*. All right, why not."

He headed downstairs next, seeking the calm sanctity of the cave. Except it hadn't been very calm ever since Winter had started messing with the stone.

The dwarf was hard at work, surrounded by a pile of tools and parts. He wasn't alone. A tall, slender Light Elf teenager named Finch was peering over his shoulder.

"And this, I'm told, is called a smart-sleeve." Winter demonstrated by holding up the membrane and stretching it a few times. "It can conduct electricity into or out of pretty much anything you put it on. Our gracious, humble, and not-so-sweet-smelling host, Henry Neumann, invented it."

Finch looked over with awe. "You created this device, Mr. Neumann?"

"Just call me Henry. Hearing 'Mr. Neumann' makes me feel like a hip high school science teacher." Henry picked up a nearby granola bar wrapper, wadded it up, and bounced it off Winter's head. "I guess that might not be the worst thing to feel like, though."

Winter scowled at him. "Don't interrupt a man while he's working."

Henry laughed. "Tell that to the kids upstairs. It sounds like we're hosting a bull run up there today. Looks like you've got an apprentice."

Winter grinned and patted Finch on the arm. "The kid has the gift of curiosity. That's a Light Elf for you. They can't stand it when things are going on that they don't understand. I guess they're like humans in that way. Eh, Finch?"

"Easy, Winter." Henry leaned on the table, grabbing some potato chips from a nearby bag and munching on them. "Don't insult Finch by comparing him to my kind. Are you making any progress?"

"Aye." Winter finished tightening the smart-sleeve around the stone and stepped aside to let Henry see. "Look at how I've capped the terminals. See the wire running between them?"

Henry stared in disbelief. "So, you're feeding the magical energy out of the stone and right back into it? That's your big idea?"

"Think about it." Winter tapped a finger against Henry's temple. "The stone ordinarily requires a great deal of input before it opens up and starts channeling energy. Perhaps Ellie has some Pictish blood in her that allows her to activate the stone more easily. I don't know. What I *do* know is that my design should make it possible, theoretically speaking of course, for *anyone* to achieve what Ellie does."

"How so?"

"Well, by feeding the stone's energy back into it, we can create a feedback loop. Sort of like me eating through tubs of ice cream. I scarf them down, and the next time I look in the freezer, they're back."

"That's because I keep buying more."

Winter waved that off. "Whatever. The stone is a conduit, right? It can pull magical energy through and translate it into some other form. So it's not like there's a limited supply of energy. When we feed the energy back in, it will eventually cause an overload which will make the stone unstable, priming it so that activation requires much less effort."

Henry picked up the stone, his hands squeaking on the rubbery sleeve. "But it still needs to be activated."

"Right. Bear with me on this." Winter took the stone from Henry, holding it high above his head. "The Picts must have had some way of activating these stones, right? They were supposed to be weapons. So, what if it's something about fighting that allows the activation? It's only a hunch, but something tells me the stone will work when you need it to."

"That's it?" Henry sighed. "After all these tests, that's where we're at?"

Winter lowered the stone, shrugging. "I'm a genius, not a miracle worker. I'm still running tests. So far, no explosion like you had in your lab in Seattle. I guess that means I'm the better tinkerer, right?"

He held out his hand to Finch, and the two of them engaged in a fast, elaborate secret handshake. Henry laughed and shook his head. "I'm going upstairs to get a snack. Just keep working. If Stryker resurfaces, you can bet he'll have some more secret weapons up his sleeves. I intend on having one of my own."

Henry went upstairs and into the kitchen. It was pandemonium inside as four teenagers carried boxes in from the front door and started unpacking them, filling every available surface with groceries.

"Uh… What?" Henry stood in the doorway and stared.

"Oh, hey, Mr. Neumann." Benji waved. "We thought we'd do something nice for you. Now you don't have to worry about shopping for a while."

Henry looked in one of the boxes and saw an industrial size package of hot dogs. "Processed meat-like products. My favorite. Thanks, though. Who paid for all this?"

Rami, the Light Elf who was bad at *Streetfighter*, set Henry's credit card on the counter and slid it over. "You did."

"Huh." Henry picked up the card and put it back in his wallet. "Didn't even realize it was missing."

Ellie walked in behind him, grabbing an apple from the mess. "You should keep better track of your financials, rich boy."

Henry paused, then pulled the card back out and handed it to her. "You might as well hold onto it. But keep the spending to the essentials. *My* definition of essentials. No more of…" He grabbed a jar of marshmallow fluff. "… Whatever this is. You could probably use this to spackle over some nail holes in the library."

Ellie laughed, tossing a bag of carrots his way. "It's not all junk, Henry. But I'll do my best."

"I guess I can't ask you to promise more than that." Henry smiled when he saw a six-pack of beer and grabbed a bottle. "Not sure how you managed to get the delivery guy to give you this. Benji, did you use your magic to make that peach fuzz on your chin look like a real beard?"

He went back into his office, twisting the cap off his beer and taking a drink. He almost spat it out, wincing as he looked at the label. "*Root* beer. Not what I was expecting to taste. I guess it is a workday."

He looked at his screen, where the same email was open that he should have replied to an hour ago. Rolling forward on his chair, he reached for the keyboard to finally get it done. That was when his phone rang.

But not just the landline on the desk. His cell phone started going at almost the same moment, buzzing in his pocket. And, if that wasn't enough, he even heard the muffled sound of his old pager going off somewhere in the depths of a desk drawer.

"What the hell is going on?" He grabbed the landline. "Henry speaking. What's up?"

"Mr. Neumann!" The frantic voice was barely recognizable as that of his assistant, Susie. "We have a problem here. Security breach. Someone's broken in. A bunch of our cameras are out, and I have no idea what's going on."

Henry got to his feet. His cell phone was still buzzing in his pocket. "I'm on my way. Just lay low, Susie, and call the police. Now! Do what you can to get a read on the situation, and keep me updated with text messages. If it comes down to it, don't hesitate to use the panic room in my office. Someone else is trying to get hold of me. I'll call you back."

He hung up and pulled out his cell phone. His gut

flipped over when he saw the name on the screen. He answered it. "Aspen, are you okay?"

There was no answer at first, only a series of shuddering breaths. When she finally answered, it was in a whisper. "Henry…someone's breaking into my house."

His blood ran cold, then hot as acid. Fur prickled down the back of his neck. "Where are you? Are you safe? Can you get out?"

"No…I'm in my bedroom closet."

"Shit!" Henry whipped around, running out of the office and back toward the library. "Did you call the cops? Do you need me to?"

"I already did. I don't know how long they're going to take to get here. Please…"

Henry pulled open the hidden cave entrance and sprinted down the steps. "Don't worry, Aspen. Everything's going to be fine. I promise. Hang up now. Don't make any more noise."

She ended the call, and Henry quickly stuffed the phone back into his pocket as he burst out into the cave. Winter and Finch were messing around in his squat rack, climbing around like monkeys. They dropped to the floor and stared as Henry grabbed every weapon in his arsenal.

"What's going on, muscles?" Winter asked.

Henry grabbed a fresh wind grenade and shoved it into his belt pouch. "I might have to choose between saving my sister or saving the company I've worked my ass off to build."

Winter rushed over, rifling through keys and tossing Henry the one for the new Suzuki Hayabusa. "Here. This should get you to wherever you're going as fast as possible. Just don't crash this time. Which one are you going for?"

Henry frowned, wiping sweat from his face. "Aspen. And I'm not going to crash."

Winter nodded, handing an earpiece over. "Your assistant has already piped what's left of your office security feeds over. I'll try to keep you apprised. Go save her, laddy."

Henry ran for the Hayabusa, hopped onto the seat, and started the engine. He raced out of the cave and down the tunnel. He drove out through the gates way before they were open, clipping his side mirrors.

He didn't care. He'd wreck every motorcycle in the world if it got him to Aspen a second sooner.

Ellie listened to Henry's frantic voice through his office door. She stepped back when he ran through. He didn't see her as he turned and made a beeline for the cave. Ellie ran back to the kitchen and beckoned to the others, then followed him down.

By the time they reached the cave, Henry was already racing out on the back of his motorcycle. Winter and Finch were watching him go in stunned silence. Ellie dashed past them and grabbed whatever Henry hadn't taken, including a new prototype take on the umbrella gun. This one was shaped like a golf club.

Winter came up behind her. "What are you doing now, lass?"

"What's right," she replied simply. "I overheard Henry's conversation. I assume he's going for his sister."

Winter crossed his arms. "You don't need to worry yourself about that. Henry wants you all to stay put for now and keep safe until he figures out what—"

"What to do with us?" Ellie interrupted him, shaking her head. "We agreed to come under his protection, but we're not going to sit around when there's something useful we could be doing."

Winter started to talk again, but he looked around and noticed that the whole group of teenagers was staring at him. "Well, it seems to me that I'm surrounded by budding magicals driven by foolish adolescent bravado. You remind me of myself once upon a time. And sometimes even now, when I see a good-looking lady and convince myself I have a chance. Fine, then. Go on. Just don't do anything so foolishly heroic that not even I could condone it."

He put his hands in his pockets and walked upstairs, turning a blind eye. When he reached the kitchen, a troubling thought occurred to him and he rushed back downstairs. By then, the teenagers were already gone, and the security feeds from Neumann Tower were all dead.

CHAPTER TWENTY-EIGHT

Aspen lived in Ruston, a suburb to the west of Tacoma. Henry reached her home off Winnifred Street in record time. Not wanting to waste a single second, he tore over the wide grassy median and positioned himself in the bike lane. The door of a parked car sprang open in front of him, and Henry had to dodge at the last second. If not for his shifter reflexes, he would have crashed and broken his promise to Winter.

"Look out, moron!" the guy from the car yelled.

Henry growled quietly, "If I wasn't in such a hurry…"

He turned off at Aspen's driveway and ditched his bike into the grass of her front yard. Running for the front door, he saw that it was open by half an inch. The damage to the frame was minimal. Surgical. Whoever had broken in was an expert.

Henry left his helmet face shield down as he slowly entered the house. He stepped wide over the linoleum floor to reach the carpeted hall, creeping toward Aspen's bedroom.

There was a man inside, rifling around in her dresser. He seemed to have no aim except to make as big of a mess as possible, grabbing armloads of clothing and tossing them over his shoulder. He scattered her jewelry and threw perfume bottles against the walls, smashing them.

Henry watched the burglar at work for a second, then shifted his eyes toward the closet. The door was still shut, but he thought he saw it wiggle a bit. Maybe Aspen was inside and her whereabouts still a secret. It wouldn't stay that way for long.

"Looks like I got here just in time."

The burglar didn't seem startled as he turned toward Henry, wearing a cheap Halloween mask of a generic monster. The kind of mask made of flimsy plastic, with an elastic band that held it to your face. It was a total mismatch to his professional methodology and that he dressed much more nicely than any petty thief Henry had ever seen.

Something wasn't right here.

The burglar laughed. "You're just in time. Enjoying the show?"

Before Henry could muster a response, the burglar charged toward him, leaping over the bed. Henry caught the man by the throat, turning and slamming him to the floor. He reared back, delivering a heavy punch to the man's jaw that knocked him out cold.

As the burglar twitched on the floor, Henry ripped open the closet and saw his sister crouched behind some luggage, holding a huge chef's knife.

She gave her brother a shaky smile. "I was going to stab him if he opened that door."

"No need for any blood, sis. Although I might have put him in a coma. Do you think you can forget about your Hippocratic Oath for a second do me a favor?"

She took his hand and let him pull her out of the closet. "Sure. I guess so."

"Good. Get in your car and head for my place. Winter and the kids are there."

"Actually," Winter said into Henry's ear. "It's just me."

Henry sighed. "Scratch that. It's just Winter. But go anyway. And stay put until I get home. Go!" He gave his sister a shove. That was all it took for her to start running. She detoured into the kitchen to drop her knife on the counter, and then she was out the door. Henry went to the front window to watch and ensure she got away. "All right Winter, what's this about you being alone?"

"I might have made a mistake, Henry. Those kids...they can be persuasive. Or maybe I'm a big softy. Anyway, to make a long story short, they're gone and so is your Hummer. Amazing how many teenagers you can cram in one of those things. They didn't say where they were going, but it's safe to assume they're heading for your office. They're going to need you. I suspect it might be a setup. An ambush."

Henry let the window blinds fall and went to check on the burglar. *I knew it was too easy.* The guy was still now, lying peacefully next to the bed. "I was starting to think the same thing. It's no coincidence that my office and my sister's house got broken into at the same time. I'm going to need you to call the cops and send them over here, by the way. An ambulance, too."

"Hm. I guess that means you took care of business. Good lad. I'll make the call, don't you worry."

Henry narrowed his eyes. "Winter, what's that noise? It sounds an awful lot like waves."

"Oh, that? It's white noise. I turned a YouTube video on. I find it helps keep my anxiety in check. Being the guy back at home base isn't as stress-free as it seems. Which is where I am, of course. Back at home base. Not sure why I'd be anywhere else."

Henry almost said something, but he realized he was wasting time. "I'm heading for the office, Winter. I'll keep you posted."

Seattle traffic was just as backed up as Henry expected for midafternoon, but he took advantage of his motorcycle's small footprint and wove through it all. Things started to change as he got closer to the intersection of Fifth and Young, where Neumann Tower was.

He soon reached a police barricade, where a Seattle deputy held up a hand to stop him. "No one's coming through here just yet, chief. We've got a situation at Neumann Tower. Gas leak. Could be dangerous."

Henry flipped up his face shield, hoping the recognition would help. The deputy showed no sign of knowing who he was. "I'm Henry Neumann. I own that tower, and I need to get through."

"No can do, sir. Sorry. You'll have to wait while we get things under control."

Henry shook his head. "I know it's not a gas leak. That's

the oldest lie in the book. Just let me through."

The deputy refused to relent, so Henry pretended like he was giving up and drove away. He turned back and punched the throttle, aiming for a narrow slot between the cop car and the wooden barrier. He barely managed to squeeze through and was racing toward Neumann Tower before the deputy could react.

Smoke rolled from the shattered front glass of the lobby. Henry drove straight up the steps and inside, crunching over the glass. A few firefighters were inside, helping workers and receptionists to their feet.

"Hey, you can't be in here!" one yelled. "Especially not on that rice rocket! Wait…is that racist?"

Henry rolled past them and punched the elevator button. The doors opened, and he pushed the motorcycle inside, riding it up to the top floor.

When the doors opened again, Susie was kneeling on the floor, wiping tears from her eyes.

Henry leaned the bike on the elevator's threshold so it wouldn't leave and ran toward her. He crouched at her side. "Susie! What happened? Are you all right?"

She nodded. "He didn't hurt me. But he was so frightening, Mr. Neumann."

Henry's blood ran cold. "Stryker."

Susie nodded again. "He told me his name. And he said…he was looking for something with these markings. He said if he found out you were hiding it from him, he'd be back. And your company would never recover."

She pulled a piece of paper out of her pocket and handed it to him. It bore the same symbols Charlie had shown him, the ones that would be on a vessel holding the life essence of dead Picts.

"He's gone now?" Henry asked.

"He left ten minutes ago. I'm sorry, Henry, but…"

He grabbed her arm. "What, Susie? Tell me."

"Those kids were here. Along with that odd girl who broke in before. I think he took them."

Henry stood fast. "Fuck! Are you sure you're all right, Susie? The cops are here. Firefighters are making their way through the building. You'll be safe. I have to go."

He hopped onto his bike and backed it into the elevator. Once in the lobby, he raced through the thin smoke back onto the street.

The same deputy was there, bent over and trying to catch his breath. One of his hands was grabbing the tailpipe of an old Harley-Davidson chopper, complete with a sidecar and a mounted machine gun.

"Holy shit." Henry moved around the chopper, taking it in. "Is this what you had under that tarp this whole time?"

Winter grinned from the driver's seat. "Nothing wrong with having a secret project. I knew there might come a time when you'd need more help in the field, and that day came earlier than expected. By the way…" He pulled the stone out of a side satchel and handed it to Henry. "I've done about as much as I can with this thing, for now. Preliminary test results were promising. I'll let you find out what that means for yourself."

Henry tucked the stone into a larger pouch on his belt. "Nice work, Winter. You can head back home now. I need my eyes and ears."

"Bullshit, laddy. You need my muscles and my unique

ass-kicking abilities. Didn't I tell you I used to be a warrior? You're not the only one with brains *and* brawn. Besides, it was me who let those kids run off on their fool's errand. I'll admit, I was starting to like those young morons. They remind me of myself a bit."

Henry shrugged. "All right, then. But how do we find them?"

Winter smiled, showing Henry his phone. "One of those little blighters grabbed a GPS strip before they left. Has to be Finch. Smart one. Or maybe Ellie. She's probably cleverer than the two of us put together."

"Then let's stop talking and go help them." Henry turned the bike around, getting ready to drive off.

"Wait!" the deputy shouted. "You can't just leave!"

Winter gave the man a confused look. "First you don't want us inside the barricade, and now you don't want us to go *out*side. Make up your mind!"

They rode off, ignoring the deputy's cries.

CHAPTER TWENTY-NINE

T he teenagers' GPS blip finally stopped moving once it reached the old Fisher Flour Mill on Harbor Island. Henry and Winter took the West Seattle Bridge and turned off onto Klickitat Avenue, riding up the ramp past a park and a couple of operational businesses.

They came to the deserted mill. With its waterfront location and silo-like megastructure, it greatly resembled the Terminal 86 grain facility.

"I guess Stryker has a certain type of place where he likes duking it out." Henry throttled back as they came down off the ramp and doubled back along Sixteenth.

"Creepy industrial complexes." Winter's voice would have been inaudible over the wind, but he was still coming in through Henry's earpiece. "Let's hope we can turn this mill into his final resting place. I don't know about you, but I think the Picts had their time."

"Couldn't agree more, my friend."

They wove through some rusting old train cars and

entered the mill's main lot. It funneled them through a corridor, the walls of which were shipping containers.

Henry kept looking around, trying to catch a glimpse of Stryker or some of his zombified warrior friends. However, there was nothing. "Where's that blip at?"

"In the water," Winter grunted. "Stryker must have found the strip and tossed it in. Hopefully, he didn't throw the teenager in with it. Do you think they've moved on already?"

"Not likely. He must have come to this island for a reason. Maybe he wanted a dead end. Somewhere he could make a stand against me."

Henry narrowed his eyes as the cold wind whipped around inside his helmet. He barely caught sight of a faint shimmer in the air in front of him. With a fraction of a second to spare, he ditched the bike to the side, hitting the asphalt and skidding along it.

Still sliding, he looked back and watched as Winter rode straight at the steel cable strung across the road. It was at Henry's neck level and surely would have decapitated him if he kept riding. Winter went straight under it with no problem.

Henry finally slid to a stop, reaching out to let Winter help him up.

"Nice driving, laddy! And I'm being sarcastic. What was that about? Did you hit a pebble or something?"

"Didn't you see the wire?" Henry shook his head and dusted himself off. "Thank God you're so short. It might be smarter to go on foot from here. At least for me. I'll keep going this way and try to draw Stryker's attention."

Winter nodded, revving his engine. "I'll mosey my way around the back. See what kind of trouble I can get into."

They parted ways. Henry headed for the mill's main structure at a jog, keeping his eye out for more traps. In a moment he was through into the broad expanse of the empty parking lot. There were smaller buildings dotted around, as well as old trucks and more shipping containers.

Stryker and his friends could be hiding behind any of them.

"I'm here!" Henry announced, spreading his arms wide. "This is what you wanted, right? To lure me in like a fish on a hook? Well, you got your wish. You might as well come out and gloat."

Henry faced the road and the ramp he had been driving on a short while ago. He thought maybe Stryker had moved away, but not very far. He might be watching from a distance, laughing at Henry's desperation.

Henry felt a sudden heat against the back of his neck and dove forward. The fireball singed up along the back of his neck, burning some of his hair as it spun away across the parking lot and finally exploded against a section of fence.

Flipping onto his back, Henry launched himself to his feet and pulled out his umbrella gun.

"It may be a clever contraption." Stryker strode out of the shadows of an outbuilding, smiling. "But that firearm is of no use against me. You don't think, in the hundreds of years I've lived, I've found a way to defend myself against any weapon a non-magical could devise?"

Henry fired a shot. Stryker clasped his hands together

and threw them wide, stretching a magical membrane that caught the bullet and turned it to dust.

"That's not Pictish magic, is it?" Henry asked.

"No, it is not." Stryker kept stepping forward as calmly as though he were approaching a kitten. "Our original magic all worked via one of our stone conduits. I've learned some more tricks in my time. Never underestimate a man driven by the holiest of motives, Henry."

Henry looked around, searching for any sign of the teens. "What motive is that?"

"The redemption of my people, of course. We were killed by unholy means, well before our time. I will ensure that we all have our peace. I respect you, Henry, but I won't allow you to get in my way."

"Too late." Henry sidestepped toward a shipping container. "I already have."

Stryker grinned. "I will chop you down like summer wheat."

"I don't think so. Wheat can't hit back. Or dodge."

Henry leaped for the cover of the container, getting behind it as Stryker's next fireball fizzled out against its side. He rolled to his feet and dashed into the cool shadows of a concrete structure. He ran upstairs, passed graffiti and trash, praying he was going the right way.

An undead Pictish warrior stepped onto a landing ahead of him, barring the way with a spear. Henry delivered an enhanced punch to the undead man's groin, shattering his dusty pelvis. He grabbed the warrior in both hands, throwing him headlong through a broken window. The warrior plummeted two stories to the ground, shattering into a dozen pieces.

Henry dusted his hands. "Guess this means I'm going the right way."

Henry watched through the window as Winter zoomed into view. The dwarf steered with one hand, using the other to hold down the trigger of the mounted machine gun. A volley of bullets flew at Stryker, who deflected and blocked every one.

"Don't do anything too stupid," Henry warned the dwarf. He continued up the stairs.

After the battle at the grain facility, Stryker didn't have many warriors left. Only two more met Henry on the stairs. The stairwell acted as a choke point, forcing them to come at him one at a time. He took them both down with ease, pulling one's head off and stomping the skull of the other one into dust.

At the top of the stairs, he came into a room where the teens were bound and gagged with magical rope. Henry freed Ellie first, and she helped him get the rest of them untied.

He didn't notice the other warriors in the room until Wexell pointed them out. There were four of them, standing sentry in the shadows. Between them, resting atop a wooden crate, was…something. Henry couldn't make it out.

"Why aren't they attacking?" he muttered.

"I think they have a different duty. Let's see if this wakes them up. Norman." Ellie nodded.

A dark-haired Light Elf stepped forward, shooting fireballs at the warriors. Either they had been working on their skills, or they were properly fueled by anger because their magic was more powerful than what Henry had dealt with before. The warriors went up in flames, dancing around in pain before collapsing into heaps of burning leather.

"Let's see what they were guarding." Henry stepped toward the crate, picking up the object resting on it. It was a wooden box, sealed all around with wax. Carved on its lid were the symbols Henry had been looking for. "I guess Stryker already found some of his missing essences. Here, Ellie." He handed it to the girl. "Keep this safe. And stay right here."

She shook her head. "No way. We want to help. We *can* help."

"You can help by not dying. You already tried to face Stryker once today, and look what happened. I'll be all right. I've got my secret weapon. Don't worry. I'll give you a chance to redeem yourselves later."

Henry ran out of the room. He half-expected the kids to follow him despite his words, but when he looked up at the bottom of the stairs, he didn't see them.

"Huh. They decided to listen. If one miracle can happen, why not two? Time to take Stryker down."

As he came back outside, Winter screeched to a stop before him, pulling uselessly on the machine gun trigger. "I went dry! Didn't put a dent in the bastard! Hop in, laddy."

Henry jumped into the sidecar without question, holding on tight as Winter whipped the bike around and hauled ass.

Stryker was coming toward them, down the narrow lane between two buildings. The Pict seemed unworried, and Henry began to doubt that this game of chicken would go well for himself and the dwarf. So he moved, standing in the sidecar and planting his feet wide to keep his balance. He took out a wind grenade, aiming and throwing it toward Stryker's feet.

It turned out to be a bad move. Stryker formed another magical shield, causing the grenade to bounce back and hit the front wheel of the chopper.

The Harley flew off the ground, doing half a barrel roll. It started to fall, less than a second away from crushing Henry and Winter beneath it.

Henry let himself begin to transform, his muscles gaining size and strength and his reflexes sharpening further. He grabbed Winter in both arms, holding the dwarf against his chest as he kicked away from the Harley and landed on his shoulder. The two of them rolled away as the bike hit the ground and tumbled, flipping over twice before stopping against a shipping container.

It all happened so fast that Henry didn't even have time to transform all the way. He was back to his human form a second later. The button on his pants had popped off, and his shirt had ripped in a few places.

"Winter, are you okay?"

The dwarf pushed himself away from Henry, drawing a deep breath. "I'm fine. Please don't smother me in those big, meaty mammaries."

Henry sighed and pushed the man away. They got to their feet and faced Stryker.

The Pict was standing in the same spot as before, watching them with mild curiosity. "As you can see, my earlier claim was correct. There is nothing you can do against me. I have an answer for everything."

"Oh yeah?" Winter took a step forward. "What's the capital of Kazakhstan?"

"Shut up." Stryker flicked a fireball at the dwarf.

Winter tried to dodge, but the fireball hit him in the shoulder and spun him around. He fell to the ground, groaning in pain, smoke erupting from his arm.

"Bastard!" Henry growled, charging toward the Pict. Fireballs flew at him. He ducked one, jumped over another, and sent a punch flying at Stryker's face.

Stryker spun to the side, kicking Henry in the back and making him sprawl. Stryker grabbed the back of his shirt at the base of his neck and held him down.

"Good idea. Play dead."

"Why play when you can die for real?" Henry turned over, slamming his foot against Stryker's shin. The Pict grunted but somehow stayed standing.

He grabbed Henry in both hands and picked him up in a display of superhuman strength. Henry felt as helpless as a puppy when Stryker carried him inside the building and threw him against the corner.

Henry hit hard, the breath shooting out of him. He had no time to recover before Stryker's boot landed against the side of his face, knocking him loopy. The taste of blood filled his mouth.

"You may be under the false impression that I need magic to win against you." Stryker kicked again, this time smashing a couple of Henry's ribs. "That is simply not the case. I can dismantle you with my bare hands, Henry. In fact, that is the preferred method."

Henry accepted the blows. It was easy to play up his

suffering because the kicks hurt like hell. He fought to stay lucid, slowly reaching for his belt.

"Wait… I have… something…"

Stryker stopped kicking and leaned down, smiling serenely. "What's that? You have something to say? Perhaps you'll admit where you're keeping the rest of the essence. Will you allow me to put my people to rest finally?"

"We both…know that's not what you want," Henry wheezed. "You're mad with power, Stryker. I know your type. Besides, I have no clue where the rest of the essence is."

Stryker frowned. "Then what is it you'd like to say? Care to beg for my mercy?"

"No." Henry pulled the stone out. "Just letting you get even closer."

He squeezed, connecting the terminals of the smart-sleeve. For a second he was afraid nothing would happen, that his gambit was for nothing and Stryker would win. Then he felt the heat and saw the light shooting out from between his fingers.

"No." Stryker stepped back, his eyes going wide. "No! You fool, do you realize the power that you're playing with? You have no idea what you're doing!"

"You're right." Henry got to his feet, holding the stone out. "I don't. Maybe you should start running."

Stryker turned and rushed for the exit. Henry smiled, and the smile became a snarl as the transformation took over. The stone dropped to the floor, falling as his hand turned to a paw, but it no longer needed the input of his anger and fear. It had achieved a self-sustaining reaction.

Energy exploded from it, shooting out in starburst rays that stung Henry's eyes. He turned away, huddling against the corner. The last thing he saw before shutting his eyes was the light enveloping Stryker. The Pict screamed, shielding his face with both hands as he dropped to his knees.

Then Henry passed out in a wash of pain.

***

Consciousness returned in fits and starts. He saw Stryker lying motionless. He faded out again, and when he came back, he saw several more Pictish warriors lifting Stryker from the ground and carrying him away. Henry tried to crawl toward them, tried to call out, but he was barely able to move a muscle. The last thing he saw before fading out again was his arm, back in human form, reaching out for Stryker.

Suddenly he was awake again, and Winter was there, helping him up. "That's it, laddy. Just sit there and get hold of yourself. You're all right. I think. Oh, maybe we should do this..."

He grabbed the shredded remains of Henry's clothes and draped them over his crotch.

"Thanks, Winter." Henry patted the man on the arm, eliciting a hiss of pain. "Oh! Sorry. Forgot about the burn. Is it bad?"

"I'll live." Winter stood. The teenagers came up behind him, all staring down at Henry. Ellie was at the front, holding the wax-sealed box. "Stryker got away," Winter went on, "but he didn't manage to get his hands back on this."

Henry smiled. "All in all, I think it's safe to say we won this time."

Winter and the teens shared a look. All at once, they burst out laughing.

"Aye, laddy. It's safe to say. Now we should get some clothes back on you and cover up those muscles. You're making us all look bad."

CHAPTER THIRTY

Three days passed. Aspen stayed at Henry's house that whole time, tending to all their battle wounds and getting to know the teenagers. On the second day, they took part in a board game tournament of *Munchkin* and its various expansion packs, which turned into a raucous good time. By the third day, it was clear that everyone was itching for a purpose.

Henry and Winter sat together in the library, sipping some whiskey Charlie had lent to them.

Winter sighed. "Stryker's still out there."

"Do you think so? I'm hoping he succumbed to his injuries and died. The only reason the stone didn't kill me was that I was in wolf form."

"Right. But you're not an immortal, magical Pict." Winter drained his glass and set it down roughly on an end table. "Stryker will be licking his wounds. Recovering the way we are. He's certain to be plotting his next move. It would be nice if everything was neat and wrapped up, laddy, but we both know that's not the case."

Henry nodded, staring into space. "He'll be back in the game pretty soon, trying to find the missing essence. He knows I have some of it now." He glanced at the safe where they were keeping the sealed box. "We haven't seen the end of him."

Winter stood, slapping his knees. "We need to find that essence before he does. The race is on, Henry. I'd better get back to Oriceran now. Check in with my contacts at the Dark Market and see if they have any information for me."

"Do you have to leave right now?" a voice asked from the doorway. They both turned and saw Ellie standing there.

"I suppose not," Winter grunted.

Ellie stepped inside the library. "Good. I hoped I could talk to both of you. Henry, you said you'd give us a chance to redeem ourselves. Did you only say that to get us to do what you wanted?"

Henry shook his head. "No. I have an idea for you. Something you and your friends—" Winter shot him a look. "I mean, something you and your *family* can do."

Ellie walked toward him eagerly. "Great! What is it?"

Henry stood, beckoning as he headed out of the library and down the hall. Ellie called for everyone to join them, and a moment later a whole entourage of teenagers followed them out of the house.

Henry led the way out onto Circle Drive. "Look around, kids. What do you see?"

"Trees," Finch said.

"A gravel road," Benji added.

"Some recycling bins," Ellie replied.

Henry shook his head. "Think deeper. Think *bigger*. You

see a vast world full of hiding places. Full of darkness and evil. This is my home, and until I find you all a permanent place to live, it's your home as well. With Stryker in the wind, it won't be long until Bremerton becomes a hot spot. So I'd like all of you to keep an eye on things in this city. Pretend the whole place is your secret hideout, and you want to keep everything safe and secure. Got it?"

They all nodded.

"Can we use the cave?" Finch asked.

"Only if Winter is there, and only if he approves." Henry nudged his dwarf friend. "I'm giving you another shot. Don't let them drive off in my Hummer and get themselves kidnapped again."

"Aye. You have my word, Henry."

He laughed, turning to the teens. "What are you waiting for? Off you go."

They looked at each other, then took off down the street, laughing as they went.

Winter nudged Henry in the side. "I don't believe you for a second, muscles."

"About what?"

"About finding them another place to live."

Henry shrugged. "I know it's a big house, but that's still a lot of teenagers to be running around. I like things quiet."

"Keep telling yourself that." Winter dusted his hands, letting out a sigh. "I suppose I should head down into the cave in case any of them need to get in contact with me. What are you going to do?"

Henry stretched side to side, testing his bruised ribs. "I think it's time to get a workout in. Just some light weights."

They headed inside and went downstairs, where they

drifted away to their separate activities. Henry couldn't help but think of Stryker as he loaded up the barbell for a few sets of squats. Anger fueled him, and before long he was doing fast reps with three plates on each side.

Winter reached up over the dividing wall separating the gym from the command center, waving. "Henry, I may have something here."

Henry racked the bar and walked over, his legs feeling weak and wobbly from the heavy weight. Winter was on the magical dark web, looking at an anonymous post someone had made in a forum to discuss magical artifacts.

Looking for more information on Pictish symbols. Is it true they were a magical race? I heard they possessed powerful artifacts. I'm attaching a picture of some symbols I have found. I'd like to know more about them. Please, can anyone tell me something?

Winter opened the attachment. It was an image showing a scattered grouping of twenty Pictish symbols. Henry scanned through them, then reached out and touched the screen. "These are the three Charlie showed me."

"Aye, so they are." Winter scratched his beard, narrowing his eyes. "Do you think it's Stryker?"

"It could be him, playing dumb. Fishing for any information he can get. If it *is* Stryker, I think it's safe to say he's feeling desperate. We might have him on the ropes here."

"But we have to find him before we can deliver the knockout punch," Winter pointed out.

"Exactly. If he gets desperate enough, he'll come to us.

With the kids patrolling the streets, we'll know he's coming ahead of time."

Winter kicked back in his chair, putting his feet on the desk. "So it's a waiting game. My favorite kind. Lots of time for snacks."

"Don't get too comfy. We need to stay proactive. We know firsthand the kind of damage Stryker can do, and I'd rather not have him showing up at my doorstep. Or my sister's. I'd like to find this guy and nail him before he has a chance to catch his breath."

Henry stomped back over to the barbell and loaded up another plate on each side. He positioned himself under it, drawing deep breaths as he prepared to move the heavy load. Sometimes he let himself start to shift before doing his heaviest sets. It provided an extra boost. But today, he made himself stay human.

He was already strong, but he knew he had to become stronger.

"I'll get you, Stryker. And I'll make you wish you died along with the rest of your people."

Get sneak peeks, exclusive giveaways, behind the scenes content, and more. PLUS you'll be notified of special **one day only fan pricing** on new releases.

Sign up today to get free stories.

Visit: https://marthacarr.com/read-free-stories/

Summer is almost upon us. My first big trip in life was at the start of summer to Longport, New Jersey. The pearl of Absecon Island. I was six years old and we lived in Philadelphia. My father had gotten a job as the summer rector at the Church of the Redeemer. Dad had been an engineer in World War II fixing radios and then later worked as an engineer for the government. He was very, very particular about things and was the only one who was allowed to pack the old green Chevrolet station wagon. We always had used cars kept alive by Dad - no air conditioning - until 1968 when he bought his first new car of his life. A Ford Galaxy 500, aqua blue with air conditioning, which my mother hated and was always trying to turn down. It was bigger than a Cadillac and one of the first to have shoulder straps - separate from the lap belt. Probably not safe.

Anyway, Dad would carefully pack the station wagon with enough for two adults and four kids and then stuff my brother, Jeff and myself, the two smallest, sat in the back with the suitcases. Linda and Cary sat in the middle. My oldest sister, Diana spent her summers in Virginia and never came with us. I don't know why.

When I was two and she was twelve and we lived in Little Washington, Virginia she was shipped off to boarding school at St. Margaret's in Tappahannock. The storyline was she was too smart for the public schools but that was a lie. And when we moved to Philadelphia no one bothered to try and fetch her. I only saw her in the summers. Later in life she would tell me how much she hated the school. Family mysteries that never get solved.

Dad had carefully mapped out the route to Longport on a yellow legal pad in longhand. He was MapQuest before there was an internet. He had details like - at the .8 mile marker move to the right lane. When he died there was a metal filing cabinet, and one drawer was full of those yellow legal pads with directions to everywhere he'd ever been. When one of us needed directions, he would photo-copy them from the master files. I don't know what became of them.

On the road we had either warm peanut butter and jelly sandwiches or warm tomato and mayonnaise sandwiches. Both on Wonder Bread and smushy in the middle. By the time we left at the end of July it was already swampy hot in Philadelphia and we had no air conditioning. It was nice to be leaving the suburbs and the city behind for a while.

My brother and I would entertain ourselves by trying to get the big trucks to blow their air whistles or by making faces at passing cars. Linda would bully my parents into playing Motown, which I loved. They weren't easily bullied but in those days Linda was fierce and single-minded. She once stabbed me in the hand with a pen during Twister. Always angry is how we thought of her.

The drive took four or five hours, but it felt like forever until we hit route 40 in New Jersey and the open farmland. We always stopped at a roadside farmstand for Jersey tomatoes and peaches. Once Dad went out on his own and got caught up in a Concord grape pick all you can field and came home with bushels. The seat of his pants was even dotted with purple from where he sat on a few. We ended up pushing grapes on anyone and everyone.

I loved it when we got to the old rickety wooden bridge that crossed into Longport and I could smell the ocean, finally. The Atlantic Ocean has a strong fish scent that might bothersome, but it was wonderful to me. Once we got to Longport my parents stopped wondering where we were. Frankly, they didn't wonder much at all in Philadelphia either, but they really didn't care there. I was free to roam for hours till dark, even at six years old and would often take Jeff with me, just like home. We were known as M&J then. Find one of us, you found the other.

I shared the back bedroom with my brother, and shared a room with him back home, and from there we could hear the ocean. That part of the island was only a block wide with the bay on one side and the ocean on the other. We would stay there till just past my birthday when I got to put pennies in an old lighthouse that lit up with each penny and a cake after church with my name on it and all the other September birthdays. And then packing up again to head back to the city. Another school year awaited. More adventures to follow.

AUTHOR NOTES - MICHAEL ANDERLE

MAY 13, 2022

Thank you for not only reading this book but these author notes as well!

For those who are reading something of mine or a collaboration, I have a few books under my belt. But...

Let's get to the good part of the author's notes, the stuff related to this story.

So, here we begin a new series where we left off ... No, *that's not right.*

Have you SEEN the cover? This is not at ALL like we left off. Normally, I don't have any of the ladies in the company say, "I found my new BB!"

Me: What's a BB?

Lady: Book Boyfriend.

Me: The cover guy?

Lady: ...

Me: Ok, I'm being dense. Duly noted.

I have been wondering not only what our present readers will think of the cover but what they will think of the story. Further, if you found the story because of the cover, I'd like to know.

Did the simpering man-hunk do the trick? If so, we can do more simpering man-hunk covers for you. We know the two artists who took the pictures. I have no shame about putting something fans want on the cover, and I am not (very) jealous of his looks.

If you are a fan of the cover, feel free to mention it in the review section of the book. I can pass your "book boyfriend" vote to Martha and "Lady X" (technically, there are TWO Lady Xs, but I'd like to keep this simple.)

I do hope you have enjoy this series. If you are into urban fantasy, fantasy, sci-fi, action-adventure, epic fantasy, and other stuff, check out my other books.

See you at the end of the next book!

Ad Aeternitatem,

Michael

CONNECT WITH THE AUTHORS

Martha Carr Social
Website:
http://www.marthacarr.com
Facebook:
https://www.facebook.com/groups/MarthaCarrFans/

Michael Anderle

Website: http://lmbpn.com

Email List: http://lmbpn.com/email/

https://www.facebook.com/LMBPNPublishing

https://twitter.com/MichaelAnderle

https://www.instagram.com/lmbpn_publishing/

https://www.bookbub.com/authors/michael-anderle